# Sophie's
## Friendship Fiasco

## Also by Nancy Rue

*You! A Christian Girl's Guide to Growing Up*
*Girl Politics*
*Everyone Tells Me to Be Myself ... but I Don't Know Who I Am*

### Sophie's World Series
*Meet Sophie (Book One)*
*Sophie Steps Up (Book Two)*
*Sophie and Friends (Book Three)*
*Sophie's Friendship Fiasco (Book Four)*
*Sophie Flakes Out (Book Five)*
*Sophie's Drama (Book Six)*

### The Lucy Series
*Lucy Doesn't Wear Pink (Book One)*
*Lucy Out of Bounds (Book Two)*
*Lucy's Perfect Summer (Book Three)*
*Lucy Finds Her Way (Book Four)*

## Other books in the growing Faithgirlz!™ library

### Bibles
*The Faithgirlz! Bible*
*NIV Faithgirlz! Backpack Bible*

### Faithgirlz! Bible Studies
*Secret Power of Love*
*Secret Power of Joy*
*Secret Power of Goodness*
*Secret Power of Grace*

# Fiction

## From Sadie's Sketchbook

*Shades of Truth (Book One)*
*Flickering Hope (Book Two)*
*Waves of Light (Book Three)*
*Brilliant Hues (Book Four)*

## The Girls of Harbor View

*Girl Power (Book One)*
*Take Charge (Book Two)*
*Raising Faith (Book Three)*
*Secret Admirer (Book Four)*

## Boarding School Mysteries

*Vanished (Book One)*
*Betrayed (Book Two)*
*Burned (Book Three)*
*Poisoned (Book Four)*

# Nonfiction

*Faithgirlz! Handbook*
*Faithgirlz Journal*
*Food, Faith, and Fun! Faithgirlz Cookbook*
*No Boys Allowed*
*What's a Girl to Do?*
*Girlz Rock*
*Chick Chat*
*Real Girls of the Bible*
*My Beautiful Daughter*
*Whatever!*

## Check out www.faithgirlz.com

the beauty of believing

# Sophie's
## Friendship Fiasco

**2 BOOKS IN 1**
Includes *Sophie's Friendship Fiasco*
and *Sophie and the New Girl*

## Nancy Rue

ZONDER**kidz**

ZONDERVAN.com/
AUTHORTRACKER
*follow your favorite authors*

*Dedicated to the original Corn Flake Girls*
*of Drexel Hill, Pennsylvania:*

Brittany, Stephanie M., Lorraine, Jenny, Allison, Sarah,
Julie, Stephanie R., Lauren, Lindsay, and Amanda.

ZONDERKIDZ

www.zonderkidz.com

*Sophie's Friendship Fiasco*
Copyright © 2009, 2013 by Nancy Rue

*Sophie and the New Girl*
Copyright © 2009 by Nancy Rue

This title is also available as a Zondervan ebook.
Visit www.zondervan.com/ebooks

Requests for information should be addressed to:
Zonderkidz, 5300 Patterson Ave. SE, Grand Rapids, Michigan 49530

ISBN 978-0310-73853-4

Published in association with the literary agency of Alive Communications, Inc., 7680 Goddard Street, Suite 200, Colorado Springs, CO 80920. www.alivecommunucations.com

Zonderkidz is a trademark of Zondervan.

*Interior art direction and design: Sarah Molegraaf*
*Cover illustrator: Steve James*

*Printed in the United States*

13 14 15 16 17 18 19 20 21 22 23 24 25 26 27 28 /DCI/ 22 21 20 19 18 17 16 15 14 13 12 11 10 9 8 7 6 5 4 3 2 1

*So we fix our eyes not on what is seen,*
*but on what is unseen.*
*For what is seen is temporary,*
*but what is unseen is eternal.*

—2 Corinthians 4:18

# Sophie's Friendship Fiasco

# One

Sophie LaCroix groaned out loud in the hallway of Great Marsh Middle School. "Can I just say I loathe PE class?" she said.

"Is *loathe* a Fiona word?" Kitty said as she linked her arm through Sophie's. She giggled, the way she did at the end of almost every sentence.

"What's it mean?" said Maggie, who hardly ever giggled.

Fiona pushed aside the stubborn strip of golden-brown hair that was always falling over one eye and continued to lead the way down the hall toward the PE locker room. "It means 'hate,'" she said.

"Only it sounds smarter," said Darbie, who had an Irish accent. She gave a firm nod, making her own reddish bangs dance on her forehead.

"I don't feel very smart in this class," Sophie said. "Coach Yates is always yelling at me—and every time I try to explain something to her, my voice comes out all squeaky."

The Corn Flakes grinned at each other.

"Your voice always comes out all squeaky," Maggie said in her that's-a-fact way.

"That's just you, Soph," Fiona said. "You're just you, and we're all just us."

Sophie managed a little bit of a smile. Just being them was what made them the Corn Flakes. *Other* people might think they were ditzy and flaky and say the things they did were corny. But the Corn Flakes knew better.

"Hey, Cue Ball!" somebody yelled. Sophie felt her smile snap away.

"Get Kitty into the locker room!" Darbie said.

Willoughby and Fiona unlatched Kitty from Sophie, and Maggie shoved the three of them through the door with Darbie on their heels, just as Sophie felt her quilted hat being plucked off her head. She grabbed at her glasses so they wouldn't go too.

"Catch, Eddie!" Colton Messik cried.

Sophie saw Eddie Wornom's belly bulge out from under his shirt as he jumped up and caught Sophie's hat. *Ewww*, she thought. Eddie hurled it at Tod Ravelli, whose face came to its usual point as he slam-dunked the hat into the trash can.

"Score!" Colton's grin seemed to spread from one stuck-out ear to the other. "Hey, Cue Ball," he said to Sophie. "You're bald!"

*Like you haven't told me that a bazillion times*, Sophie thought.

She waited until the boys had shoved each other into their locker room before she went calmly to the trash can and fished out her hat.

*At least they didn't get to Kitty*, she told herself as she pushed it down over her shaved head. *That's all that matters*. After all, she couldn't expect Fruit Loops like them to understand how a Corn Flake could part with all her hair to keep a sick friend from being the only girl in the whole school who was bald.

When Sophie got to her locker, the other Corn Flakes were almost changed into their PE clothes. Willoughby slung her arm around Sophie's shoulder and pressed their cheeks together, her almost-dark curls tickling Sophie's face. She was the only one of them who was short enough to do that—and even she was a few inches taller than tiny Sophie. "You're the best," she said in her bouncy voice.

"Trash can again?" Fiona said.

Sophie rolled her eyes.

Maggie shook her head at Kitty, so hard that her Cuban-dark hair splashed against her cheeks. "Boys are just lame."

There was a grunt from a few lockers down. Julia Cummings, the tall leader of the Corn Pops, tossed back her auburn hair.

"Someday you'll grow up and change your mind," Julia said.

She smirked at Anne-Stuart, one of her fellow "popular" girls, who gave the usual juicy sniff. She was pale and thin, and Sophie had never known her not to need a Kleenex.

"Grow up?" said B.J., the chubby-cheeked Corn Pop. "I don't *think* so."

A girl who had strawberry-blonde hair trailing down her back laughed—*way* loud—and looked at Julia like a puppy waiting for a treat. She was Cassandra Combs, the newest Corn Pop wannabe.

Sophie hoped the Pops would leave, but they just went back to putting on lip gloss. Sophie went into slow motion as she turned to the locker she and Kitty shared, dialing each number on the lock with precise care.

"You're gonna be late one of these days," Maggie said.

Willoughby went into the arm motions for a cheer. "Class won't be so bad today, Soph. All we're doing is running the track, and if you keep going Coach Yates won't yell at you."

"Coach Hates," Fiona put in.

Sophie kept her eyes away from them. "It takes me longer because I'm helping Kitty," she said.

Kitty peeled off her bright pink T-shirt, revealing the tiny "porthole" in her chest just above her bra. Kitty had leukemia, and the hole was where a tiny tube had been inserted so the doctors could give her the chemotherapy medicine—which hopefully would stop her disease—through the tube instead of having to give her shots. Sophie crowded in close until Kitty pulled on the white tee with GMMS—for Great Marsh Middle School—sprawled across the front in the red and blue school colors.

"Thanks, Sophie," Kitty whispered as she slipped off the quilted hat that matched Sophie's. Sophie replaced it at lightning speed with a red bandanna.

Only when Kitty's bald head was covered did Sophie step back. So far most of the Corn Pops hadn't seen the hole or gotten a close-up view of Kitty's head, and Sophie wanted to keep it that way. Even though chemotherapy had made all Kitty's hair fall out, Sophie and the Corn Flakes thought Kitty's naked head made her blue eyes seem bigger and bluer than ever and her tiny nose look even more like a piece of fine china.

But Sophie knew there would be no end to the Corn Pops' blurting out things like, "I wouldn't even come to school if I looked like that!"

Just as she always did, Sophie whipped off her own cap like a knight removing his armored helmet at the end of a tournament, revealing her peach-fuzzed head before she tied on her bandanna.

Kitty giggled. "You're so brave, Sophie."

"They can't hurt me," Sophie said. "Besides, it's only hair."

"Or lack of," Fiona said. She stood up from tying her tennis shoes. "You coming?"

"I'm not ready yet," Sophie said. "I was helping Ki—"

"You were foostering about, is what you were doing," Darbie said.

Maggie gave a matter-of-fact nod. "You're gonna get detention if you aren't there when Coach Yates blows her whistle."

"Your father will take your camera," Fiona put in, "and then we won't be able to make our next movie— "

"I'm *coming!*" Sophie snapped. All five pairs of eyes widened, and Sophie softened her voice. "You guys go ahead, okay?"

The Flakes left. So did the Pops, finally. Sophie could now get into her gym clothes without them seeing that, unlike every other seventh-grade girl on earth, she didn't even wear a bra yet. She still looked exactly the way she had in sixth grade. It didn't take much to imagine what the Corn Pops would do if they saw that.

Sophie put her PE shirt between her teeth, letting it hang in front of her while she unbuttoned her top. She would just have time to wriggle out of the blouse, yank the shirt over her head, and tear outside to get in line before roll check started.

Just as she parted her teeth and let go of the T-shirt, Sophie heard sneakers squeal to a stop on the floor a few feet away. Cassandra was staring at Sophie's bare chest, mouth open so her pale blue braces gleamed.

"Oh, my gosh!" she said. "I thought you were a boy!"

Somehow Sophie got her shirt pulled on and ran past Cassandra and out to her line just as Coach Yates was ending the long toot on her whistle. The coach, her too-tight, graying ponytail pinching her face, gave Sophie a look with a warning in it. Sophie was just glad she didn't yell. They'd found out the first day that this lady could bellow like an elephant. What really stunk was that they had her for PE *and* sixth period Life Skills. That was a lot of bellowing.

Coach Yates blasted out the order for them to run twice around the track, and Cassandra gathered the Corn Pops around herself. They took two steps and exploded into high-pitched shrieks and turned around to gawk at Sophie's chest. She was sure they were going to rush up to her and rip off her T-shirt just to check out Cassandra's story.

"Now what are they up to?" Darbie said at Sophie's elbow.

"Something heinous, guaranteed," Fiona said.

Sophie moaned inside. Fiona's favorite word for evil, *heinous*, was perfect for this situation.

"I know exactly what they're doing," Willoughby said. "Don't forget I was a Corn Pop before you guys saved me from them." She nodded wisely. "Cassie's trying to pass one of their tests for being accepted into the Corn Pops. She has to tell them something they can use for ammunition."

Sophie's stomach went into an immediate knot.

"What do you think it is?" Kitty said.

"What was yours when you got into the Corn Pops, Willoughby?" Sophie said quickly. The Corn Flakes shared everything, but this situation was way too embarrassing, even in front of her best friends on the planet. Her heart started to knot up too.

"You don't even want to know," Willoughby said.

"Let's get a move on, ladies—or you'll be doing three laps!"

They all broke into a run at the sound of the coach's roar, except for Kitty, who only had to walk as far as she could. Sophie peeked back at her over her shoulder. Kitty looked so small and puffy-faced and quivery all by herself. She and the rest of the Flakes had tried hanging back with her before, but Coach Hates had said a big-time NO to that.

"No Corn Pop better say an evil word to Kitty," Fiona said.

"We can't do anything evil back to them if they do," Maggie said.

"Our blasted code," Darbie said. "Sometimes it's a bit of a bother."

The Code was actually the thing Sophie loved most about the Corn Flakes. They had vowed never to put anybody down, even though people did it to them. The also vowed not to fight back or give in to bullies, and instead take back their power to be themselves. And they promised to talk to Jesus and obey God's Word, because God gave them the power to be who they were made to be. The Code made Sophie feel noble, like a maiden from medieval times who was as honorable as any knight of the Round Table—

*Her name was Aurora, and she was the leader of six young maidens. She had led them to the Code and they lived by it, vanquishing vixens and villains with sheer goodness.*

Willoughby gave Sophie a poke that brought her out of her dream world. She was pointing at the Corn Pops, who were a half lap behind them. They all had their heads leaning toward Cassandra, who still appeared to be enchanting them with her tale.

*There isn't THAT much to tell about one flat chest*, Sophie thought.

"I think Cassie passed her first test," Willoughby said.

"So what's her next one?" Fiona said.

"Now she has to do something about whatever she just told them."

Sophie swallowed hard.

"They're gonna get in trouble if they do anything to *us*," Maggie said. Sweat was making plastered-down sideburns in front of her ears. "After all the stuff they got caught for at the end of last year."

Fiona turned around to run backward so she could face them. "That was a whole different school though. The teachers here don't know about all that. The Pops are starting over with a clean slate."

"No fair," Maggie said. "We have to keep them from making fun of Kitty."

Sophie put a hand on her knotty side. They could protect their Kitty, she knew. But she wasn't sure how she was going to protect *herself* now that Cassie had seen—

But then she shook her head. *It doesn't matter*, she thought. *I won't LET it matter. They can't hurt me.* She tried to ignore the knot that was now twisting the *rest* of her insides like a whole bag of pretzels.

*I will hold up the Code like a Shield of Honor before me, Aurora vowed to herself. And I will turn my thoughts to another, more noble cause—which surely I will find, because I always do—*

"This probably sounds lame next to having leukemia," Willoughby said, "but I'm scared about cheerleading tryouts."

Sophie pulled her mind back to the Flakes. "Why?" she said. "You're good."

"We should know," Fiona said. "We've been watching you practice twenty-four/seven."

"You're *so* gonna make it," Sophie said.

Willoughby shook her head. "You know the Pops will try to make me mess up."

"Yeah," Maggie said from several steps behind them. She was now puffing like a train. "They hate you worse than any of us right now because you dumped them."

Willoughby pushed a bunch of curls up from her neck. "If one of you would try out with me, I wouldn't be so scared of what they might do."

"Not me," Maggie said.

"You don't want me either," Darbie said. "With my long legs, I'll make a bags of the whole thing."

Fiona was already shaking her head. "I'd end up getting right in their faces if they even looked at you wrong."

"Sophie?" Willoughby said. "What about you?"

A laugh gurgled up out of Sophie's throat. "Are you kidding me?"

"I need *somebody*." Willoughby's voice quivered. "I can't do it by myself, and I want this really, really bad—"

*Aurora drew in a breath, and with it came the courage she was so known for. I don't know the dance, she thought. But I must be at the side of my fellow maiden in her distress. Until she learns the power of the Code, I must stand by her—*

Fiona snapped her fingers in Sophie's face. "Where did you go, Soph?"

"You have a new character, don't you?" Darbie said.

Without even hesitating, Sophie said, "Aurora—medieval maiden."

"Our next Corn Flakes production!" Fiona said.

Maggie grunted behind them. "Don't say anything else. We don't have the Treasure Book with us to write stuff down."

"But what about the cheerleading tryouts?" Willoughby said.

Sophie smiled what she hoped was an Aurora smile. "I'm there for you," she said.

Willoughby shrieked in that way that always made Sophie think of a poodle yipping. She tried to hug Sophie while they were running. They both got an extra half a lap from Coach Hates.

At the end of class, Kitty was all proud that she'd walked a quarter of the way around *one* lap. The Flakes carried her into the locker room, yelling, "Kitty rocks!"

Sophie ran in ahead of them to clear a space on the bench so they could set Kitty's wobbly self down. Something caught her eye as she rounded the corner. On Sophie's locker door were two wads of cotton stuck on with duct tape, and above them was a piece of paper with a message scrawled across it: *Use these under your shirt until you get some real ones!*

Behind her the Flakes were rounding the corner. Sophie's hand flew up to yank it off, but the tape wouldn't let go.

"What is *that*?" Darbie said.

Sophie got the cotton balls and the paper down just as the Corn Pops also came around the corner. When they saw Sophie, they smothered their mouths with their hands. Cassie sidled up to her and spit through her braces, "I'll show you where to put them."

The other three Pops collapsed in a heap as Sophie's Flakes looked on, baffled. Only Cassie's narrow face was Corn Pop cool.

"I know where to put them," Sophie said. She stuck the taped side of both cotton balls under her nose like a mustache and turned to the Flakes.

"You look like Albert Einstein!" Fiona said. The rest of the Flakes cackled.

Behind them, the Pops laughed even harder, but Sophie pretended they weren't there. She just helped Kitty out of her shirt without anybody seeing her porthole, keeping the cotton balls stuffed under her nose the whole time. Kitty giggled until her cap was safely back on her head.

But Fiona held Sophie back on the way to fourth-period math. Her bow of a mouth was pulled into a small pink knot. "Are they teasing you about not having a bra that's padded out to here like they have?" She held her hands six inches from her chest.

"You knew?" Sophie said.

"Hello! I'm your best friend! So who saw? Cassie?"

Sophie nodded.

"Figures," Fiona said. "She tries to make herself look like Jennifer Lopez or somebody."

Sophie laughed. "We're not supposed to say evil stuff about them."

"Even if it's true?"

"That's the Code," Sophie said.

Fiona sighed. "I know," she said. Then she gave Sophie a sideways grin. "But you have to admit: you got them with the mustache."

Sophie grinned back. Yeah, she definitely had.

# TWO

But as soon as Fiona and Sophie went into Miss Imes' math room, all mirth—as Fiona called it—disappeared. Sophie dreaded this class almost as much as she did PE.

She had barely dropped into her seat when Miss Imes said, "Sophie."

She was standing over Sophie's desk. With her dark eyebrows shooting like arrows toward her short, almost-white hair, Miss Imes pointed to her head and mouthed, *Off.*

This was the only class where the teacher made Sophie stick to the no-hats-in-class school rule. Kitty was allowed to keep hers on in the fourth-period section because she had a medical reason. Miss Imes had told Sophie the first day that she didn't qualify for that. Slowly Sophie slid her cap off and put it in her lap.

"Hey, Cue Ball," Colton Messik whispered.

Sophie ignored him and adjusted her glasses as she stared, unseeing, at the board.

"If it weren't for your face, I wouldn't be able to tell the front of your head from the back."

*I can't WAIT to tell Fiona how hilarious he is,* Sophie thought, rolling her eyes.

"Yeah, it's pretty weird back here," Colton whispered on. "It's like your nose is missing. And your eyes. Dude, somebody stole your face!"

*I wish somebody would steal YOURS,* Sophie thought. This would be so much easier if Kitty were in their class, instead of her and Maggie and Willoughby being in another seventh-grade section for academics. Sophie always felt braver when she was showing Kitty how to handle these ignorant little children.

*Aurora slid her Sword of Vengeance back into its sheath and lowered her head. "Father," she whispered to God, "please forgive me for my evil thoughts." Aurora knew that revenge belonged to God alone. Her job was to protect her maidens by teaching them to live by the Code. A Code that came from the Father himself. With her eyes closed and her face turned up to the Light, she could feel his strength coming into her again—*

"Sophie LaCroix."

Sophie opened her eyes. Miss Imes was scowling down at her.

"Class," she said. Her voice was brisk and pointy like her eyebrows. "Your first test is this Friday, and I warn you, if you are not prepared, you will most definitely fail it. You came to me highly recommended, and I expect top work. So far, with the exception of Tod and Fiona, very few of you are giving me that. Am I clear?"

Sophie nodded. After all, Miss Imes might as well have just *said* she was talking right to her.

*I would LOVE to give you top work,* Sophie thought as she hunkered down over her paper. *But I've hardly understood a thing you've ever put up on the board. I'm lost!*

*Lost in a sea of numbers that even she, Aurora, could not navigate—*

Sophie felt something tickle the back of her head. She forced herself not to turn around.

*No wonder I'm having trouble concentrating in here*, she thought. *I wish I could sit next to Fiona. She'd help me focus.*

But Miss Imes had scoffed at that suggestion when they'd made it the first day. "I don't think much math would get done," she'd said. "And besides, Fiona is going to be working ahead of the class. She has an excellent mind for mathematics."

Sophie felt the tickle on the back of her head again, but she simply wrote down the next problem and stared at it. For at least three minutes. She could hear Fiona coughing, the way she always did when she saw that Sophie might be drifting off into dream world. But it wasn't that this time. Sophie just didn't get it.

And heaven knew what Colton was still brushing against her head. The thought of him touching her made her feel like things were crawling under her skin.

*Oh, gross—he isn't BLOWING on me, is he?* Sophie thought with horror.

She couldn't stop herself this time. She slid her hand across the back of her head and flicked it a few times, like she was shooing a fly. The room erupted.

Miss Imes glared over the top of her half-glasses. The classroom went as still as a morgue. When she looked down again, Sophie started to pick up her pencil. But there was something black on the palm of her hand. It was smeared with something. Like ink.

She whirled around in time to see Colton passing a black Sharpie over his shoulder to Anne-Stuart, who smothered a thick laugh. Colton had been writing on the back of her head with a *Sharpie*? What was now permanently engraved on her scalp for every hyena in middle school to go into hysterics over?

Sophie wasn't sure what she would have done if the bell hadn't rung at that exact moment. She clapped her hat onto her head and mowed down three people trying to get to the door. Miss Imes met her there.

"Your citizenship grade is falling, Sophie," she said. "You'd better get serious."

When Sophie got out into the hall, Fiona was leaning against the outside railing next to Darbie, holding a piece of paper with a smiley face on it.

"I can't smile!" Sophie said.

"No, *eejit*," Darbie said, pronouncing "idiot" in her Irish way. "That's what Colton drew on the back of your noggin!"

"Can you get it off?" Sophie said.

They scurried for the restroom, the minutes before the next bell ticking away. Fiona scrubbed Sophie's head with soap and a paper towel, until Darbie announced that it wasn't budging.

"We'll all be getting detention if we don't get to lunch," she said.

Sophie punched her cap back on and they ran for the cafeteria. Maggie, Willoughby, and Kitty were waiting, and before Sophie could even sit down, Darbie said, "The Loops are being eejits again." She pulled up the back of Sophie's hat just enough for the Flakes to take a peek.

Flake eyes bulged and hands came up to mouths. But all Sophie saw was Kitty, staring in horror.

"You don't think he'll try to do that to ME, do you?" she said.

"No way," Maggie said. "We'll protect you."

Sophie squeezed out a giggle that she hoped was convincing. "Colton is *so* not an artist," she said. "Is this lame or what?"

A slow smile broke across Darbie's face. "He made a bags of it, that's for sure."

Fiona nudged Kitty. "You draw way better than him."

Sophie felt an idea pop up like a spring. "Can you make it look better, Kitty?" she said. "Anybody have any Sharpies?"

"I do." Maggie dug into her backpack. "What colors do you want?"

Sandwiches were left uneaten as Kitty went to work on the back of Sophie's head, amid much coaching from the other Flakes.

"Bigger lips!" Willoughby said.

"More eyelashes, Kitty," Fiona told her. "And draw in glasses too."

When Kitty was finished, they declared it was good enough for a TV cartoon.

"I wish I could do it on myself!" Kitty said. She giggled.

Darbie drew her eyebrows together. "I just wish we could drop the Code for once and do something back to those black-guards," she said.

Darbie pronounced it "blaggards," which Sophie loved, but she shook her head.

"No way," Sophie said. "Then we're as heinous as they are. I'm never breaking the Code no matter what happens. Besides—" She shrugged. "This is all small stuff."

"You're so good, Sophie," Darbie said.

Sophie trailed Fiona and Darbie on the way to science, her mind spinning. It was cool that Darbie thought she was good. Still, she was really glad they were going to their girls' group Bible study after school. She needed a good boost.

Mr. Stires, their science teacher, was at the door, cheerfully greeting them with his shiny bald head and his toothbrush mustache. As soon as Sophie was past him, she felt something tug at her backpack, and suddenly all her books were pouring out of it onto the floor. She leaned over to pick them up, and her hat fell too.

"Dude!" said Colton Messik from behind her. She felt him poke at the back of her head. "I didn't do *that* face!"

"Lemme see." Tod stepped on Sophie's science book to get behind her.

Sophie turned her head to give Tod a full view and then looked back at him. Everything came to a point at his nose, until he started to laugh.

"No, man," he said to Colton, "you can't draw that good. That is cool!"

"Shut up!" Colton said. He punched Tod in the side with his fist. "It's not funny!"

"Yeah, it is. Hey, Julia, check it out!"

Anne-Stuart arrived behind Sophie with Julia, and Sophie ducked her head forward so she wouldn't get nose gunk all over her when Anne-Stuart snuffled.

"That's cuter than your real face," Julia said to Sophie with an actual giggle.

"I know," Sophie said. "I'm thinking of having it done the same way." She grinned. "But I'm not going to let Colton do it."

By now the entire class was crowded around Sophie's head. Right in front were Darbie and Fiona, who were giving her thumbs-ups and jerking their heads toward the Loops and Pops. Sophie had to agree that their usual enemies were looking impressed.

Except for Colton, who gave Tod a shove. "It's lame, man—it's stupid."

Tod, Julia, and Anne-Stuart stared at him, and Sophie watched the realization spring into their eyes one by one: they had forgotten they were supposed to think everything Sophie and her friends did was dumb.

"That is, like, such an immature thing to do," Julia said, tossing her mane.

"But it's so Sophie," Anne-Stuart said.

Tod pointed his finger at Sophie and gave a hard laugh. "Lame again," he said.

*Aurora pushed away the inner knot that strained against her brocade gown. I have nobler causes, she reminded herself. I must protect the sickly Katrina, and the happy Willow, who so much wants to dance. The words of vixens and villains cannot hurt me.*

Sophie felt a smile, the kind Fiona always described as wispy, spread across her face. *The Code of the Medieval Maidens* was going to be such a great film.

The minute the Corn Flakes got to the Bible study room at church after school, Fiona made Sophie take off her hat so Dr. Peter could see her decorated scalp. His eyes twinkled behind his glasses, which he pushed up by wrinkling his nose.

"That's a hoot!" he said. He ran his hand over the back of his head. "The barber cut mine so short this time, I could have one of those done too."

"You can't do it," Maggie said, her voice Maggie-factual. "You're a grown-up."

He grinned at her. "Don't spread that around," he said.

He lowered himself into a beanbag chair like the ones all the girls were sitting in—Gill and her friend Harley, who were two of the very-cool athletic girls the Corn Flakes called Wheaties, plus Fiona, Maggie, Willoughby, Darbie, and Sophie. Kitty wasn't with them. She was too tired at the end of the school day to do anything except take a nap.

But Kitty's pink beanbag was there beside Sophie's purple one, as empty as the Kitty-place inside Sophie. She always tried to make sure Kitty got to Bible study. When she had first found out she had leukemia, Kitty had been afraid she would die and not go to heaven. Sophie and Dr. Peter had been helping her get to know Jesus so she wouldn't be afraid of that anymore. Dr. Peter even went to Kitty's house and taught her the lessons when she couldn't be in class. Still, Sophie wanted her there, right beside her, so she could be sure Kitty was getting it—

"All right, ladies," Dr. Peter said. "Open up your Bibles to Luke 22:31–34."

Sophie picked up the Bible with the purple cover. All their Bible covers matched their beanbags—that's how amazing Dr. Peter was. She was totally ready to put herself right into the story they were about to read, which was the way Dr. Peter taught them. With any luck, it would help her with the Corn Pop/Fruit Loop situation, not to mention Miss Imes and Coach Yates—

"Now," Dr. Peter said, "we're at the end of Jesus' time with his disciples, and they're having their last supper together. Let's try to imagine—"

Sophie didn't even have to hear the rest of the instructions. Dr. Peter had been her special therapist for all of sixth grade, and he had taught her how to put herself in the Bible stories to help with all the heinous things she'd had to deal with back then. Now that he was their Bible-study teacher, she got to work on it even more.

Sophie closed her eyes and decided to be Simon Peter himself. It wasn't even that hard to pretend she was a boy anymore.

Something poked at Sophie's insides. *"I thought you were a boy!"* Cassie New Pop had said. *"Use these until you get some real ones."*

"Everybody ready?" Dr. Peter said.

Sophie replaced the Cassie thoughts with an image of herself, sitting on the floor near Jesus.

*Jesus is so easy to listen to,* Sophie/Simon thought. *Not only is everything he says like warm bread in my mouth, but his eyes—his eyes are always so kind, even when they're stern. Sophie/Simon could never get enough of the way Jesus looked at her—as if no matter how much she messed up, he would help her be better—*

"Jesus has told them that one of them is going to turn him over to the people who want to kill him," Dr. Peter said. His voice sounded far away. "And that has shaken everybody up pretty good."

*"I would never do that!"* Sophie/Simon shouted to herself.

"And now Jesus is going to tell Simon Peter that Satan will test the disciples, especially him."

Dr. Peter began to read. Sophie kept her eyes shut tight and her mind wrapped around Simon Peter, his bread still in his hand as he listened—

"'Simon, Simon,'" Dr. Peter read, "'Satan has asked to sift you as wheat. But I have prayed for you, Simon, that your faith may not fail. And when you have turned back, strengthen your brothers.'"

*Sophie/Simon felt her neck go stiff, and she dropped the bread onto the plate.*

"'Lord, I am ready to go with you to prison and to death,'" Dr. Peter read.

*Sophie/Simon's heart was beating hard as Jesus turned to her.*

"'I tell you, Peter, before the rooster crows today, you will deny three times that you know me.'"

*Sophie/Simon shook her head, over and over, even as Jesus looked into her with his kind eyes.*

"You're kidding, right?" Fiona said.

Gill raised her hand. "There's no way he said he didn't know Jesus. Couldn't happen."

"You're going to find out in your homework reading," Dr. Peter said. "But let's talk about this some. Do any of you think you would deny you knew Jesus?"

"How about NO!" Sophie said. The rest of the girls shook their heads.

Dr. Peter sat forward in his beanbag. "You're right. You don't deny him—but all of us mess up on letting him be as important in our lives as we should."

."Mess up how?" Fiona said.

"Sometimes we get too busy to pray," Dr. Peter said.

Sophie knew she was okay there. Every night she imagined Jesus, the way Dr. Peter had taught her to, and talked to him. Sometimes she even did it during the day.

"Not reading the Bible is another one."

"We're good on that one," Willoughby said. "We're here!" Sophie thought she was going to break into a cheer.

"Okay, here's another one. When we worry and try to fix everything on our own, we're denying that God can help us and that he wants to help us."

There were head shakes and head bobs. Sophie scratched under her nose. *I really don't worry that much*, she thought. *God gave us our Code and we follow it, so we're really okay—except in PE—and math—*

There was a thinking silence.

"Just think about it and watch for it," Dr. Peter said. His eyes twinkled. "Nobody has to confess right now."

Fiona grinned at him. "That's good, because I could be here for days!"

*Amid the laughter, Aurora stroked her Shield of Truth. Was it really so amusing, she wondered, to think of one's denials of the*

*Code? She sighed from the depths of her golden soul. There was much to teach the maidens. But leading them into Truth would be the noblest thing she had ever done. Even though she didn't know where to start, she knew God would show her how. Hadn't she already been guided to dance beside the maiden Willow so she wouldn't have to dance alone? Hadn't she already stood up to the villains and vixens for the maiden Katrina, all with the Spirit of Mirth? What was there she could not do as long as she stayed with the Code—which she most certainly would?*

"You going to sit here all day like Miss Muffet on her tuffet?"

Sophie blinked up at her own reflection in Dr. Peter's glasses. The room was empty, and the Flakes' voices were fading down the hall.

"Not Miss Muffet," Sophie said. "The medieval maiden Aurora."

Dr. Peter broke into a grin. "Are you working on a new film?"

"It's not just a film. I think it's going to teach the rest of the Flakes how important it is to stick to our Code—you know the one."

Dr. Peter nodded. In the last year, Sophie had told him all about everything Corn Flake.

"I can't wait to see how it turns out," Dr. Peter said. He squatted down beside her. "Just be sure you're giving Jesus equal imagination time. Especially if you feel like you're escaping into the maiden Aurora when you shouldn't be."

"I'm not," Sophie said. "I'm getting all my assignments done—well, except math, but I'm gonna try harder—and I'm getting along with Daddy and Lacie and everything."

He stood up, nodding, and Sophie scrambled out of the beanbag. "Just one more thing," he said. "Be sure you do the assignment for this class as soon as you can, okay? Because, Sophie-Lophie-Loodle, I think you just might be put to the test."

"Okay," Sophie said.

But on the way out of the room, she chewed on her lower lip. What assignment was he talking about?

# Three

Sophie was going to ask Fiona about the Bible study homework during first period the next day when they got to their combined English/History class. But Ms. Hess, one of their two team teachers, was writing on the board in handwriting as bubbly as her voice:

*Essay Assignment: YOUR Code of Honor*

All other thoughts left Sophie's head. *I could write that essay in my sleep!* she thought.

As soon as the bell rang, Colton Messik stopped trying to nudge Sophie's tweed newsboy cap off with his pencil and said, "What's a Code of Honor?"

*You wouldn't know one if it bit your head off*, Sophie thought. For Pete's sake — they had only been studying the legends and the history of medieval times for three weeks. She had wondered more than once how Colton had ever gotten into this special honors block in the first place.

Ms. Hess' dimples appeared like two finger pokes in whipped cream. "Just to refresh your memory," she said, "King Arthur wrote one for his Knights of the Round Table so they would realize, for one thing, that might didn't make right. What else was in the Code, class?"

As usual, she was pronouncing her words very clearly, as if her lips were made of rubber. Their other team teacher, Mrs. Clayton, barely moved *her* mouth at *all* when she talked. It was as if the words were coming out of her long narrow nose with its horn-flare nostrils.

"Let's hear it," she trumpeted out.

Julia raised her hand. "Do what you ought to in spite of your fear?" she said. She cocked her head, letting one side of her thick tresses slide over a green eye. That, Sophie knew, wasn't for the teacher's benefit. It was for Tod Ravelli's. He and Julia were "going out"—although Sophie could never figure out exactly where they were "going." They were both twelve.

"Good job, Julia," Ms. Hess said.

Sophie looked quickly to see if she was talking about Julia's answer or her flirting techniques.

"What else?" Mrs. Clayton said. "Educate Colton."

*No problem!* Sophie thought. She shot her hand up. "Work for justice rather than power. Your word—"

"*—is your most valuable possession!*" Aurora cried out. She held up her shield. "*Never take advantage of weakness but rescue the innocent—*"

Sophie could hear somebody coughing, and she looked over at Fiona. She was hacking herself blue and pointing at Sophie's literature book—which she was holding in front of her in a shield-like fashion. She lowered it and hoped her face wasn't turning as red as it felt.

Mrs. Clayton gave Sophie a long look before she said, "Good," and turned to the class. "Now, in this essay we want you to describe the Code of Honor that you live by. We also want you to include the things that make it hard for you to stay true to those principles."

"What if I don't have any principles?" Tod said without raising his hand. His brown spiky hair always stuck up farther than anything else on his short self anyway.

"You just make it up as you go along, huh, Tod?" Ms. Hess said.

The dimples appeared again. Between those, and the fact that Ms. Hess wore about a size 2 and had her ash-blonde hair flipping up from a crooked part, it was hard to tell her from the eighth graders.

"Works for me" Tod said. Then he leaned way across Darbie so he could high-five Colton.

"Tell us all about it in your paper," Mrs. Clayton said to Tod. She didn't bubble and dimple like Ms. Hess. She had blonde cemented hair and blue eyes like bullets. But she did twitch a smile at him. What, Sophie wondered, did teachers see in that kid?

"Let's get started," Mrs. Clayton said.

"How long can we make it?" Anne-Stuart said.

"Would you like it typed on the computer?" Julia said.

"Longhand is fine, and no more than two pages. You two are such perfectionists!" Ms. Hess shook her head at Mrs. Clayton, so that her zebra earrings wiggled back and forth.

*There they go with the I'm-such-a-perfect-student routine again*, Sophie thought.

She and the Corn Flakes had already figured out what that was about. Ms. Hess was the cheerleading adviser, so she would be one of the judges at the tryouts. The Pops weren't going to take any chances of her finding out what they were *really* like.

Sophie looked at her paper and scratched under her nose with her gel pen. It was going to be easy to write what her Code of Honor was. But when it came to the things that got in the way of living the Code, it was going to mean telling how heinous the Corn Pops and Fruit Loops had been to them.

Wasn't that breaking the first rule of the Code: don't put other people down?

She closed her eyes and let Aurora come into view. She was bound to have some answers …

Sophie's dad brought home dinner in two steaming boxes from Anna's Pizza that night.

"You kids are wearing your mother out," Daddy said. He deposited the boxes on the big square coffee table in the family room and nodded toward Mama, who was curled up on the couch. "She's too tired to cook."

Six-year-old Zeke let out a first-grader-style yelp and dove for the cheese and pepperoni. But Sophie and her older sister, Lacie, looked at each other with puzzled eyes.

*Mama was too tired to cook?* Sophie thought. *Mama cooks when she's been up all night with one of us that's barfing!*

"Okay, what's wrong?" Lacie said.

"She's taking the night off," Daddy said. He directed his dark blue eyes at Lacie. "Give your mother a piece."

"Uh, no," Mama said. She lifted one side of her upper lip. "Just some crust."

*Oh,* Sophie thought. *SHE's the one who was barfing all night.*

Come to think of it, Mama's face was pretty much as pale as her highlighted curls. And she didn't look so much wispy — the way people said she and Sophie both did — as she did puny. Yeah, that was the stomach flu all right.

Lacie and Zeke, on the other hand, both had dark hair and deep blue eyes like Daddy, and they were big-boned the way he was. Daddy had even started wearing his hair like Zeke's, stuck out in short, every-which-way spikes.

*Daddy's the one that needs a hat*, Sophie thought. While she reached for a piece of pizza, she automatically put her hand up to keep her cap from sliding off. It wasn't there.

She had forgotten to put it back on when she came downstairs. Oops. Mama and Daddy hadn't seen her other face yesterday. She'd kind of been hoping it would just wear off before they did.

"Hey—cooool!" Zeke poked a pizza-greasy finger at Sophie's scalp. "I want that on my head!"

"Do I want to know what he's talking about?" Daddy said.

Lacie turned Sophie around and let out a husky laugh. "No, you don't," she said.

Daddy took Sophie's head in his hands. She could feel his eyes boring into Kitty's drawing.

*Please, God, make him think it's funny!* Sophie thought.

"I think it's gonna make the Corn Pops and them stop teasing Kitty," Sophie said. "You know—we're showing them that they're not getting to us."

"That game plan could backfire," Daddy said. He was going into sports talk. Not a good sign.

He and Mama looked at each other and had a parent conversation without saying a word. Not a good sign either.

"What about your teachers?" Mama said. She was sitting up farther on the couch. *Definitely* not a good sign.

"None of my teachers have even noticed," Sophie said. "They all let me wear my hat except Miss Imes."

Lacie coughed.

"What?" Daddy said to her.

"Nothing. Choked on a pepperoni."

Daddy scratched his head. "We just don't want you creating a distraction in the classroom, Soph. We're all for you standing up for Kitty and making this easier for her, but you need to play your own zone too. You see what I'm saying?"

Sophie didn't, but she'd get Lacie to explain it later. She was athletic. She got the sports-talk thing.

"I'll make sure I'm not a distraction," Sophie said.

"You know you lose the video camera if you get into any trouble—" Daddy said.

"Ugh."

They all looked at Mama, who was closing the lids on the pizza boxes. "Would everybody mind taking their pizza to their rooms to eat? I just can't stand the smell right now."

Sophie was more than happy to grab a piece and escape to her bedroom and end *that* conversation.

Besides, she had to write her paper for Ms. Hess and Mrs. Clayton. If she was going to be such a loser in math, she had to make up for it in English, or her video camera was going to wind up in Daddy's closet.

As long as she didn't make worse than a B in any subject or get into trouble, she was allowed to use her video camera for Corn Flake Productions. If she messed that up, the camera was history for a while. She had never lost it yet in a whole year. Well, except for that one time . . .

Sophie ate the pepperoni off the pizza and propped herself against a pile of pillows on her pink bedspread. With her notebook on her lap and the gauzy bed curtains cozying her into her own world, Sophie knew just how to get around putting down the Pops and Flakes in her paper. All other thoughts faded with the mist that hung over Camelot.

*With her pen dipping in and out of the ink like a bird at a feeder, Aurora wrote lavishly of her beloved Code, the words streaming across the page, trying to keep up with her thoughts.*

*And then she grew troubled. Sir Peter had seemed to doubt her that day, talking about a test she would face. Didn't he realize that she had mastered all that he had taught her?*

*Aurora set down her pen and went to her window, winding herself up in the veil of curtains that muted the moonlight. He will see, she thought, that I—and all of my maidens—are ready to stand up to any test that is put before us.*

"You are totally going to pull those down one of these days."

Sophie peeked out of the curtains to see Lacie sprawling across her bed. Sophie unwound herself, frowning.

"I'm doing my homework," she said as she joined Lacie among the pillows.

"I get it," Lacie said dryly. "Look. Let me give you some advice about Miss Imes."

"I heard you choking when I said her name," Sophie said. "Do you think she'll give me a detention if she sees my head?"

"Nah. Show me in the school handbook where it says that's against the rules. But—"

"I hate 'buts,'" Sophie said.

"If she sees it, she's going to think it's a distraction too. Just keep a low profile."

"How do I do that?"

"Do all your work. Don't pass notes or talk. Ace all your tests. Piece of cake."

*Maybe for you*, Sophie thought. Just as it was occurring to her that—du-uh—maybe Lacie could actually help her with math, Lacie said, "Same goes for Coach Yates."

"Coach Hates," Sophie said.

Lacie grinned as she went for the door. "You got it," she said.

Sophie smiled to herself when she finished her paper, with a pen-flourish, and turned out the light.

As soon as she took off her glasses and snuggled under the covers and closed her eyes, there was Jesus in her mind. She could just "see" him looking at her with his kind eyes, and she knew she could ask him anything she wanted to.

"Jesus?" she whispered. "Thanks for giving us the Code and for giving me so many friends who believe in it—and in you, of course. And could you just help me with whatever test Dr. Peter thinks I'm gonna get? Especially if it's a math test. They're the worst. And getting dressed for PE. I need help there."

She let out a long Sophie-to-Jesus sigh and waited. If she let her imagination give her an answer, it would be, *Sure, Sophie—next test, A—guaranteed. And when you wake up tomorrow, you'll have breasts like everybody else.*

But Dr. Peter had also taught her that she shouldn't put words into Jesus' mouth, because they would just be what she *wanted* him to say. Jesus always answered somehow if she just listened and paid attention. He was always nudging her forward to do something she didn't think she could manage alone. With Jesus there, she really wasn't doing it by herself.

She wriggled down farther under the covers. *As long as I follow the Code, I'm okay,* she thought sleepily. *And I always, always will.*

# Four

The next day, when all the Code of Honor papers had been turned in, Mrs. Clayton told them to turn to page sixty-four in their literature books and read.

"This is the place in the legend," she blared out, "where he discovers that something vital to the success of his Round Table has completely been forgotten."

Sophie dug hungrily in her backpack for her book. There was bound to be more good stuff in the Arthur legend for the Corn Flakes to use in their film. *We need to get started*, she thought.

When Sophie sat back up, book in hand, her pen was on the floor, and Colton's foot was suspiciously close to it. Sophie held on to her pink-and-black-plaid hat with one hand and bent to retrieve the pen with the other. Colton gave it another nudge with his toe, pushing it out of reach. When Sophie let go of her hat so she could hold on to her desk with one hand and snatch up the pen with the other, *of course* Colton snatched her cap.

There were a few snickers close by. As Sophie turned around to get the hat back, she caught Fiona's look. There was a devilish gleam in her eyes as she held up her notebook, where she'd scrawled *Repeat yesterday*.

Sophie shifted her gaze to Colton, who was twirling her hat on his finger. Make a joke out of it? Was that what Fiona meant?

"You know what, Colton?" Sophie said out loud. "You really ought to get some new material." She grinned at him. "I'm over the knock-the-hat-off thing."

He watched her lips as she spoke, and Sophie noticed his ears sticking out on the sides of his head in that way Anne-Stuart always said was "SO cute!" *Ewww*. Sophie lifted the hat from his finger and perched it on her head.

"If you really want to wear it, you can," she said, "but I don't think it's your color."

The class roared, and Sophie turned back around, fixing her most innocent gaze on Mrs. Clayton, who was turning from the board to face them.

"All right," the teacher trumpeted out of her nose, "this is not Comedy Central. Get to work, people."

Ms. Hess was nodding. Even the pumpkin faces dangling from her earrings looked disapproving. When they turned to each other to exchange teacher glances, Colton hissed, "Real funny, Cue Ball. You're killin' me."

Sophie didn't answer. She was too busy watching Julia and Anne-Stuart give each other stunned glances. Sophie smiled smugly at Fiona.

When the bell rang at the end of their two-hour block, both Fiona and Darbie hurried over to Sophie, faces shining.

"That was *class*, Sophie!" Darbie said.

"Come on," Fiona said. She dragged Sophie toward the door. "I can't wait to tell Maggie and them."

"I wish we coulda been there!" Willoughby said when they were jogging around the track, minus Kitty. She gave one of her like-a-poodle laughs that sounded as if she had been there. The usual cartwheel came next.

"I have a question though," Maggie said. She had to talk between huffs. "Is it against the Corn Flake Code to make people laugh at those guys?"

"I don't see how," Fiona said. "We're not supposed to give them back what they give us, but since when were they ever as funny as we are?"

Darbie snorted. "If they tried, they'd make a bags of it for sure."

"We're not supposed to hurt people's feelings," Maggie said.

"Who says we're hurting their feelings?" Fiona said.

"They don't have feelings!" Willoughby said.

Darbie elbowed Sophie as they started the second lap. "Are you slagging them to hurt their feelings?"

"No," Sophie said. "Honest."

"Then why are you doing it?" Maggie said.

By now she had slowed to a walk and was several steps behind. They all slowed with her.

"I'm doing it," Sophie said, "so that maybe they'll see they aren't getting to us and they'll stop. It's to protect us." Sophie glanced over her shoulder at the lone figure three rows up on the bleachers whose back was curved like a lost puppy's.

"Oh," Darbie said. She looked at Kitty too. "It's decided then: funny comebacks—"

"They're called 'retorts,'" Fiona put in.

"—are not against the Corn Flake Code, as long as they don't hurt people and they're used only for our protection." Darbie ended with a definite nod.

"Yes!" Willoughby said.

They high-fived and broke into a run so they could get done and tell Kitty. Maybe at last, Sophie thought, this *was* a way to teach the Corn Pops. A way that was Code-worthy.

So, armed with Aurora's Spirit of Mirth, Sophie plunged fearlessly into territory she would have run cowering from before.

When chubby Fruit Loop Eddie Wornom lunged for Kitty's hat in the hall, Sophie told him he was three yards short of a touchdown. Sometimes it paid to have a sports freak for a father. Everyone laughed. Except Eddie.

When Colton pretended to throw up on their table in the cafeteria and left a rubber thing that looked like he really *had* upchucked, Sophie picked it up and said, "Uh, Colton? You left your lunch here. Did you make it yourself?"

And when Tod tried to imitate Darbie's accent during the lab experiment in fifth-period science class, Sophie asked him—oh so politely—if he had an impediment stuck in his throat. She loved it when he had to ask Julia what an "impediment" was. Julia didn't know either, which gave Fiona a chance to instruct them. Tod wasn't amused.

Once Sophie was on a roll, the rest of the Flakes joined in.

Darbie could be hilarious with her Irish slang, and Fiona's vocabulary seemed to strike most people as funny. Willoughby had a sense of the silly that cracked kids up, especially when she practically did a cartwheel after everything she said.

Kitty usually giggled so much she didn't have a chance to chime in. Maggie never did get the hang of it, so she just got the Corn Flakes Treasure Book that Fiona always kept and wrote everything down in there, in case they ever wanted to use any of it in a film.

But one of the best scenes happened without the Corn Flakes even planning it.

"I'm going to look like a moron at these tryouts today," Sophie said on Thursday during sixth period.

"I've seen you cheer, Soph," Fiona said. "I think you're right."

"So what are you going to do, Sophie?" Darbie said.

Sophie felt a slow grin easing onto her face. "The same thing we've *been* doing," she said.

So after school, with most of the seventh graders watching from the bleachers in the gym, Sophie cheered the cheer Willoughby had tried to teach her, only with her arms flapping and her legs tangling up. The goofy grin (Fiona said later) made Ronald McDonald look depressed. Sophie's final cartwheel and splits landed her upside down, glasses and toboggan hat sailing off, feet kicking in the air—but she was still yelling, "GO! FIGHT! WIN!" She got a standing ovation.

But even better than *that* was what Sophie hadn't expected. B.J. was called up next, and she was laughing so hard, she had to start over twice. Anne-Stuart's laughter put her into bronchial spasms, and she had to wait until last to go. Cassie kept it together until her final cartwheel, when she careened into the judges. The whole crowd howled because they thought she'd done it on purpose, just to outdo Sophie. It was obvious from the way Julia was twitching her pom-pom back and forth like a cat's tail that she was not pleased with any of them.

Only seven people made the squad. Cassie wasn't one of them. The rest of the Corn Pops made it, and so did Willoughby and three girls who had come to GMMS from different elementary schools. Willoughby told Sophie later that Ms. Hess said a few judges actually voted for Sophie, but that she had said she wasn't having Bozo the Clown on her squad.

Sophie didn't care about that because Kitty was still laughing—like she hadn't laughed in a long time.

*Yes!* Sophie thought. *I think I'm passing the test.*

"I actually think the Fruit Loops are starting to lay off us," Fiona said to Sophie before first period Friday morning. "We have them quaking in their Nikes."

In class, Ms. Hess told them to look up the definitions for next week's vocabulary words and write a sample sentence for each one.

"And you don't need to try to be funny," she said, American flags standing at attention on her earlobes.

"Aw, man!" Colton said.

But Sophie was sure from the way Ms. Hess moved her rubbery mouth in her direction that she was talking about her. Looking as studious as she could, Sophie wrote down the first word—*Virile: characteristic of an adult male; manly; masculine.*

*I wonder what the female word is?* Sophie thought.

*Aurora looked at herself in the mirror, gazing at her finely toned muscles, studying the strength of her jaw. She was all woman, from her intelligent forehead to the chest that breathed only good. But as she slowly smiled at herself, she knew she would never wreak vengeance on the villains and vixens by making them quake. It would be purely through the Spirit of Mirth, the Shield of Truth, the Strength of the Code—*

*Aurora laughed her soft laugh. Her power was in being a maiden of the Code. The six maidens were strong. "But girls are girls," she said to the mist. "They are not merely soft boys—"*

"I know that; thanks," said Colton behind her.

There was a hard chuckle from another corner. "You know it now that she *told* you!" Tod said.

"Shut UP!" Colton said.

"You would know that," Anne-Stuart whispered to Sophie, "Little Boy LaCroix."

"Enough!" Mrs. Clayton blared.

Sophie looked away and pretended to be intent on the next vocabulary word. Inside, she was stinging.

*If they can't hurt me,* she thought, *how come I feel like a swarm of bees just attacked me?*

She blinked at the word list. *Chivalry* came next.

*A code of honorable behavior,* she wrote.

Just like the Corn Flake Code.

*Take back the power to be yourself.*

*Yes,* she told herself. *Just laugh it off.*

At the end of the period Colton unzipped her back-pack—again—so that everything fell out of it when she picked it up.

"I told you," she said to him as he walked backward out of the room, smirking at her, "you need some new material."

She waved the Flakes on and collected her books. It actually didn't bother her that much. If she timed it just right, she would be slipping into the locker room just as everybody else was leaving. She could still make it out to the line before Coach Hates blew that evil whistle. She wasn't sure she could laugh that off yet.

The only problem was that she wouldn't be there to help Kitty with her bandanna. One of the other Flakes could do it, but Sophie liked to make sure.

*Okay, stop it,* Sophie told herself as she double-timed it toward the locker room door. Which was really worse: her getting teased because she didn't need a bra, or Kitty getting a hard time because of her leukemia? *Well, duh,* Sophie thought.

She broke into a half-run, only to skid to a stop in front of the locker room. There was a computer-printed sign on the door that read:

```
The boys' showers are not working.
The locker rooms have been switched for
today.
All girls go to the boys' locker room.
```

*That makes sense,* Sophie thought as she headed for the other room. The girls hardly ever took showers in PE, but if the boys didn't—*Ewww.* Sophie pulled open the door of the boys' locker room and stepped inside. It was quiet, and it smelled like gross dirty socks and boy sweat, which burned a person's nose way more than girl sweat.

"Hello?" she said.

Her voice echoed back to her in its high-pitched-ness. Everybody must already be out on the field, and she was later than she thought.

Sophie hitched her backpack up some more and hurried around a tiled wall. Six feet from her, a boy was just pulling his shirt down over his hairy armpits.

Before she could turn and flee, a man even bigger than Daddy was blocking her, and from every side it seemed.

He had a shaved head and an eyebrow that went all the way across his forehead. His picture, she thought, must be next to the word *virile* in the dictionary. Only when Sophie spotted the whistle hanging from his neck did she realize he was one of the boys' coaches. She didn't know his name.

"Where do you think you're going?" he said.

Sophie nearly choked. His voice was almost as high-pitched as hers was. It didn't sound like it should be coming out of his barrel chest.

"You think it's funny, walking into the boys' locker room?" he said.

A giggle inched upward with every word he said. Sophie slapped her hand over her mouth.

Coach Virile narrowed his eyes into two pencil points. "What were you planning to do in here?"

Sophie sucked back the giggle. "Um, get dressed for PE," she said.

She tried to make her voice deeper, but she could see it didn't work. His eyes went from pencils to pins.

"If you're mocking me, you've got some hard time coming," he said.

"I'm not mocking you, honest!" Sophie said. "That's just the way I talk!"

*Ewww.* Even worse.

Sophie jerked her thumb toward the door. "The sign on the girls' locker room said we were changing in here today."

He *glowered*—a Fiona-word that was made for the way his one eyebrow hooded his eyes. He went out the door and down the few steps to the next door, with Sophie close behind. He ripped off the sign with two fingers.

"You actually thought this was for real?" he said in his soprano-like voice.

"I guess I did," Sophie said. "Silly me, huh?"

Sophie wanted to bite back the words as soon as they were out of her mouth. Coach Virile's sense of humor was obviously not as big as he was.

"Funny how nobody else took the bait," he said. "Who's your teacher?"

"Coach Hates—um—Yates!"

The eyebrow lowered. "You just don't know when to quit, do you? Get on to class—I'll be talking to Coach Yates."

*I'm toast,* Sophie thought as she dragged herself into the *right* locker room. The place was empty, and she knew that Coach Yates had long since called the roll by now. With visions of detention lurking in her mind, Sophie pulled open her locker. A piece of paper floated out:

Little Boy LaCroix,

In the future, please change in the Boys' Locker Room — where you BELONG!

*I TRIED to change in there,* she wanted to say to the Pops. *Thanks to you.*

# Five

When Sophie got to the field, Coach Virile and Coach Yates were standing together. They bored their eyes into her at the same time.

"You got it handled?" Coach Virile said to Coach Yates.

Coach Yates nodded as Coach Virile jogged off to the boys' field, making the earth quake as he went.

"Somebody put a sign up, huh?" Coach Yates yelled.

Sophie knew putting her hands over her ears would *not* be a good idea. She nodded.

Coach Yates shifted her voice up to the next yell-level. "Admit it, LaCroix: you did it yourself. You're the little class clown—making a joke out of the cheerleading tryouts, getting the back of your head painted."

*How does she know about all that?* Sophie thought.

"I think you need a little attitude check." Coach Yates ran her eyes down her clipboard, face pinched by the ponytail as always. "Detention," she said. "After school—Wednesday. Be here."

She made a huge *T* next to Sophie's name. "It's not looking good for your citizenship grade," she said. "So I'd start adjusting before Wednesday. Four laps. Right now."

Sophie mumbled a "Sorry" and headed for the track. The other Flakes were finished running, and Sophie felt alone without them.

*And I'm going to be even MORE alone when Daddy takes my camera and we can't make our medieval film—plus, I'll probably get grounded for LIFE.*

But even that wasn't the worst.

When she got to math class, Miss Imes had written on the board: TODAY IS FRIDAY. YOU KNOW WHAT THAT MEANS.

"No!" Sophie said out loud. "Not the test!"

"Yes, the test!" Anne-Stuart said, in a voice that sounded like a stuffy-nosed version of Sophie's.

"Wait a minute though." Julia was cocking her head at Anne-Stuart. "Don't boys *like* math?"

Then they both turned to Sophie, barely hiding their smirks.

When Miss Imes passed out the tests and Sophie looked at hers, her heart took a dive for her knees. There wasn't a problem on there she knew how to do, and she'd totally forgotten to ask Lacie for help. There was only one thing to do.

*Dear Miss Imes,* Sophie wrote at the bottom of the test paper. *Something very strange has occurred, because I don't know how to do any of these problems. Maybe the math part of my brain got erased and it's been replaced by a more creative force. Or maybe I'm just dumb. I think I need help.*

When everybody passed their papers up, Sophie put hers on the bottom of the stack.

"All right, class," Miss Imes said, "I'm going to pass these out again, and we're going to grade them together. Please let me know if you get your own paper."

*Dear Lord,* Sophie thought, *PLEASE let Fiona or Darbie or one of the Wheaties get mine. PLEASE!*

But what if the Lord wouldn't give her a yes? After all, she realized with a lump in her throat, she hadn't imagined Jesus in two days. Every nerve was practically poking out of her pores as Sophie watched Miss Imes pass out the papers. When she got to the last one, she stopped, looked more closely at the sheet, and placed it facedown on Sophie's desk. "We'll talk after class," she said. The eyebrows were pointing.

While everyone else checked answers, Sophie tried not to give up hope of ever seeing her video camera again. Maybe Miss Imes hadn't read her whole note. Maybe when she saw that Sophie was asking for help, she wouldn't shoot her eyebrows into her scalp.

When the rest of the class left for lunch, with Fiona and Darbie mouthing questions at Sophie as they trailed out, Sophie tried to get Aurora in mind on her way to Miss Imes's desk, but the medieval maiden didn't show up.

"You're in trouble, aren't you, Sophie?" Miss Imes said.

*No*, Sophie thought, *I'm just math-retarded.*

"I know math is just not some people's thing," Miss Imes said. "But anyone can learn what I'm teaching in here."

Although Sophie wanted to say, *Anyone except me!*, she just nodded.

"But the further behind a student gets," Miss Imes went on, "the harder it is to catch up." She put on her half-glasses. "You haven't scored better than a D on a quiz in here yet, have you?"

"No, ma'am," Sophie said.

Miss Imes looked at Sophie over the tops of the half-glasses. "Do you WANT to pass the tests?"

"Yes, ma'am!" Sophie said. And then she completely lost her mind and said, "I'd like to drive right past every one of them!"

Miss Imes looked as surprised as Sophie felt. But she recovered first and said, "I keep the parents of my seventh graders very well informed of any difficulties their children are having—and your parents need to hear from me on a number of levels. Not the least of which is your attempt to amuse the entire class with that other face you're wearing."

Sophie couldn't swallow. It felt like there was a hippopotamus in her throat.

Miss Imes took off the glasses and folded them neatly. "But I am going to give you one more chance to prove to me that your failure is not simply because you fool around too much. I am going to assign you an in-class tutor."

Sophie gulped over the hippo. "I'll prove it," she said. "Fiona knows how to help me."

"What makes you think it's going to be Fiona?" Miss Imes said. She nodded toward the door. "You'd better go to lunch."

*No,* Sophie thought as she dragged herself to the cafeteria, *I'd better go to a dungeon and have them lock me up there so Daddy can't find me.*

When Sophie got to the Flakes' table, Maggie had the purple Treasure Book open.

"We need to get started on our film," Fiona said. "Before we go nuts."

Sophie sagged into a seat. "There might not *be* another film," she said.

"Miss Imes," Maggie said.

Sophie nodded miserably. "I'm failing in there, and she's gonna call my parents unless I pass the next quiz. She's giving me a tutor. Only she said it might not be Fiona."

Kitty slipped her hand into Sophie's and gave it a weak squeeze.

"Who's she gonna give you then?" Willoughby said. "Fiona's the smartest person in this whole school in math."

"She's gonna give me to you, Soph," Fiona said. Her little bow mouth was firm. "She's just trying to scare you."

"Work you into a dither for the entire weekend," Darbie said.

"I say we go on with the film," Fiona said.

"We can meet at my house tomorrow for the whole day," Darbie said.

They were all looking at Sophie as if the next words out of her mouth would decide whether they gave up on life as they knew it. Kitty's face was the most hopeful.

"I love you guys," Sophie said.

"We're the best, the best, the best," Kitty said. Her voice cracked as she threw her arms around Sophie. "I don't know how I would stand it right now if it weren't for you."

After that, how could Sophie even think about Miss Imes or detention or what Daddy was going to say?

Sophie, Fiona, Willoughby, and Maggie went to Darbie's that night and slept over, although Kitty's mom didn't let her come until the next morning. The Corn Flakes all promised her that they wouldn't have a bit of fun before she got there. They did, but they tried not to talk about that in front of Kitty when they were finally all together eating Darbie's aunt Emily's pancakes. They already had a movie name for her when she got there, though—the maiden Katrina.

Maggie, it had also been decided the night before, was Maid Magdalena the Dark.

Darbie was named Lady Patricia the Irish, and Willoughby chose just plain Willow. She started making up medieval cheers about her character immediately.

The only possible name for Fiona was Lady of the Rapier. She said a "rapier" was a slender sword with two edges so it could cut both ways. That's how sharp the Rapier's wit would be.

Sophie, naturally, was Aurora.

"Aurora the Mighty," Kitty said. She giggled, but the trust in her blue eyes made Sophie feel like she just might *be* mighty.

Once they got started acting out scenes and Maggie wrote them into the script, the Corn Flakes killed themselves — *killed* themselves — laughing all day. They stayed true to their Code, which didn't allow for anything that could hurt somebody's feelings or be mean. So when they came up with things like, "Excuse me, but have you a large fly on your nose? Oh, I'm sorry — that's a wart!" they crossed them out. But the jokes were really hard to part with.

Fiona kept their literature and history books open in front of her and Darbie's computer constantly online so she could keep the film medieval-accurate. She was the one who came up with the need for a jousting tournament scene, where four of the maidens thrust wrapping-paper rolls at dummies of villains and vixens they constructed from stacks of pillows. They shouted their best one-liners while the rescued maiden Katrina clapped and threw roses at the winner.

Maggie got it all with Sophie's camera, and when they crowded around its little digital window to see their work, Kitty laughed so hard, Sophie thought she was going to lose her breath. It wasn't the noble, serious film Sophie had imagined. But if it meant Kitty could have something to look forward to besides more chemotherapy and more throwing up and more being too tired to play, it couldn't be goofy enough.

Sophie *had* to keep that camera. That was why, when she was back home in her own bed that night, she remembered Miss Imes and Coach Yates. She couldn't think of anything funny OR noble that she would be capable of to deal with them. Or to keep Mama and Daddy from finding out. It was an old feeling—that one she used to get, long before she met Fiona and before the Corn Flakes started. Long before she met Dr. Peter and learned to imagine Jesus. It was a heavy feeling that meant, *I CAN'T do this. I CAN'T!*

The hippo-sized lump reappeared in her throat. Praying. Imagining Jesus. She wasn't doing any of that these days. How could she make sure Kitty knew him when she herself felt like he was now living in another town?

Sophie closed her eyes and tried to see Jesus with his kind eyes. The Jesus who never acted like he had someplace else to be. The Jesus who helped.

It took a long time for her to get a picture of him in her mind. Longer than it ever had before. And when he did come into focus, eyes as kind as ever, Sophie's eyes sprang open.

She couldn't look at him. And she wasn't sure why.

# Six

🌸 🏠 ☀️

The next morning Mama was too sick to go to Sunday school, and Daddy tried to fix breakfast and get Zeke ready. Except there was no milk in the house and no way to comb Zeke's hair the way Mama did it. Zeke went wearing one of Daddy's ball caps that even covered his nose and hollered about wanting Spider-Man waffles. When they arrived at the church forty-five minutes late, Sophie hung out in the hall outside the Sunday school room because she was too embarrassed to go in so long after class had started. She couldn't shake the feeling that Jesus was very far away—maybe even as far away as the thirteenth century. Dr. Peter found her as he strolled down the corridor with a cup of coffee.

"Sophie-Lophie-Loodle!" he said. He shot a puzzled look at the classroom door.

"I'm too late," Sophie said.

"You're looking a little—what does Fiona always say?" He chuckled. "Vexed. Are you vexed?"

*Yes!* Sophie wanted to say. *I feel like I went off someplace and left Jesus, and now I can't look at him because I know he's not happy with me and I don't even know why—*

And yet even as Dr. Peter waited quietly, sipping his coffee and steaming up his glasses, she couldn't say any of it. There was just too much crowding to get out.

"You don't *have* to talk about it," Dr. Peter said.

"Do you think Jesus has a sense of humor?" Sophie blurted out.

Dr. Peter stopped in mid-sip and blinked. "Well," he said, "when we think of God and Jesus as one, sure—I mean, God has to have a sense of what's funny to create a rhinoceros—or my hair." He patted his curls, all gelled down for Sunday.

Sophie shook her head. "I mean, like, did Jesus ever say funny things to get people to think or, like, make them back off and stop being stupid?"

Dr. Peter took a really long drink out of his cup and said, "There isn't anything like that in the Gospel stories. But, then, we don't know everything he said when he wasn't busy teaching and healing and all that ..."

Sophie looked down at her boot tops and up through the bill of her denim ball cap, everywhere but at Dr. Peter. It was the first time ever that she didn't want him to see what was in her eyes.

The door to the middle school room opened, and the Corn Flakes and the two Wheaties burst out. They surrounded Sophie and Dr. Peter with questions and squeals and the need to display Kitty in a trucker hat with "I Love Jesus" embroidered on it.

"My dad bought it for me to wear when I go back in the hospital Wednesday for my chemo," she said. "It'll make me feel like I'm with you guys."

"Back in the hospital?" Sophie said. Her heart was already pounding and heading for her throat.

"I like the hat," Dr. Peter said to Kitty.

"I think we should all get them," Darbie said.

"But not shave our heads," Willoughby whispered to Sophie while the rest of the girls went on chattering. "The Pops are giving me enough trouble without that."

"How come you didn't tell us?" Sophie said.

Willoughby shrugged. "My problems aren't as bad as Kitty's," she said. "They're not talking to me at cheerleading practice, and every time I make a suggestion, they just act like I didn't even say anything. The girls who didn't go through elementary with us act like they're afraid of the Pops, so they ignore me too. *Plus*, Cassie is there watching every practice, and she's always pointing at me and rolling her eyes." Willoughby hugged Sophie's arm. "I try to just laugh, but it's hard when you're not there."

"All right," Dr. Peter said, "who's working on the Bible study assignment?"

"Me!" Kitty said.

Everybody else nodded too, and Sophie bobbed her head right along with them. But she was careful to keep her eyes away from Dr. Peter's.

*I WILL do it*, she thought. *Just as soon as I find out what it is!*

As soon as the worship service was over, Fiona dragged Sophie aside.

"Did you tell your dad about needing help in math yet?" she said.

"No," Sophie said. "He might take the camera away from me right now, and we don't have that much time left with Kitty."

"Don't worry about it," Fiona said. "I'm gonna go in before school tomorrow and convince Miss Imes that I'm the absolutely best tutor you could ever have and that you will totally ace the next quiz with my help." Her magic-gray eyes were shining. "I'll sit there until she sees it my way."

"You would do that?" Sophie said.

"Hello! I'm your best friend."

"I wish you knew a way to get me out of detention," Sophie said.

Fiona's eyes shone. "You'll make Coach Hates see how awesome you are, Soph. You always end up doing that."

Sophie couldn't even nod.

"I think I totally won Miss Imes over," Fiona told Sophie during PE the next day.

But before Sophie could even start to hope, Coach Yates yelled, "LaCroix! Don't forget you have detention after school Wednesday."

Sophie realized something she hadn't before, something that made things even worse. "Does it have to be Wednesday?" she said. "I have Bible study after school on Wednesdays. Could I come in during lunch or something?"

Coach Yates looked down at her, face ponytail-pinched. "Bible study?" she said. "I don't think it's doing you any good, LaCroix—not the way you keep pushing everything. Wednesday's the only day I hold detention. Be here, or expect an F in citizenship. Now, give me six laps."

Sophie couldn't catch up with the other Flakes, and Coach Yates barked at them when she saw them slowing down. So Sophie ran around the track six times alone, until her side felt like it had been stabbed and her thoughts were in a tangle.

*At least I won't have to have my Bible assignment done, not that I even know what it is. And Mama is REALLY gonna be upset that I have to miss Bible study because I got in trouble. Mama? What about Daddy?*

Not only that, but Kitty was going to leave, and then Sophie wouldn't have her to think about instead of all the other stuff. And what if Kitty didn't get all the things she needed to know about Jesus and she got more sick and—Sophie pulled away from that thought and went to, *I'm going to be the only one with a bald head in the whole school now.*

*But that's not what's important.*

Then why did she get that big lump in her throat when the Pops called her Little Boy LaCroix?

Sophie didn't feel any closer to untangling that knotted mess when she got to math class. She pulled off her blue-knit twirl cap as she walked into the room and went to her desk without even looking at a Corn Pop or a Fruit Loop, just in case one of them wanted to start in. But before she could sit down, Miss Imes said to her, "I'm putting you in the back with your tutor."

At least she was keeping her voice low. Sophie was grateful for that. And being in the last row with Fiona was going to make life way better.

"Tod Ravelli will be working with you," Miss Imes said.

Sophie's mouth fell open so far she could taste chalk dust.

*"Tod?"* Sophie said.

Miss Imes whipped off her half-glasses. Her eyebrows threatened to shoot right off her face. "If there is any more arguing, I will assume you don't want help, and I will be on the telephone to your parents."

Sophie couldn't even get out a "Yes, ma'am." She just nodded and struggled to swallow the hippopotamus that was in her throat again. She collected her backpack and made her way blindly to the back of the room. Out of the corner of her eye, she could see Fiona waving her hand to be called on.

"It's a done deal, Fiona," Miss Imes said.

Tod joined Sophie after a quick conference with Miss Imes, all tough and swaggering, winking at Julia as he passed her.

*Why isn't he saying he doesn't want to sit with me?* Sophie thought. He was up to something.

Tod plopped himself into the next desk and scooted it closer to Sophie. She tried not to shudder.

"So where's your book, Soapy?" he said.

Sophie was careful not to take her eyes off him as she pulled out her math book. He slouched against the back of the chair and made a big *L* on his forehead with his thumb and index finger for Colton's benefit. Colton made one back.

But Sophie could feel somebody else staring at her. Julia. Her green eyes seemed to be made of steel at the moment as she bored them into Tod. He looked at her and whispered, "What?"

*He's stupider than I thought,* Sophie said to herself. *She's mad because he's sitting so close to me, and he can't even see that.*

"All right, class, Sophie and Tod are not on display for your entertainment," Miss Imes said. "Eyes this way, please."

As the class turned reluctantly to the board, Fiona gave Sophie one last glance that clearly said, *Don't be mad at me. I really tried.*

"So, like, I'm gonna teach you some shortcuts."

Sophie stared at Tod. She could smell grape gum on his breath.

"Why?" she said.

"Because the faster you get it, the faster I don't have to sit back here with you anymore."

That was the first familiar thing that had happened all day, and Sophie grabbed at it.

"I want to get that done, like, yesterday," she said.

Tod poked at a problem on the open page of his book with his pencil. "I'll show you how to do this one *way* easier than the way Imes explains it. All you do is—"

Tod completed the problem in three short steps. Sophie stared at it.

"You don't even get *that*?" Tod said.

"I get it," Sophie said. She blinked. "It just can't be that easy."

"Don't believe me then. Just keep flunking."

"No!" Sophie said. "I'll try it."

She wrote down the numbers, followed Tod's steps, and came up with an answer.

"Right?" she said.

"Dude," Tod said. "You're not as dumb as everybody says you are."

"Give me another one," Sophie said.

He did. She worked it, and she got it right.

After five more correct answers, the hippo in Sophie's throat started to swim off somewhere. But then she caught it by the tail.

"How come you know the easy way and Miss Imes doesn't?" Sophie said.

Tod gave her a pointy look. "She knows it — duh. But she's a teacher. She has to make it hard, or they don't pay her."

"So I guess you aren't getting paid," Sophie said.

"Like she's really gonna give me cash," Tod said. He leaned in even closer. Sophie could practically feel Julia stabbing her in the temple with her eyes. "But if you don't pass the next test, I get a D in citizenship. I forgot to tell you that part."

"When did you start caring about your citizenship grade?" Sophie said.

"When I found out you can't play sports if you get below a B. Stupid rule. Anyways, you gotta pass the quiz, so do ten more of these just like I showed you, and I'll tell you if you get the right answers."

Sophie gnawed at her eraser. It was way hard to trust Tod. When had he ever done anything for a Corn Flake?

But one thing they all knew: the Fruit Loops practically breathed sports. If Tod wasn't going to be able to play football or something because she failed, he was going to make sure she didn't.

Besides, not being a total moron on a math problem felt, as Fiona would say, blissful. That day, and the next day too.

# Seven

❋ 🕊 ❋

"Tod is still a heinous creature," Sophie told the Flakes at their Tuesday afternoon movie rehearsal at Fiona's house. "But he's really teaching me. I'm SO gonna pass that math quiz tomorrow."

"Will you call me in the hospital and tell me?" Kitty said. She was sitting listlessly on top of a pile of cushions, pulling the petals off the silk rose she was holding.

"I will call you every day and tell you every single detail," Sophie said.

"I'll email you," Fiona said. "We have a high-speed Internet connection."

Kitty pulled out three petals at once. "But I want to be *here*. And what about our movie?"

Sophie could barely talk over the lump in her throat, but she managed to say, "That's why we're filming all your parts today—so you won't miss anything."

"Let's do it with the hats on," Darbie said. "That'll be class!"

Maggie pulled out the cone-shaped hats her mom, who always made their costumes, had put together. They were all covered in shiny couch-like material and had trailing chiffon veils. With those on their heads, the jousting tournament scene came alive, although they were definitely going to need a way to keep them in place. Darbie took the point of Maggie's right in the armpit when it flew off. Nobody could stop laughing. Especially not Kitty.

"Do you promise you'll send me a DVD when it's all finished?" Kitty said. Her blue eyes were filmy.

*I HAVE to get everything fixed so I can keep the camera,* Sophie thought fiercely. *And I will.*

"Okay, Maggie," she said. "Let's shoot that scene again—"

For the first time in her whole seventh-grade experience, Sophie was looking forward to going to math class Wednesday. By that time, she had imagined over and over the look on Miss Imes's face when she saw all the problems done right on Sophie's paper, and now she was going to *see* it.

And, Sophie thought, Miss Imes was going to see Aurora/Sophie, the girl who didn't act out on purpose, the girl who only wanted to protect her friends from villains and vixens without becoming one herself.

In fact, that seemed to be working. Nobody had picked on them for two days, except for what Willoughby was going through at practice. And even though that was Corn Pop-heinous, at least they had a new mission. It made being without Kitty a little easier.

*Protecting Willoughby is our next challenge,* Sophie decided. *Right after I ace this test.*

It was with the confidence of Aurora herself that Sophie attacked her math quiz, brandishing her sword—pencil. She was one of the first people to turn hers in, right behind Tod.

"Hey, Miz I," Tod said.

"Yes, Mr. R," Miss Imes said.

"Would you grade Soapy's right now so I can see how she did?"

Miss Imes's eyebrows pointed up. " 'Soapy'?" she said.

To Sophie's horror, Tod flung his arm around her shoulders. "That's my pet name for her," he said.

His skin was clammy on her neck, and Sophie couldn't help gasping. She was pretty sure she heard Julia gasp too.

"Have a seat, Romeo," Miss Imes said in a dry voice. "And I'll call you up when I've checked your paper."

Sophie was barely back in her desk when Miss Imes scraped her chair back and called Sophie's name as she charged for the door. Sophie followed her out, and Miss Imes shut the door behind her. The teacher's whole face seemed to be pointing upward.

"What is *this*?" Miss Imes said.

She held up Sophie's quiz. There was a large red F at the top. Sophie was sure her heart stopped.

"I thought you were paying attention to Tod," Miss Imes said.

Sophie shook her head as she stared at her paper. She had never felt more bald.

"I did listen to him!" she said. "And after he showed me the easy way to do the problems, I've been getting all the answers right!"

Miss Imes pulled another paper out from behind Sophie's. It was Tod's, and it had a huge A+ on it.

"Tod got all the answers correct. You got none of them right. Obviously, you didn't do it the way he showed you."

Sophie pulled her face closer to Tod's paper. "*He* didn't do it the way he showed me!"

"Are you saying he taught you wrong?" Miss Imes said.

"No—he wouldn't do that because—!"

"Because he obviously likes you. The whole nickname thing—"

"It's not that!" Sophie said. Her voice, she knew, was going so high it was almost off the scale. "If I don't pass, he gets a D in citizenship, and then he can't play sports!"

Miss Imes took off her half-glasses and drilled her eyes into Sophie's. "Where on earth did you get an idea like that?"

"Tod told me," Sophie said.

"I would never put that kind of responsibility on a student. Are you sure you heard him right?"

Sophie's shoulders nearly met in the middle. "I should have known," she said. It was only the hippo in her throat that kept her from crying. Her voice barely came out.

"Should have known what?" Miss Imes said.

"That he would try to trick me—but I didn't think he'd think of something like that—I bet it was Julia or Anne-Stuart who thought of it—"

Sophie stopped herself and listened to the Code shatter to the ground. She bit her lip, and wished she could bite back the rest of it.

Miss Imes crossed her arms, the quizzes still dangling from one hand along with her glasses.

"So," Miss Imes said, "there's some sort of war going on among you kids?"

"It's their war, not ours," Sophie said.

"And do you really think this is the way to fight it?" Miss Imes glanced again at Sophie's quiz. "You can't pull it off the way your friends do. Fiona, Darbie, Maggie, Willoughby, even poor little Kitty—they're all managing to keep their math grades up while they're following you around stirring things up with a stick."

"All we want," Sophie managed to say, "is for people not to harass other people. Especially Kitty."

"I'm just not seeing anybody doing any harassing. All I've seen is you clowning around in my class." Miss Imes put her glasses back on and looked over the quizzes yet again. "It really is your word against Tod's though," she said. She sighed. "I'll look into it. In the meantime, here's what we're going to do. I am going to allow you to retake the quiz tomorrow. If you pass, I will throw this quiz away. I trust you'll be getting help from Fiona outside of class, since Tod obviously didn't do the job."

"But you said Fiona couldn't be my tutor."

There was another sigh. "Just because I said you couldn't work with Fiona in class doesn't mean you can't seek her help outside. I don't understand why you didn't do that before things got this bad for you. Although I suppose you two can't settle down to anything together anytime except to joke your way through your 'war.'"

"I'm dumb in math!" Sophie cried. "And there's a Code, and I can't break it — but I have to protect — "

She stopped, because the words were coming out in pieces all chopped up by sobs. She knew she wasn't making any sense.

Miss Imes pulled a tissue out of her sleeve and handed it to her. "Use this until you get to the restroom to wash your face," she said. Her voice was a little softer. "Go ahead and have the rest of your cry while you're in there."

Sophie nodded. She could hardly see as she turned to go.

"Sophie."

Sophie stopped and waited, but she didn't look back.

"Just be honest," Miss Imes said. "Then maybe we can get somewhere."

71

*Why?* Sophie thought as she half-ran to the girls' restroom. *You wouldn't believe me anyway.*

*Aurora choked back her tears as she leaned against the castle wall. There was no time to cry. And there was no time to defend herself. There was only the crusade—to stop the villains and vixens—*

*But all the Codes in the world didn't seem to be enough. For the first time in her life as a mighty maiden of the Court, she felt unable to defend herself.*

Sophie stayed in the restroom until class was over. She didn't want to see Tod and the rest of them looking all innocent and disgusting. The Flakes would be waiting for her, and they would figure something out over lunch.

*My maidens! The thought was like a shaft of light coming into Aurora's heart. They will be waiting there for me, and they will vouch for my character. I have taught them well!*

All of them were pulled into a knot at the end of the math hall when Sophie got there. And even Fiona was white-faced.

"It's okay," Sophie said. She attempted a smile. "Tod taught me wrong, and she's going to let me take the test over—"

"She did take him out in the hall," Darbie said. But she didn't really look at Sophie.

"What's going on?" Sophie said.

"Miss Imes yelled at us," Fiona said.

"She didn't exactly yell," Maggie said. "She just said we would all be in trouble if we kept 'doing battle.'" Maggie's face darkened. "Even if the stuff we did wasn't against the rules in the handbook."

"Um, you guys?" They all turned to Willoughby. She looked like an egg about to crack open. "I have to go," she said. And she took off running.

"*What?*" Sophie said.

"She's afraid she's gonna get kicked off the cheerleading squad if she gets in trouble," Maggie said. "She's probably right."

Sophie's throat got thick as she watched Willoughby's retreating figure. "What did you tell Miss Imes?"

"Nothing," Fiona said. "What was the point in arguing?"

"Because I'm in trouble!" Sophie said. "She thinks I'm the biggest liar and troublemaker on the planet, but she would have believed it if you'd told her I wasn't!"

"If we argued with her, that would only make it worse." Fiona drew closer to Sophie, and so did the rest of them. "It's okay, Soph. We're still gonna do what we've been doing. We just have to be careful not to do it in front of her, or you'll get your camera taken away and we won't be able to make movies and—"

"I can't, Sophie," Darbie said. "I can't!"

Sophie looked at Darbie in time to see her face crumple. Her knees sagged, and Sophie knew she would have dropped right down to the floor if Maggie hadn't caught her.

"It was fine when we were just playing and making flicks," Darbie said between globby sobs, "but when she started talking about war—I got scared. I've seen enough war—"

A door opened down the hall, and everyone stiffened.

"Come on," Maggie whispered as she lifted Darbie up by her armpits. "We *are* gonna get in trouble if we keep standing here."

Fiona and Maggie swept Darbie off to the cafeteria. But Sophie didn't follow them.

When she had stared at their backs until they disappeared, she threw her lunch into the first trashcan she found and went to the outside courtyard and sat on a bench.

*Could I get in trouble for THIS too?* she thought. She pulled herself into a ball.

*How come everything is suddenly about not getting in trouble? I thought we were all about the Code—*

*I cannot be discouraged, Aurora told herself. They have all run like frightened rabbits, and there is nothing to laugh about now—no Spirit of Mirth. But I must be strong.*

*She ran her hand across the smooth scalp she had been so happy to shave—for the Code. It had been a drastic move, one she had never expected Willow or Magdalena or Patricia or even her faithful Rapier to make for the maiden Katrina. But she had never regretted it, even now that Katrina was gone and no longer needed their protection.*

*"I would do the same for any of them!" she cried. "I would do anything to defend the Code we have worked so hard to form! I would march right up to any villain—"*

From afar a bell tolled. Sophie only shook herself out of Aurora's world long enough to get to science class and settle in her seat. Just as she was about to return to her vow to uphold the Code against any odds, a folded piece of paper appeared on her desk

"We'll be moving to the lab in just a few minutes," Mr. Stires said in his always-cheerful voice. "I want you to get out two sheets of paper and a pencil and be ready—"

Sophie opened the note, folded into an origami bird as only Fiona did it, and read: *Are you mad at us? Please don't be.*

Sophie looked up at Fiona, who was blinking like a kitten from over the top of her backpack. She didn't even have time to say yes or no before Mr. Stires began herding them into the lab area.

*How can I be angry with you, my friend? Aurora thought. I would die for you! I would march up to any villain and face him dead-on before I would abandon you to his evils—*

*Even as the thoughts galloped through Aurora's mind on gallant steeds, she caught sight of one of the smaller villains, the Ridiculous Tod of Loop Land. He had a javelin in his hand, and as he pulled his*

*arm back, Aurora knew he meant ill will. Plunging forth through a crowd of innocent members of the court, she dived for the now-flying spear and caught it in midair. Clutching it to her bosom—which was larger than any other maiden's in the kingdom—she crumpled to the ground with the skirts of her gown piled around her—*

"I'm glad you're so enthusiastic," Mr. Stires said. "But there's no need to knock yourself out getting there. We'll wait for you."

Sophie scrambled to her feet. Miss Imes said all the teachers were saying things about her. Maybe even happy Mr. Stires.

Only when Sophie was standing up again did she realize she was holding a paper airplane that looked like it had been folded and unfolded a bunch of times. She glanced around. Where had it come from?

As soon as she got to her lab station, Sophie unfolded it. There were several different colors of ink used in as many different handwritings. Sophie recognized Anne-Stuart's curlicue letters as the first one.

WE'VE GOT THAT BUNCH OF GOOD GIRLS NOW, she had written.

ONE MORE TO GO AND THEY'RE DONE, somebody else had added.

IT'S GONNA BE SO EASY. THEY'RE NOTHING WITHOUT LBL, said the next one.

YEAH, BUT WE STILL HAVE TO WATCH HER.

THEY WILL GO DOWN.

DO IT FOR CASSIE.

"Let's get started," Mr. Stires sang out.

Sophie stuffed the note into the pocket of her jeans and tried to concentrate on the making-cotton-candy lab. It was hard with the words shouting in her head: *ONE MORE TO GO AND THEY'RE DONE.*

*The Good Girls, that's us,* she thought. *Who else would it be?*

THEY'RE NOTHING WITHOUT LBL, one of them had said. That was her, she knew—Little Boy LaCroix. *So they really did plan that whole thing so I'd be scared to get in more trouble with Miss Imes,* she thought. *They even got Tod in on it.*

But who was the ONE MORE TO GO?

# Eight

It didn't take long to find out. At the end of science class, an announcement was made over the intercom for all cheerleaders to come to the office.

"Our uniforms are here!" Anne-Stuart said.

She bounced toward the door, corn-silk hair flying, before the bell even rang, and latched on to Julia on the way out.

"B.J.!" Julia shouted in the direction of the hallway. "Wait up!"

Sophie got to the doorway just as the three of them took off down the hall, squealing. And leaving Willoughby in their dust. Sophie watched her try to catch up, everything on her drooping as she fell farther behind.

"Why didn't they wait for you, Willoughby?" somebody called out.

It was Cassie, using the Corn Pop I'm-your-friend-right-now voice.

Willoughby just walked faster, legs stiff. But Julia, now about to turn the corner in the hall, whipped her head around with a toss of her ponytail, and called back, "Oh, sor-ry, Willoughby. We forgot about *you*." With another toss she was gone.

Sophie felt a nudge on her arm as Fiona pushed her in the other direction. "We can't be late to sixth period if all the teachers are gonna be holding surveillance on us."

Sophie didn't even ask her what *surveillance* meant. She was too busy watching Darbie work her way through the hallway crowd ahead of them like a burrowing dachshund.

*I can't do it, Sophie!* Darbie had said.

Sophie followed Fiona, bumped by elbows and backpacks and unhappy thoughts.

*Who IS going to do it, then?*

The Pops were after Willoughby because she made cheerleader instead of Cassie. Would Aurora just let it go because teachers didn't understand?

*"No!" Aurora cried. Her noble, womanly arm came up, fist clenched in the air. "I will uphold the Code, even if I have to do it alone!"*

*Alone? You never have to do it alone. Listen to me—*

"Hey, get off me, Cue Ball!"

Sophie stumbled forward, one leg tangled in Colton Messik's too-big pant leg. She could feel them both going down—until something grabbed at the straps of her backpack and yanked her back to her feet. Colton, who was still staggering around to get his balance, looked up and said, "Hey, Coach. How's it going?"

"Get up, Messik," said a familiar high-pitched-for-a-man voice.

Sophie closed her eyes and prepared to die. Coach Virile. He was still holding on to her straps, and Sophie could feel his one big eyebrow looming over her.

"Thanks," she said without looking up at him. Maybe he wouldn't recognize her.

"Let's get to class, people. And try not to kill each other while you're doing it."

Everybody else scattered like ants, which Sophie would have loved to do if Coach Virile wasn't holding her captive. Even when he let go as the hall emptied, she didn't move.

"For such a little thing you sure get yourself into some big messes, don't you?" he said.

"I don't try to," she said to the floor.

"Hey."

It was a command to look at him. Sophie obeyed. Just as she'd suspected, his eyebrow was hooding his face. But his eyes weren't poking at her like pencil points this time. They looked surprised. He folded his arms, like two large hams.

"You okay?" he said.

Sophie couldn't answer. Coach Virile hunched his shoulders to get closer to her level. "If somebody's giving you trouble," he said, "don't go it alone. There are people here who can —"

Sophie didn't hear the rest. *Don't go it alone. That* drowned everything else out.

"Coach Yates," Coach Virile was now calling into the Life Skills classroom. "I held this one up. You mind if I have a minute with Colton Messik?"

"Please," Coach Yates said, "and any of the rest of them you want to take off my hands."

A few minutes later, Willoughby, Julia, Anne-Stuart, and B.J. returned. The Pops looked like they'd just been to Disney World. Willoughby looked like she was coming back from a year at the state prison. Sophie kept her eyes on the Pops. Julia nodded to Anne-Stuart, who turned around to look at Cassie. A sly smile appeared on Anne-Stuart's face, and as she tilted her head ever so slightly toward Willoughby, she turned a thumb up for Cassie to see.

*Thank you,* Cassie mouthed to her.

*A sizzle went through Aurora's veins. The vixens were trying to take Willow down, remove her from the Dance. But what could she do now? Everyone was watching, waiting for Aurora to make a false move. Even the maidens were too frightened to act. Could she go it alone?*

*That word rankled like a chain in her mind. It wasn't a word she was accustomed to. And now she was hearing it from unexpected places.*

*Aurora raised her head. There was no time to ponder that now. If she was going to know what to do for Willow, she needed more information. And there was only one way to get it.*

The bell rang, and Sophie headed for the door with a purpose. Coach Yates stopped her with a different one.

"I'll see you in ten minutes in my office, LaCroix," she said.

Outside in the hall, Sophie leaned against the wall and tried to think. The Flakes stood around her.

"You couldn't talk her out of it, huh?" Fiona said. Her voice seemed stiff.

"Does your mom know?" Maggie said.

Sophie shook her head. "You guys go ahead with—who's driving today?"

"Aunt Emily," Darbie said. She was already backing away.

"I'm not going. I have cheerleading," Willoughby said. "Ms. Hess said we can't miss any practices before the assembly Monday."

Sophie felt an idea forming. "The rest of you just go," she said, "and I'll take the last bus home and tell Mama then."

Willoughby was watching Sophie closely. "You sure are calm about it. I'd be bawling my eyes out."

"It'll be okay," Sophie said.

Heads nodded woodenly. Sophie only let herself feel a little bit of a sting as she watched them go. Then she pulled herself up to what height she could reach and marched off to detention. If it worked out the way she hoped, it could be a very good thing for the maidens and their Code.

The cheerleaders were all changing into their shorts and tennies when Sophie passed through the locker room on her way to Coach Yates' office. So far, so good.

When Coach Yates told her she had to go up and down the bleachers in the gym and pick up trash, that was a plus as well.

Just as Willoughby had told them she always did, Cassie was sitting in the bleachers, twisting her long, very-straight hair around her hand and watching wistfully as the cheerleaders gathered for practice.

*It is an excellent plan, Aurora said to herself. I cannot hold back.*

So Sophie snapped open the big black garbage bag Coach Yates had given her and zipped up and down her assigned rows of bleachers, collecting discarded handouts and empty candy wrappers and broken pencils. It left the other detention-ites looking like slackers.

She made absolutely sure she had covered her whole area before she went back to clean up the row where Cassie was sitting. Then she became so slow and thorough, Mr. Clean himself could have come in behind her with a white glove.

When Sophie got within a few feet of Cassie, she ran her hand under the bench in front of her and made a disgusted noise.

"How foul is that?" she said.

"What?" Cassie said.

"Big old nasty wad of gum," Sophie said. "That's just disgusting."

"Do you have to get it off?" Cassie said. She curled back her lip, blue braces showing.

"Yeah," Sophie said. "Don't ever get detention."

"I don't plan to," Cassie said.

Her eyes returned to the Pops, who weren't cheering but standing in a bunch squabbling. The girls Sophie didn't know were huddled a little apart from them. Sophie forced herself not to search out Willoughby.

*I might not be able to go through with it if I see her crying*, she thought.

"It doesn't sound like it's going so well," Sophie said, as she pretended to scrape off the nonexistent wad of gum with her thumbnail.

"It would be if Willoughby could actually cheer," Cassie said. Then she darted her eyes to Sophie. "I know she's your friend, but she totally can't do the moves."

"Really?" Sophie said. She chose her words carefully. *No lying*, she told herself. *Just get Cassie talking.*

"Haven't you been watching?" Cassie said. "It's not even that hard, but she's all falling down and stuff."

Sophie shrugged. "I don't know that much about cheering. You saw me at the tryouts."

Cassie snorted. "Why did you try out anyway?" she said, curling her lip again. Julia, Sophie decided, had really been working with her.

"Just for fun," Sophie said. "And so Willoughby wouldn't be nervous."

There was another snort. "If she was that nervous at tryouts, how is she ever gonna stand up in front of the whole school and cheer Monday at the assembly? Of course she'll mess up. We'll make sure—"

Cassie stopped. Sophie glanced up to see her narrow face flush.

"You think she'll mess up?" Sophie said.

Cassie turned toward the gym floor where Ms. Hess had arrived. The group was finally lined up, hands on hips. When the music started, they went into their routine, arms in perfect straight lines, voices husky, hips making circles over their fast-moving feet. Sophie had to admit, she was impressed with the way they were all in time with each other, as if the same puppeteer were moving them all. Including Willoughby.

"Willoughby looks good to me," Sophie said to Cassie.

"Yeah, well—just wait 'til Monday. She's going to look like a moron."

Sophie looked at Cassie, who had her eyes glued on the cheerleaders. Eyes that gleamed like tomorrow was Christmas.

"So she looks good now, but she's going to look like a moron Monday," Sophie said. "Okay—whatever."

Cassie's mouth opened, and then she gave Sophie a sharp look. "Aren't you and Willoughby really close?" she said.

Sophie sucked in air. This was the hard part—the part where she had to decide.

"You guys *are* close," Cassie said. Her words were like accusing fingers. "You're like best friends."

"Not so much," Sophie said. "In fact, Willoughby isn't talking to me as much now, not since lunchtime today."

*That's not a total lie*, she shouted at herself. *I can't help her if I don't do this!*

Cassie nodded. "Julia and them said she's that way. They said she used to hang out with them all the time, and then she just dumped them and started being friends with y'all."

"Uh-huh," Sophie said.

"It's totally going to bite her in the behind Monday," Cassie said, "when she makes an idiot out of herself at the assembly and Ms. Hess takes her off the squad."

Sophie picked up her garbage bag and nodded. She climbed down the bleachers, and over her shoulder she lied again: "Nice talking to you, Cassie."

Sophie turned in her garbage bag to Coach Yates and promised she would be on time to every class and not try to entertain everybody anymore. Coach Yates didn't exactly look convinced. Sophie tried not to think about that as she went to a bench out front to wait for the late bus. She had to think about Willoughby.

*So now I know they're trying to make Willoughby mess up at the assembly so Ms. Hess will take her off the squad and put Cassie on. But HOW are they going to do it?*

Sophie didn't care what Cassie Corn Pop said. Willoughby knew that routine like she was born doing it.

She had to find out their plan. And the only way to do that was to stay as close as she could to the Pops and gather information.

*That isn't gonna look TOO suspicious!* Sophie thought. *They're gonna know I'm up to something—unless—*

Sophie shook her head, nearly knocking off her cap. She'd already made Cassie think she and Willoughby weren't that close anymore, and it didn't feel good.

What felt worse was that maybe it wasn't a lie. The Flakes had been too scared to stand up for her with Miss Imes, and they'd acted all stiff and weird after school. Even though Sophie almost understood, it made her feel coldly alone.

*"We are not alone,"* Aurora said. *"Just like King Arthur, we are forgetting something very important."*

"Hey, Soapy—"

That definitely wasn't it.

"Hey, Cue Ball—"

Sophie looked at a wall of smiling faces that didn't usually smile at her.

"Stop calling her lame names, y'all," Julia said. "We've outgrown that."

"Not only that—" B.J. gave Tod a shove, which landed him almost in Sophie's lap, which set Colton and Eddie off into boy-steria, which made Julia say, "To-od—make them quit!" It stopped only when Tod punched Eddie in the stomach.

Anne-Stuart sat down next to Sophie, her pale blue eyes wide and serious. "Cassie said y'all were talking during cheerleading practice."

*Careful*, Sophie told herself. "Uh-huh," she said.

Julia joined her on the other side. "She told you that Willoughby is going to mess up at the assembly when we do our cheer."

"And we totally know you're gonna go tell her—" B.J. started to say.

"Shut UP!" the rest of them shouted at her.

Anne-Stuart put her hand on Sophie's arm. Sophie imagined it rotting her skin.

"Willoughby's going to mess up on her own," Anne-Stuart said. "We aren't going to make her."

Julia tossed her ponytail. "We don't even want her to. We just know she will. And if you tell her what Cassie said, she'll just be all nervous and mess up worse and then we'll *all* look bad."

*And we wouldn't want THAT now, would we?* Sophie wanted to say to her. But she waited. She could tell there was more by the way B.J. was holding on to Tod, who was edging away like he had to go to the bathroom.

"I know we all used to hate each other," Julia went on. "Your friends and ours."

*When did that change?* Sophie thought.

"But we think that's immature now," Anne-Stuart said. "Especially what Tod did to you in math."

She sniffed up a nose-full in B.J.'s direction, and B.J. thrust Tod forward again. He stopped just short of Sophie's toes.

"You're busted, man!" Colton said. Eddie clapped like an ape.

"Shut UP!" Tod said.

"Tell her, Tod," Julia said.

Tod crossed his arms and smirked at Sophie. "I'm sorry you got messed up on the test. I didn't teach you that good."

"Hel-lo!" Sophie said. "You told me the wrong way to do it on purpose!"

"I was just messing around," Tod said.

"But he's sorry now," Julia said. "And he wants to teach you the right way so you'll do good on the re-test."

"Why?" Sophie said.

The Pops looked at each other. Tod looked at them. Colton and Eddie just looked like they were bored.

"Well," Julia said. "It's like you do us a favor and we do you a favor. Instead of fighting all the time."

"So let me get this straight," Sophie said. "I do you a favor by not telling Willoughby that you think she's gonna mess up at the assembly so she won't get all nervous and really mess up—and you do me a favor by helping me pass the test that Tod made me fail in the first place."

There was another exchange of looks, and then Julia said, "Yeah. That's basically it."

Sophie would have laughed at them if something hadn't been niggling in the back of her mind. There was a hole the Pops and the Loops obviously didn't see.

"Okay," Sophie said. "If I make an A on the re-test, I won't tell Willoughby."

"An A?" Tod said. "It'll never happen."

"Then I guess the deal's off," Sophie said.

She started to get up, but Julia grabbed her sleeve. "Tod will make sure you ace it," she said, never taking her green eyes off him. "Right, baby?"

"I'm gonna puke!" Eddie said.

For the first time ever, Sophie had to agree with him. But Tod just nodded.

"He'll call you tonight, Sophie," Anne-Stuart said.

"One more thing," Julia said in a low voice. "When you talk to Tod on the phone tonight, it's just going to be about math, okay?"

"What else would I talk to him about?" Sophie said.

Julia smiled icily. "That's just what I wanted to hear," she said.

# Nine

✳ ⬠ ✺

The late bus pulled up, and Sophie shook the Pops off and headed for it. The hole she'd seen was gaping in her mind: What was to stop her from telling Willoughby that the Pops were definitely up to something—*after* she aced the math test?

And then what was to stop her from keeping her camera and bringing the Flakes back together? There was more to find out, and she was going to. Nothing could stop her now except lack of information.

Nothing except the fact that mothers had some kind of foolproof hotline.

The minute Sophie got inside the kitchen door, Mama dropped a lid on a pot and turned to Sophie with a disappointed face.

"Why didn't you tell me you had detention today?" she said.

*Evidently somebody did*, Sophie thought. But she couldn't really blame the Flakes. It wasn't part of the Code to lie for each other.

"One thing we've always been able to rely on is your honesty, Soph," Mama said. Her eyes looked so sad, Sophie just wished she'd yell, although she knew she'd be able to count on Daddy for that later.

"This is the truth, Mama," Sophie said. "I kept thinking I could get it changed."

Mama opened the pot and stirred for an endless minute, and then she said, "What did you get detention for?"

Sophie wanted to groan. "I accidentally went into the boys' locker room."

"Were you daydreaming, Soph?"

"That wasn't the reason!" Sophie said.

"Then what was it?" That came from Daddy, who was in the doorway. Sophie didn't even want to know how long he had been there.

Sophie opened her mouth, and then she closed it. *I can't tell DADDY somebody played a joke on me because I'm breast-retarded!* she thought. There had just been too much to deal with that day to go there.

So she looked at the floor and said, "Yeah, I guess maybe that was the reason."

"Then you know what that means," Daddy said.

Sophie nodded miserably. "I'll get it and bring it to you."

But even as Sophie deposited the video camera into Daddy's hands and dragged herself back to her room to flop on her bed, that wasn't what made her want to hurl her glasses across the room and sob into her pillow. It was the sick feeling that flooded over her, that made her refuse spaghetti dinner. Even after she realized that Mama was actually cooking again, she stayed in her room. What if Daddy asked about her grades too? What if she couldn't find out what the Pops were planning for Willoughby? What if her Flakes kept acting stiff and funky?

"Hey, Soph—" Lacie popped her head in the doorway, phone in hand. "It's for you." Her eyes were dancing. "It's a boy," she whispered loudly.

"He's helping me with my math," Sophie said. She snatched the phone from Lacie.

"Why are you getting math help from some absurd little creep?" Lacie said as she exited. "Hel-lo—I'm an algebra whiz!"

Sophie was sure she was going to be sick to her stomach.

"Hello?" she said into the phone.

"It's me," Tod said.

"I know."

"So—I gotta teach you."

Sophie squeezed the receiver. "How do I know you aren't going to mess with me again?"

"Because Miss Imes said if I do, I'm busted."

"You already tried that with me," Sophie said.

"For real this time," Tod said. "She never said I'd get a D in citizenship if you messed up—but she did say I had to try helping you again now. But don't tell Julia I told you that. She thinks I'm doing it for her."

"So start teaching me," Sophie said. "I can't be on the line after nine."

It was hard doing it over the phone, but after about twenty times with the formula that had always escaped her, Sophie finally started getting the problems right.

"Do you swear these are the right answers?" Sophie said when he'd told her she'd gotten three correct in a row.

"Look it up in the back of the book, moron," he said. "All the odd ones are there."

Sophie did. He was right. And so was she.

Just to be on the safe side, when they hung up, Sophie went into Lacie's room to get her to check her work.

"Oh, now you want my help," Lacie said. "Okay—I get it. Boys are cuter than sisters."

*Ewww!* Sophie wanted to cry. But she forced herself to nod.

Lacie looked over the paper and then up at Sophie. "Nice job, Soph," she said. "Hey, and let me give you a hint about squaring numbers. Here's a trick—"

By the time she was finished, the only thing Sophie could think was: *Why didn't I ask her for help sooner?*

*Or Daddy? Or Fiona?*

*Why did I try to do it by myself?* she asked herself as she climbed into bed.

*By myself. Alone.*

*Again.*

Sophie closed her eyes, and through the tears that stung at her, she could see each of her Flakes alone too. Kitty in the hospital. Darbie trying to fall asleep with thoughts about war in her head again. Maggie reading the middle-school handbook with a flashlight under the covers, so she wouldn't get in trouble with Miss Imes. Fiona trying to find the right words for it all. Willoughby crying into her pillow—

The tears spilled over. When the door creaked open and Mama tiptoed over to kiss her on the cheek, Sophie pretended she was asleep.

"Soph?" Mama whispered. "Is there something you want to talk about, Dream Girl?"

Sophie stayed still as a stone, and Mama tiptoed back out. Sophie didn't really go to sleep until she made a decision. *I don't want to be alone anymore. Tomorrow I'm going to tell Willoughby BEFORE I even take the test.*

*And then I'm going to find out what the Pops are really up to.*

*And then the Corn Flakes will be okay again.*

"Don't forget one thing," Aurora whispered to her—

Whatever it was, it was lost in Sophie's dreams.

The next morning Sophie headed straight to Willoughby's locker, but she barely got to the locker hall before she was surrounded by Corn Pops—minus Cassie.

"Thank you, Sophie," Julia said as she hooked her arm through Sophie's. Anne-Stuart did the same on the other side. B.J. danced in front of them as they made their way toward the stairs.

"For what?" Sophie said. She tried to stop, but her feet were barely touching the ground. "Where are you taking me?"

"Thank you for not trying to get Tod away from me," Julia said. "He said y'all only talked about math."

"Where are we *going*?"

"We're taking you to our place where we always hang out."

"We can talk there," Anne-Stuart said.

"It's way cool," B.J. said. She turned around and led the way down the steps and across the grass toward the gym.

"You can put me down," Sophie said. "I'm not gonna run." No way. This was perfect. She was sure to find out something now that she could tell Willoughby.

But Anne-Stuart and Julia didn't let go of her as they hauled her into the gym and wriggled her and themselves through a space between the bleachers and the wall, which led to an under-the-seats hideaway. Anne-Stuart wafted a hand toward four tumbling mats, arranged in the cracked light like it was somebody's living room.

"Cool, huh?" B.J. said.

"Have a seat," Julia said. B.J. gave Sophie a push that knocked her onto one of the mats. The smiles were gone, and Julia's narrow gaze, striped by the light coming in between the benches, made her look almost cross-eyed.

"I wish the assembly was before the re-test," Julia said. She squatted down in front of Sophie. "But it's not, and that means you could tell Willoughby, now that you know how to do the math problems."

*Shameless wenches!* Sophie thought. *They figured it out.*

"We have to make sure you don't tell," Anne-Stuart said.

"Okay," Sophie said, shrugging casually. "I won't."

"Not good enough," B.J. said.

Anne-Stuart gave a particularly juicy sniff. "If you tell Willoughby what Cassie blabbed to you, we will tell Miss Imes that we saw you cheating on the re-test."

"How would I cheat?" Sophie said. "I'm the only one taking it!"

"Easy," B.J. said. She was all but licking her chops.

Anne-Stuart pulled a Sharpie out of the front pocket of her backpack. B.J. grabbed Sophie's hand, twisting it until Sophie's palm faced upward.

"Miss Imes will see your cheat sheet right on your hand," Anne-Stuart said as she poised the tip of the Sharpie over Sophie's skin. "What's that formula again, Julia?"

"It's A squared ..."

Anne-Stuart dug an *A* with a tiny 2 up and to the right of it onto Sophie's palm. Sophie tried to pull away, but B.J. had a grip on her.

"—plus B squared ..."

"Stop it! Let go of me!"

"—equals ..."

"I said *stop!*"

"Hey, down there. What's the deal?" Something big banged on the bleachers above them. It had to be Coach Virile. Sophie would know that too-high-for-a-giant voice anywhere.

# Ten

"Come out of there!" Coach Virile said.

B.J. let go of Sophie's hand enough for her to pull away from Anne-Stuart's pen. Even as she rubbed her palm frantically on the side of her jeans, Sophie snatched up her backpack and wriggled out from under the bleachers.

Coach Virile looked at her. Then he banged on the bench again. "Come on out—let's go, ladies."

"Coming, Coach Nanini!" Julia purred.

Three Corn Pop bodies slithered out, and three kitty-cat faces softened up at the big coach. All Sophie could do was look at her palm. It was a smeary mess of black ink, but the partial formula still wavered its way through her handprint in permanent ink.

"Who gave you permission to go under there?" said the coach.

"We didn't know we needed permission," Julia said. Her eyes widened as she looked at the other two, who blinked in innocence.

"So I'm telling you that you do need permission," Coach Virile said. "And I'm telling you that I'm not giving it to you, and neither is anybody else."

"We're sorry!" Julia said.

"Totally," B.J. said.

Anne-Stuart gave a sniff Sophie was sure was supposed to sound tearful.

Coach Virile hooded his eyebrow in Sophie's direction. "What about you, Little Bit?"

Sophie put her hand behind her back. "I was invited in," she said. "I didn't know it was against the rules either."

She knew if Maggie were there she would say, "It isn't in the handbook."

"We'll find a legal place to meet, Coach," Julia said. She tilted her head at him the same way she did at Tod.

The three Pops turned to go, but Coach put up a meaty hand. "We're not done here," he said. "What was going on under there? Sounded like somebody was under duress."

The Corn Pops looked at him blankly. It was obvious to Sophie that they didn't even know what *duress* meant. She did, because she had been the one under it.

"We were just doing our girl thing," Julia said, once again cocking her head.

"Which is why I'm glad I'm not a girl," Coach Virile said. "Go on—get out of here."

"By-ee!" Julia sang out. And then the three of them ran like they had a pack of dogs after them.

Sophie didn't move. She knew they were going to be around some corner waiting for her with their Sharpie.

"What's in your hand, Little Bit?"

Sophie squeezed her fist tighter behind her back.

"Nothing," she said. "They were writing something on it, and I didn't want them to." She tried to smile. "I got in enough trouble for that face on my head."

Coach Virile grunted. "You want it off?"

"Yes," Sophie said. "But it's in Sharpie."

"I've got some stuff. Come on."

Sophie didn't even hesitate, except to ask as she followed him, "Will you give me a late pass?"

"Yes," he said. "If you'll also let me give you a little advice."

He motioned for her to sit down on a bench outside the boys' locker room. Sophie sat downand waited until he came out with a bottle of something and a rag. Her heart was slamming against the inside of her chest.

He sat down next to her and dumped what looked like half the contents of the bottle into the rag and held out his hand for Sophie's. She turned her palm up, and he went after it. She was sure he didn't even look at what it said.

"I've been doing a little observing since I caught you in the boys' locker room," he said as he scrubbed. "I haven't put it all together yet, but I think you're up against something that thinks it's bigger than you."

Sophie didn't answer.

"Sometimes in life you have to face things on your own," he said, still scrubbing, "and sometimes you can't. You have to have help." He stopped rubbing, examined her palm, and went back at it. "Growing up is about learning the difference."

*But what if there's nobody there TO help?* Sophie thought. *What if your friends get scared?*

"When people try to force you to do things you don't want to do," he went on, "when they try to take away your power, that's some serious stuff."

He stopped again and surveyed Sophie's hand. "I can take away ink—but I can't take away trouble unless somebody trusts me."

Sophie could hear a question in there, but she couldn't answer it. She could only stare at her now-clean palm and cry.

"You want me to take you to Coach Yates?" Coach Virile said.

"No, sir."

"Some other teacher? Maybe a counselor?"

Sophie shook her head. What would be the point? Who would believe her?

"Talk to somebody, Little Bit," Coach Virile said. His voice was as soft as Mama's. "Because whatever you're trying to carry is just too big for you."

"I'm okay," Sophie whispered. "I just need a pass to class."

As she hurried away from him, he said something she couldn't quite hear. It sounded like "Bless your heart, Little Bit."

But she was sure she was wrong.

There was a note waiting for Sophie on her desk when she got to first period. It wasn't folded like one of Fiona's birds. "Meet us on the track third period," it said in Anne-Stuart's curlicues.

*Why?* Sophie thought. *So you can make a cheat sheet all the way up my arm?*

*Aurora shook her head. I have forgotten something—something I need in order to help fair Willow. Something more powerful than me—that will return my power to me. Aurora closed her eyes and searched. There were only kind eyes looking back at her, beckoning, pulling her—*

"All right, class," Mrs. Clayton said, "the moment you've all been waiting for." She shot her bullet gaze across the rows. "We are handing back your Honor Code papers."

"We want you to correct all the grammatical errors we've indicated," Ms. Hess said. Her dimples poked in. "And for some of you, that will take considerable time."

Wooden frog earrings danced from her lobes. *Perfect,* Sophie thought, *to go with her frog-rubbery mouth.* She automatically looked at Fiona to see if she was noticing too. But

Fiona was riveted to Mrs. Clayton, and so was Darbie, as if they were afraid to let their eyes go wandering into trouble.

"Get started," Ms. Hess said as she put the last paper in Gill's hand. "Grammar books are on the shelf if you need them."

Sophie raised her hand. "I didn't get mine back," she said.

Ms. Hess and Mrs. Clayton looked at each other.

"Did you turn one in, Sophie?" Mrs. Clayton said, voice gruff.

"Yes!" Sophie said.

"I checked it off when they first came in," Ms. Hess said. "But I don't remember grading it." She looked at Mrs. Clayton again. "Do you?"

"Okay, don't panic," Mrs. Clayton said. "We'll check through everything. It's here someplace."

Since they didn't tell her what to do while everybody else was busy correcting, Sophie drew a line under Anne-Stuart's note and picked up her pen.

*Aurora dipped into the ink and began to write. "I will meet you on the jousting field," she wrote, "but I will not have my sword or my spear. I will bring only my word that I will have no conversation with Willow before the test is put before me — or after. The maidens have all abandoned me for fear of being brought before the Court and punished, and so . . ."*

*Aurora paused, ink forming a teardrop at the end of the pen. Could she tell all these lies? How could she NOT tell them? Was this not the only way to find out the vixens' evil plan and reveal it to poor Willow before the tournament and Dance?*

*"Forgive me," she whispered, though she didn't know to whom. And then she wrote, "Since they have abandoned me, I care nothing for what happens to them now. I am on my own, a solitary lady, alone on her crusade for Truth."*

*She rolled the letter up and would have tied it with a lock of her hair except—*

Sophie pulled out one of her shoelaces and wrapped it around the spindled note. She could take one out of her PE sneakers later. As corrected papers were being turned in, Sophie passed her message over to Anne-Stuart. Then she really wanted to wash her hands.

Toward the end of the block's second hour when the class was taking turns reading, an eighth grader slipped in and handed something to Mrs. Clayton. She hurried over to Sophie's desk.

"Good news, Sophie," she said in a raspy whisper. "We must have left your paper in the teachers' workroom and someone found it. We'll get it graded and back to you Monday."

When the bell rang, Sophie headed for the door. She could see Fiona and Darbie on the other side, craning their necks to see if she was coming, but Julia blocked her way.

"Walk to PE with us, Sophie," she said.

"We don't want you to be alone, now that your friends have dumped you," Anne-Stuart said.

Their voices made Sophie think of the artificial sugar stuff Mama put in her coffee. Anne-Stuart steered Sophie out the door, her hand on the strap of Sophie's backpack. "You said you'd meet us on the track anyway," she said. "At least, I *think* that's what your note said."

"You're still weird," Julia said. They were well out of Hess-Clayton earshot now, and she dropped the Sweet'N Low voice.

Sophie wanted to jerk away from Anne-Stuart and run straight to her Corn Flakes, who were not far ahead of them, zigzagging puzzled looks back at her through the crowd.

*But if I do*, she thought, *the Pops will know I was lying about not hanging with them anymore.*

Sophie met Fiona's eyes just as the Flakes rounded the corner. *Just trust me*, she tried to say with her own.

But by the time she and the Pops made the turn, Fiona was sending her a clear message back: *This is heinous.*

Then Fiona picked up her pace, and Maggie, Darbie, and finally Willoughby hurried to keep up with her.

"They really are ditching you," Julia said into Sophie's ear. "Too bad."

"Whatever," Sophie said. The word stuck in her throat, right there with the hippopotamus.

When they got to the locker room, with Cassie and B.J. now on the scene, the Pops kept Sophie from even getting to her locker—much less her friends—until most of the girls had cleared out.

"You're going to be late," Sophie said to B.J., who was breathing Cheetos breath into her face. "You guys should go."

"Like we're going to leave you alone," Cassie said. Her voice was shrill, as if she were back to trying to impress Julia.

*She probably IS*, Sophie thought as she fumbled with her lock. *Now that she almost told me one of their secrets, she's probably back to Step Two.*

When she turned around, T-shirt in hand, they were all standing there, staring. Something in Sophie began to shrivel like a raisin. They were going to watch her expose her very-flat chest and marvel at her little-girl-ness in the presence of all their bras and lip gloss and highlighted hair.

"What's the deal?" said a voice from the end of the row of lockers.

Sophie cringed. It was Coach Yates.

*Why did she pick this day to come in here?* she thought. *Is EVERYBODY watching me now?*

"Julia, B.J., Cassie, Anne-Stuart — you all look ready to me. Let's hit the door."

"We were waiting for Sophie," Julia said, pouring the Sweet'N Low in, three pink packets at a time.

"People who wait for Sophie get tardies and detentions," Coach Yates said. Her voice went up several yell-notches. "Cheerleaders who get tardies and detentions don't cheer at assemblies."

They all ran as if they'd been shot at. Sophie turned her back to Coach Yates and put her T-shirt between her teeth.

"LaCroix," Coach said.

Sophie opened her mouth to answer and dropped her shirt on the floor.

"I haven't figured you out, but I'm working on it. Anything you want to tell me?"

Sophie shook her head.

"Okay," Coach said. "Meet me outside. I have a job for you."

Sophie would rather have been shot herself. But she got into her PE clothes and joined Coach Yates at the edge of the track.

All during class, Coach had Sophie stand beside her and write down the girls' times as they took their running tests. At the end of class, after Sophie had copied all the entries over onto another sheet in pen, everybody was already leaving the locker room. At least the Corn Pops hadn't been able to harass her, but Miss Imes was sure going to if she was late.

"I have a test next period!" Sophie said. There wasn't even time to put in a new shoelace.

"I'll tell Miss Imes you're coming," Coach Yates said.

*And she'll probably think I'm in trouble in PE again*, Sophie thought as she hurried down the hall with one shoe gaping and flopping at the heel. The only good thing about it was that the Pops were already in their seats in the math room when she arrived, and Miss Imes didn't even let her sit down before she gave her the test and put her out in the hall.

At first Sophie was sure she had forgotten the formula by now, and she stared at the problems until her eyes blurred with tears.

"*We've forgotten something*," Aurora whispered.

*Ya think?* Sophie wanted to shout at her. *The Pops won't need the formula on my hand to convince Miss Imes I cheated, because I'm gonna fail—*

"*A squared*," she could almost hear Julia saying. "*Plus—*"

"That's it!" Sophie said out loud.

She wrote the formula at the top of her paper and went to work on the problems. Some of them were the exact ones in the book that she and Tod had worked on last night. Some needed that trick Lacie had taught her. But they all worked out. She was shaking when she handed the paper to Miss Imes.

"Did Fiona help you study?" Miss Imes said as her red pencil flicked down the page.

"No," Sophie said. "Tod did."

Miss Imes smiled faintly. "That's what I wanted to hear." She wrote a large number at the top of Sophie's paper and turned it toward her. "There you are," she said. "Ninety-five. I knew you could do it if you got serious."

Sophie was sure she was going to dissolve into a puddle before she could get to her desk. On the way she tried to catch Fiona's glance, but Fiona seemed to have eyes only for the assignment she and Darbie were working on together.

As she sat down, Miss Imes stood up and said, "Tod, I want to see you out in the hall."

"Busted!" Colton crowed.

Miss Imes gave him a look that could have frozen the sun.

When the bell finally rang for lunch, Sophie was the first one to the door, even from the back of the room. She had to get to Willoughby, and she had to do it in secret so the Corn Pops wouldn't see. Their threat to tell Miss Imes she'd cheated still hung over Sophie's head like an executioner's ax.

*Aurora shook that off with a toss of her head that was so hard her pointed hat took off on the wind, its long veil trailing like a sail—*

Tod flew past her sideways, grabbing for the beanie and clutching it against him like a football as he hit the ground.

"Score!" cried Eddie Wornom, thrusting his arms above his head.

"Over here!"

Sophie whirled around to see Colton catch the hat-pass Tod threw him. He jumped straight up with it, took a shot at an imaginary basket, and dunked Sophie's wadded-up beanie over the railing and down into the front lawn below.

"I guess you better go get that, Soapy," Julia said.

"You have to get permission to go out the front door first," Anne-Stuart said.

Cassie snorted. "Good luck finding somebody to let you out at lunchtime."

Sophie considered jumping over the side, but instead headed toward the stairs.

"To-od," Julia said. "Remember—"

"*What?*" he said.

Sophie left what sounded like true love going down the toilet behind her and navigated her way through everything the

Pops had predicted. Kids passed along the way, whispering things like "Why does that girl have her head shaved?" and "Is she the one who has leukemia?" and "She should wear a hat." By the time Sophie got through all that, it was too late to go to her locker and get her lunch. She wasn't hungry anyway.

Sophie wandered back upstairs to be close to the math room when the bell rang. Maybe she'd be able to catch Willoughby heading to class and pull her away to talk someplace where the Pops couldn't see her. As she headed toward it, Sophie trailed her hand along the railing—

*Below Aurora, the sounds of the music for the ritual Dance lifted like colored scarves from the instruments. "She is going to look so LAME!" came a vixen cry.*

Sophie pulled herself down into a crouch and peered down between the bars in the railing. Julia, B.J., and Anne-Stuart were just below her in the otherwise-empty courtyard with the three cheerleaders Sophie still didn't know. All eyes were on Julia.

"Okay, once more from the beginning," she said. She bobbed her ponytail at Cassie, who was sitting on the ground next to a boom box. Cassie pushed a button, and unfamiliar music pounded as the Pops formed a line and started their routine.

*"Willoughby can't even do the moves,"* Cassie had told Sophie.

"And I guess they aren't going to help her learn them either," she whispered to herself.

But that still didn't make sense. Willoughby had been the best one at the tryouts. She practiced the routine everywhere but in the middle of Miss Imes's classroom.

As she continued to watch, Sophie could feel her eyes bulging. She'd never seen Willoughby practice *this* routine. This wasn't the one they were working on just yesterday.

The cheer ended with B.J. and Julia each putting a hand back to assist Anne-Stuart up to their shoulders, where she stood, arms raised in a *V.*

"This is where you'll come in later, Cass," Julia said.

"Yeah," B.J., said, "but for now, they'll laugh at *her* the way everybody laughed at *us* at tryouts!"

"Tell the world, B.J.," Julia said, glaring at her.

Anne-Stuart jumped down and went into a split, which opened up a space between Julia and B.J. Sophie didn't wait to see how Cassie fit into it. She crawled like a crab away from the railing and was running before she could even stand up straight. The shoe without the shoelace came off, but she kept going.

"Hey!" somebody shouted at her.

Sophie ran on, shoe squealing and sock sliding.

"I WAS watching her!" Tod yelled to somebody else.

His voice faded as Sophie took the stairs down two at a time and careened across the hall to the cafeteria door. Kids were lined up inside, ready to go to their classes when the bell rang, but Sophie was prepared to plow through all of them to get to Willoughby and tell her: *They're going to do a different cheer! They're going to make you look lame!*

Sophie skidded, arms flailing. A spattering of middle school laughter sprayed into the hall. She knew she looked like a crazy person, but she was so close—

Until somebody grabbed her and spun her around to face a Corn Pop wall.

# Eleven

Y ou little rat!" Julia shouted at her.

"We saw you spying on us!"

"You were on your way to tell her, weren't you?"

"Tell who?" Sophie said.

It was all she could think of to say, because right now if she didn't get to Willoughby, she knew the Pops would probably change their plan, maybe to something worse, and Sophie would never know how to protect Willoughby from them. She had to convince them she wasn't going near Willoughby.

"Who do you think?" B.J. said.

Sophie adjusted her glasses with a casual hand and tried not to breathe too hard. "If you're talking about Willoughby, I told you: she's not my friend anymore. None of them are."

"You're just saying that," Anne-Stuart said. "She's just saying that, Julia."

"Then why were you watching us?" Julia said. Her green eyes narrowed.

"You mean why was I looking down on the courtyard?" Sophie said. "I was pretending I was Aurora—medieval maiden—and I was in one of the castle towers."

Julia turned to Anne-Stuart and rolled her eyes. B.J. abruptly poked her in the side, and in spite of Julia's glare, whispered in her ear. Julia slowly smiled.

"So you're just weird on your own now, Soapy?" Julia said. "You really don't 'play' with your strange little friends anymore?"

She looked almost convinced. Sophie squeezed her eyes shut for a second. *Forgive me*, she thought. And then she said, "They're just a bunch of flakes. I can't wait to see Willoughby make a moron out of herself, okay? So get off me!"

Julia shrugged her shoulders and said, "Okay. We believe you."

The bell rang and the Corn Pop wall broke and disappeared. But not before Julia looked over Sophie's head and laughed, right at someone.

Sophie didn't want to turn around. She already knew who that someone was. Who they all were.

But she did turn, and she saw her beloved Flakes looking at her. The hurt in their eyes cut Sophie to her Corn Flake core.

"I didn't mean what I said!" Sophie cried. "I found something out. And I have to make them think—"

But it was as if she weren't even talking. Darbie turned white and fled with Willoughby at her heels.

"That was totally against the Code, Sophie," Maggie said.

Fiona made a hard sound, something that wasn't a laugh or a sob or anything Sophie had ever heard come out of her best friend before.

"What Code?" Fiona said. "Sophie made it up, so I guess she can un-make it anytime she wants to."

Sophie could only beg them with her eyes because she couldn't speak. Not with Fiona looking as if Sophie had run her through with a sword.

All Sophie could hear in her brain for the rest of the day was, *I denied them.*

It didn't help to tell herself that everything she'd said and done had been for the good of her maidens. In fact, by sixth period, when Aurora tried to speak, Sophie shoved her into the back of her imagination and slammed the dungeon door on her.

*I have to make them believe ME, not Aurora,* Sophie told herself. She wrote Fiona a note during sixth period and came close to dropping it into Fiona's open backpack while nobody seemed to be looking, but Eddie dived for it and Sophie had to retrieve it.

On Saturday an ache spread through Sophie like a disease. Nobody answered her emails. Nobody would talk to her on the phone, and she didn't have the heart to call Kitty. She stayed in her room, sure that Mama and Daddy thought she was pouting about not having her camera. That was fine. She didn't want them or anybody else to know how badly she'd botched everything up.

*I was only trying to protect Willoughby,* she told herself. *I had to do what I had to do.*

That was when she did cry, long and hard. Because she'd never meant for what she had to do to take her so far from the Code, and from the Corn Flakes.

"I'm sorry," she sobbed into her pillow. "I'm sorry."

She was nearly cried out before she realized that, for the first time in what seemed like a very long while, she was talking to Jesus.

With her tear-swollen eyes it was hard to see him, but somewhere in the dark hurt, he was there. His eyes were kind. They hadn't changed at all.

*Don't look at me that way!* she cried out in her heart. *I don't deserve it! I broke the whole Code you gave us! I put people down—I let them take my power—and I turned INTO them!*

Still his eyes were kind.

"Just make it so it isn't true—make it so it didn't happen—please!"

"Oh, Dream Girl, I don't think anybody can do that."

Sophie froze, and for a moment she thought it was Jesus' touch she felt.

But it was Mama, gently stroking her back. "What is it that needs undoing?" she said.

"You'll think I'm hateful!" Sophie cried.

"Sounds like you're doing a pretty good job of that yourself. Come on, let's get it out where you can look at it, huh?"

For a few minutes, Mama's words, as kind as Jesus' eyes, made Sophie cry harder. Finally she sat up, sniffling like Anne-Stuart. She blew her nose and told Mama absolutely everything, from the beginning. It wasn't until she was finished that she realized the hippo was gone. But the ache was still there.

Mama put her elfin hands on the sides of Sophie's face and looked straight into her eyes. "Sophie Rae LaCroix," she said, "I want you to promise me something."

"I'm not very good at keeping promises anymore," Sophie said.

"Keep this one. Tell me that you will never, ever again try to handle something like this by yourself." She brushed a tear from Sophie's cheek. "Sometimes we have to handle things on our own—but this was not one of those times. The Corn Pops are getting more subtle with their bullying now that they're older, and that's harder to prove. But honey, it's going deeper, and it has to stop—or you girls *are* going to become like them."

Sophie studied Mama's face, all pulled in with concern, but she could hear Coach Virile's voice, saying the same things. Coach Virile's unibrow and Mama's soft forehead holding the same thoughts? It almost made Sophie smile.

"You can come to Daddy and me. You can talk to Dr. Peter—"

The tears were there again, choking at Sophie's throat. "I can't talk to Dr. Peter now," she said. "I didn't even do the assignment he gave us. I missed his class because of detention."

"You don't have to be perfect before you can come to any of us. If you waited for that, you'd never talk to us at all! We just count on you being honest."

Sophie felt everything on her sagging as she sank against the pillows. Mama ran a hand over her head. "Does all this mean you haven't been talking to Jesus either?" she said.

Sophie could hardly look at her. "Yes. How could I do that?"

"Just the way I do and Daddy does and even Dr. Peter does—sometimes for a few minutes, sometimes for weeks, even months. It's not that we don't know he's still there. We just forget we need to go to him."

"I bet you never lost all your friends and turned into a lying Corn Pop!"

"I don't think you did either," Mama said. "But you do have some things to take care of, and Daddy and I do too."

"I don't get it," Sophie said.

"Then let's go find Daddy. We'll all sit down and see what we can figure out."

They had a meeting, the three of them, down in the kitchen over Mama's double-chocolate brownies, which Mama ate four of.

"I'm glad you're better," Sophie said to her.

Mama smiled at Daddy as she chewed. "We're going to have a LaCroix team meeting about that soon," he said. "But let's get this cleared up first."

After she and Mama and Daddy talked and came up with a plan, it looked like there might be hope. It didn't keep Sophie from sobbing while she was trying to imagine Jesus that night, but it did make it easier to face Dr. Peter the next morning.

When he greeted her with his twinkly eyes and a burst of "Sophie-Lophie-Loodle! I've missed you!" Sophie burst into tears again.

"Your mom told me what happened," he said as he located a box of Kleenex. "She said you're feeling pretty lousy."

"I think I flunked that test you were talking about," Sophie said. "I'm even having trouble looking at Jesus."

"Been there," Dr. Peter said. He opened his Bible on his lap. "So was that other Peter. Simon Peter." His voice got Dr. Peter soft and he tapped the Bible. "You ready to go back in?"

Sophie nodded and closed her eyes.

"Okay. Imagine that you are Simon and you're with Jesus when a bunch of soldiers and big muckety-mucks come to take him away."

"Do we have to read about Simon denying Jesus three times?" Sophie said. "I feel bad enough already. I know I did that too."

"Knowing it is a good start," Dr. Peter said. "The next step is to ask Jesus to forgive you."

"Will he?" Sophie said.

"When you're truly sorry—always."

"I am!" Sophie said. "I am SO sorry!"

"Tell him," Dr. Peter said.

Sophie closed her eyes, but before she could even wrap the words around her sorriness, she could see the forgiveness in those kind eyes. When she opened her own eyes, Dr. Peter was watching her.

"The next step is to ask him to help you hear him next time," he said.

Sophie nodded sadly. "BEFORE I mess up."

"Okay—come on," Dr. Peter said. "Let's skip to the good part." He fanned the pages of the Bible until he landed on a spot. "Simon's hanging out by a fire near where they've taken Jesus. He's already denied knowing Jesus twice. People keep harassing him about it, and finally somebody says he *knows*

Simon was with Jesus by their similar accents. Now, Luke twenty-two, verse sixty. Imagine—"

Sophie closed her eyes again, *and Sophie/Simon poked his freezing hands toward the fire and wished these people would just leave him alone. Everything was so confusing right now. He didn't need all these questions—*

Dr. Peter read: "'Peter replied, "Man, I don't know what you're talking about!" Just as he was speaking, the rooster crowed. The Lord turned and looked straight at Peter. Then Peter remembered the word the Lord had spoken to him: "Before the rooster crows today, you will disown me three times." And he went outside and wept bitterly.'"

Sophie didn't have to imagine that part. She was already doing it.

"I know how he feels!" she wailed. "I shouldn't have lied, no matter what!"

Dr. Peter handed Sophie another Kleenex. "Let me ask you something, Loodle," he said. "Where were all the other disciples when Simon Peter was sitting right there where people could ask him questions?"

"I don't know," Sophie said. "Hiding?"

"Yeah, they pretty much split. And why do you think he hung around?"

Sophie didn't have an answer for that one.

"Okay," Dr. Peter said. He rubbed his hands together. "Why did you hang out with Cassie when you had detention and 'spy' on the Pops when they were practicing their fool-Willoughby cheerleading routine?"

"Because I was trying to find out what they were going to do to Willoughby."

Dr. Peter was quiet. Sophie blinked at him. "Is that what Simon Peter was doing?"

"Could be. The point is, he didn't abandon Jesus completely, just like you didn't abandon Willoughby or the Code."

"But Peter ended up lying when people asked him, and so did I!"

"Don't you hate it when you're human?" Dr. Peter said. "Why did you tell the Pops that the Flakes weren't your friends anymore?"

"Because I wanted them to think I wouldn't tell Willoughby what I found out. But then all my friends believed it too!"

"That's the trouble with lying, even when we think we're doing it for the right reason. When did you feel the absolute worst about it?"

Sophie didn't even hesitate. "When I turned around and I knew they heard what I said about them and they all had this hurt look in their eyes."

Dr. Peter looked back at the Bible. " 'The Lord turned and looked straight at Peter. Then Peter remembered.' "

"But it was too late then," Sophie said.

Dr. Peter put the Bible on the floor and leaned back in his chair. "The thing is, Loodle, Simon Peter couldn't have saved Jesus no matter what he did. That wasn't his job."

"What was it then?"

"When Jesus came back after his resurrection—"

"Did he get all up in Simon Peter's face?" she said.

"Is that what you're afraid of?" Dr. Peter said.

"Yes."

"Let's see about that." He turned to the Bible. " 'Jesus said to Simon Peter, "Do you truly love me more than these?" "Yes, Lord," he said, "you know that I love you." Jesus said, "Feed my lambs." ' "

*Sophie/Simon saw Jesus' kind eyes and heard the words she wasn't expecting.*

"'Again Jesus said, "Simon son of John, do you truly love me?"
He answered, "Yes, Lord, you know that I love you." Jesus said,
"Take care of my sheep." The third time he said to him—'"

"Don't you believe me, Jesus?" Sophie burst out. "This is
the third time you've asked me that!" She bit at her lip. "I'm
sorry, Dr. Peter—go ahead."

"How many times did he deny Jesus, Loodle?"

"Three," Sophie said.

Dr. Peter was quiet, until Sophie slowly nodded her head.

"Just like you, Sophie, Simon Peter was hurt because Jesus
kept asking him. He said, 'Lord, you know all things; you
know that I love you.'"

He stopped reading. Sophie's eyes blinked open.

"So what did Jesus say?" Sophie said.

Dr. Peter's eyes looked a little wet to her. "He said, 'Feed
my sheep.' He gave Simon Peter three chances to show his
love, one for every time he had been too afraid to before. And
now he was showing him he trusted him again. He gave him
a job to do: taking care of all the people who needed to find
Jesus."

"Did Peter do it?" Sophie said.

"Until the day he died," Dr. Peter said. "I'm proud to be
named after him."

Sophie closed her eyes. She didn't see herself as Simon
Peter anymore. And she didn't see Aurora. She just saw herself—shrimpy, flat-chested, almost-bald-headed Sophie—
ready to do what she and Mama and Daddy had decided she
should do.

"I think you get it, Loodle," Dr. Peter said.

She gave him a wispy smile. "I think I do too," she said.

# Twelve

✳ ⌂ ✺

The next morning Daddy dropped her off in front of GMMS with the assurance that he and Mama would probably see her there before the day was over. Sophie breathed in a prayer and went straight to Ms. Hess' room. Sophie was sure Ms. Hess' creamy dimples flattened when she saw her. Even the silver angels dangling from her earlobes didn't look all that happy.

Sophie said, "Ms. Hess, I need to talk to you about something serious." Her voice cracked on its way up, and Sophie was sure that was the only reason Ms. Hess put down her chalk and pointed to a chair.

Sophie told her she was sorry she had messed up the cheerleading tryouts and said sarcastic things in class, and then she explained to her what she knew about the cheerleaders' plan. The angels stopped swinging against Miss Hess' cheeks. "You're making a pretty serious accusation, Sophie," she said. "Did anyone else see this go down except Cassie?"

"Tod Ravelli," Sophie said. "But I think he was supposed to be keeping me away from Willoughby so I couldn't tell her, and I guess he lost me."

Miss Hess pressed her fingers against her forehead and closed her eyes. Sophie's heart sagged. She knew what was coming next.

"I have to tell you, Sophie," Ms. Hess said, "I have my reasons not to trust you. The people you're talking about aren't perfect. But I don't see *them* clowning around in class and getting detention and trying to make fools of people." She pressed her rubbery lips together before she added, "Give me one reason why I should believe you."

"I think I have one right here." Mrs. Clayton crossed over to them from the doorway of their office, holding a paper, which she handed to Ms. Hess. Her bullet eyes were on Sophie, but they weren't shooting at her.

"Your Code of Honor paper," she said. "Is everything in here true?"

"Yes, ma'am," Sophie said.

"We didn't get a better essay than this one, Ms. Hess," Mrs. Clayton said. "And I believe in its sincerity. I think it might be time for that Round Table we've been talking about."

Ms. Hess looked up from Sophie's paper and stared at her. "I think maybe you're right," she said.

The first bell rang, and they told Sophie not to say anything to anyone else about the cheerleading thing for now. Sophie sat at her desk and pretended to get a head start on the assignment on the board while she prayed and prayed and prayed. Ms. Hess took Julia and Anne-Stuart—looking all important in their cheerleading uniforms—out of the room.

They were gone for about twenty minutes. When they returned, Julia's eyes, glittering with menace, went straight to Sophie. Then Ms. Hess called Sophie into the hall. There wasn't a dimple within a hundred miles.

"I had them do their cheer for today's assembly," she said. "They did the one I've seen them practicing."

Sophie wasn't surprised.

"But there was one little glitch that made me think." Ms. Hess stopped and fiddled with one of the angels. "I told them that had better be the cheer I see at this afternoon's assembly. Between now and then, they know that if anyone wants to speak with me privately, I'll be available."

*Aurora would go after them and slash something around and make them tell!* Sophie thought. She sucked in air. *But I just have to be Sophie and be honest and get help. That's where the power is.*

Sophie felt the hippo in her throat shrink a little. There would be no making a fool of Willoughby at the assembly. At least not the way the Pops had planned.

But as Sophie made her way through the rest of first and second periods, she knew that was only a temporary fix. What was to keep the Pops from going at her again—or at any of them—now that they were so mad their lip gloss was frying?

It was hard to keep back the tears when her Flakes all gathered around Willoughby in the locker room third period, even when Coach Yates came in again and stood at the end of the row of lockers. At least the Pops were too busy saying, "How you doing, Coach?" in their sugar-substitute voices to get to Sophie.

Sophie was all the way changed into her PE clothes before she realized she hadn't bothered to cover herself up to hide her chest. Straightening her shoulders, she tossed her bandanna back into her locker and headed outside, bare-headed. *Be honest and get help*, she kept saying to herself. *You're still there, right, Jesus?*

Out on the field Sophie stood on tiptoe and searched through the milling girls for Willoughby. But Willoughby wasn't with the other Corn Flakes. With her heart in her throat Sophie looked harder, visions of the Pops with Willoughby in some corner flashing through her mind. But none of the Pops were around either, until Coach blew her whistle and they suddenly appeared, cheeks flushed. There was still no Willoughby.

The minute Coach turned them loose to do their warm-up laps, Sophie ran straight for Fiona. It didn't matter how the Flakes treated her. It was all about Willoughby right now. When she reached them, they were gazing out in three different directions, hands shading their eyes.

"Are you looking for Willoughby?" Sophie said.

"Yes," Fiona said. "Where is she?"

"I don't know! Last time I saw her she was talking to you guys."

"She started to tell us something about the cheerleaders," Maggie said.

"Don't tell Sophie anything," Fiona said. Her voice was cold. "She's not our friend, remember?"

"Fiona, don't make a bags of it," Darbie said. She was peering intently at Sophie. "Something's wrong, isn't it, Sophie?"

Sophie told them about the fool-Willoughby cheer, and how Ms. Hess had told the cheerleaders they better do the real one at the assembly.

"That must be what she was trying to say before she disappeared," Maggie said. Her flat, practical voice was like a slap somebody needed. Fiona looked all around Sophie but not quite at her.

"I don't like the way this is sounding," Darbie said. "I think we should find her and make sure she's all right."

Fiona turned, but Sophie grabbed her arm. "I know how to do this now—not like we *were* doing it. You have to believe me."

"Why should we?" Fiona said. For a flicker of a moment her eyes had that same hurt look that had haunted Sophie all weekend.

"Fiona, can you ever lay off?" Darbie said. "Tell us what you're thinking, Sophie."

"First, we ask the Pops if they've seen Willoughby," Sophie said. "Just ask them. Don't be funny or mean or anything—"

Fiona didn't say anything.

"I'll take Julia," Sophie said. "Will you guys ask the rest of them?"

Coach Yates blew the whistle, and they scattered down the track. Julia, with her long stride, was hard to keep up with.

"Where's Willoughby?" Sophie said.

Julia didn't even look down at her. "It's not my day to watch her."

Sophie slowed down and waited for Darbie to come around to her. She and Maggie had gotten the same answers from Anne-Stuart and B.J.

"We need to ask Cassie," Sophie said.

"Fiona couldn't find her," Darbie said.

Sophie felt a little ping inside. "Fiona wanted to help?"

Darbie smiled at her. "It'll be all right, Sophie," she said. "Fiona's just stubborn, that one."

Sophie ran toward Coach Yates. The prayer in her head was hardly words now, but it was there.

"Do you know where Willoughby is, Coach?" Sophie said.

Coach Yates ran her eyes down the list on her clipboard. "She never checked in." She frowned. "I thought I saw her in the locker room though."

"She *was* in the locker room," said Maggie, suddenly at Sophie's side with Darbie and Fiona.

"You think she's cutting class?" Coach Yates said.

"No!" they all said together. It was a glorious chorus of Corn Flakes.

"If she is, she won't cheer in the assembly this afternoon," Coach Yates said.

"And that's exactly why she wouldn't cut!" Sophie said.

"All right." To Sophie's surprise, Coach Yates gave Sophie's shoulder a pat. "You girls go on and do your laps, and I'll look for her."

It was hard not to continue their search, and Darbie, Fiona, Maggie, and Sophie all swept the horizon with their eyes as they ran. Together. No one seemed to know what to say, but Sophie was afraid she wouldn't get another chance like this.

"I'm sorry I lied about you being my friends," she said. "I was trying to get information out of the Pops—and I just ended up acting like them."

"No doubt," Fiona said.

"Fiona!" Darbie barked at her.

"Well, I thought we were supposed to be honest and live by the Code."

"We didn't live by the Code when we didn't defend Sophie to Miss Imes," Maggie said.

"You've already said that like ninety times, Maggie," Fiona said.

"Maybe she should say it ninety more until you stop being so wretchedly stubborn," Darbie said. "I, for one, forgive you, Sophie. I've been desperate for you. And so has Fiona."

Actually, Fiona didn't look that desperate to Sophie. She didn't look anything, except like she was still avoiding meeting Sophie's eyes.

"All I can say," Sophie told them, "is that I learned we have to be honest and get help when we need it. Especially from God. I, like, totally stopped thinking about Jesus, and that's when I got really messed up."

Her throat was getting hippo-thick again, and she was glad the bell rang. Fiona took off like a jet toward the locker room.

"I'll talk to her, Sophie," Darbie said. "Come on, Maggie."

Once again Sophie was left without her Corn Flakes, but at least there was a tiny, birthday-candle flame of hope. She tried not to drag her feet as she headed in, but she was still near the tail end of the crowd that was pushing its way into the two locker rooms. She was wedged between a bevy of shoving boys and the wall when she heard angry voices coming from behind her, in the alcove where the water fountain was. They weren't loud, but they were familiar, and they shot into Sophie's ears like arrows.

"I'm not doing any more of your dirty work, Julia," said Tod. He spat out her name like it was a bad word. "I'm not your slave."

"Come on, Tod."

"Is it the *N* or the *O* you don't get?" Tod said. "I'm not doing it."

The crowd was thinning, and Julia lowered her voice so that Sophie had to strain to hear. "Then how are we supposed to make it look like Willoughby was hooking up with a guy instead of going to class?"

"I guess you can't," Tod said. Sophie could hear his voice moving away.

"We have to!" Julia said.

"You're psycho," Tod said.

Sophie peeled herself off the wall and dodged around the last few girls to get to Coach Yates's office. But she wasn't in there, or in the locker room.

*Coach Virile!* Sophie thought as she ran back out into the hall. She considered bursting into the boys' locker room, but she decided not to go *there* again. She had to find him, because suddenly she knew right where Willoughby was, and who was keeping her there. *Get help,* her inside voice told her. *Don't try to do this alone.* But what was she supposed to do if the help wasn't around?

Praying with nothing but big gulps of air, Sophie shoved through the doors into the gym and ran toward the bleachers. She wiggled her way between the wall and the benches and stopped inside the Pops' secret hideaway with a squeal of sneakers.

Cassie was standing up with her back to Sophie, blocking her view, but Sophie darted around her and threw her arms around a sobbing Willoughby, who was crouched on the floor.

"Too late, LaCroix," Cassie said. She sounded so much like Julia it gave Sophie a creepy chill. "She's about to be suspended for being under here with a boy when she was supposed to be in class. Bye-bye, cheerleading."

Sophie pulled Willoughby tight against her. "I don't see a boy."

"I do."

Before Sophie could even register that it was Julia talking, not Cassie, Julia grabbed her arm and wrenched her away from Willoughby.

# Thirteen

W hen are you gonna get it, Little Boy LaCroix?" Julia said. "You can't stop us. You're not GIRL enough!"

Sophie tried to pull away, but Julia grabbed at Sophie's T-shirt and yanked so hard Sophie's arm came out of the sleeve.

"They will never believe you bunch of losers!" Julia said between her teeth.

She reached over Sophie's head and clawed at her back, and Sophie could feel her T-shirt rising up to her neck. Julia's other hand was grabbing at the sleeve that was still on.

"You are the whacked-out freak losers!" Julia said, and with a final snatch she hauled the shirt over Sophie's head, knocking her glasses off and sending them flying. "They will always believe us, because we are the winners!"

She dangled the T-shirt in front of Sophie's face and laughed from someplace deep and dark.

Above them, the bleachers started to rattle. Cassie screamed.

"I think you just lost that round, Julia," said the too-high-for-a-man's voice Sophie was coming to love. "So come out with your hands up."

Cassie bolted for the opening like a bunny on the run. Julia gave Sophie one last smug look and hurled her T-shirt into the dark abyss of the bleachers.

"Good luck explaining why you're half naked," she whispered. And then she strolled toward the opening, calling out, "You are not going to believe what I found under here, Coach Nanini!"

"Let's go—all of you!"

Julia slid out, and Sophie fumbled for her glasses, squinting to see Willoughby. But she wasn't there.

"Willoughby!" Sophie said. "Come on—all we have to do is be honest. You don't have to hide!"

"I'm not hiding," said a faint little voice. "I just had to get this."

Willoughby emerged from the shadows, holding Sophie's T-shirt.

"I think you need to put this on," she said. "'Cause you don't look *anything* like a boy."

Coach Virile was already chewing Julia and Cassie out by the time Sophie pulled on her now-grimy shirt, found her glasses, and got out with Willoughby.

"The first thing you better do," he was shouting at them, "is get rid of this idea that you can do anything you want to anybody you want. That stops right here!"

"I don't think that!" Julia said. "Do I, Cassie?"

"I heard every word you said down there," Coach Virile said. "You going to call *me* a liar now?"

"No," Julia said. She flipped her ponytail toward Sophie and Willoughby. "*They* are the liars. You don't know them, but they have been trying to get us in trouble ever since sixth grade."

Coach Virile was looking at Sophie and Willoughby. "What happened, Willoughby?"

Sophie slid her hand into Willoughby's. "Just tell the truth," she said. "I didn't before, and I messed everything up."

Julia rolled her eyes. Cassie didn't seem to have the strength to roll hers. Her face was the color of Cream of Wheat.

Willoughby squeezed Sophie's hand until she was sure her fingers were going to pop off. "Before class," she said in a voice Sophie could barely hear, "they told me Ms. Hess wanted to meet with the cheerleaders again in here, and then they said they would go check me in with Coach Yates. But then just Cassie came back, and she shoved me under the bleachers and told me all this horrible stuff about my friends. Especially Sophie. And she wouldn't let me out."

Julia crossed her arms, teacher-style. "Cassie, how could you do something like that?"

"Because you made me!" Cassie said.

"Liar!"

Coach Virile stuck out his arm just as Julia lunged forward. "Give it up, Julia," he said. "It's over."

He herded Julia and Cassie across the gym, calling over his shoulder, "Little Bit, you and Willoughby go on."

Willoughby clung to Sophie like a baby koala. "Is it really over, Sophie?" she said.

Sophie nodded. But when Julia looked back from the doorway with war in her eyes, Sophie wasn't sure it was ever going to be over.

Before Sophie could explain anything to the Flakes in the locker room, a note came for her to go to the office. The secretary there directed Sophie to a room marked *Conference*.

*THIS can't be good*, she thought.

But once she got inside, she couldn't quite think anything. Around a table sat Mrs. Clayton, Ms. Hess, Miss Imes, Coach Yates, Coach Virile, and Mr. Stires, all looking somehow different away from their usual domains. She was so startled she couldn't think of the name of the curly-haired man with the equally curly beard who sat with them, although she knew he was the principal. The only thing that kept her from bolting was the sight of Mama and Daddy smiling at her.

"Welcome to the Round Table, Sophie," Mrs. Clayton said. "Please join us."

Sophie went straight to Mama and squeezed into the chair with her. Across the table, Coach Virile grinned. That was reassuring. But still she blurted out, "Am I in trouble?"

"No, Sophie, you are not," Miss Imes said. "Coach Nanini, do you want to explain?"

Coach Virile's eyebrow went into a stern line. "Little Bit, I hope you've been bullied for the last time—you and every other student in this school. It's time we did something about this power thing that's going down, and we want you to help us."

"Me?" Sophie said.

"Who better?" Coach Yates said. She pulled her whistle lanyard back and forth. "You're the feistiest little kid I ever saw."

"What do you want me to do?" Sophie said.

"Mr. Bentley?" Mrs. Clayton said.

They all looked at Mr. Principal, whose beard and mustache parted for a smile. "I think your teachers are right when they say you should be one of the students at the core of our new program to show kids how to work out their differences and put a stop to bullying at GMMS."

"Oh," Sophie said. She could feel her voice going into squeak mode with nervousness. But then the words just came out from where she'd been living them all day.

"All I know to do is be honest," she said. "And get help when you need it." She shrugged. "You have to do that so you can take back your power to be yourself."

"What did I tell you?" Mrs. Clayton said. Even Ms. Hess showed her dimples.

"That's exactly what this new program is going to be based on," Mr. Bentley said. "We're going to train you and some other core students, and our goal is that pupils at GMMS will learn how to respect the dignity of every human being."

"Like a Code of Honor," Sophie said.

"Exactly."

"We've all watched your struggles in seventh grade," Miss Imes said. Heads around the table bobbed. "But your parents have come in and shared some things with us. I read your Honor Code paper in the teachers' room, and I hope you'll forgive me, but I showed it to Mr. Stires before I turned it in. That's why I agree with everyone else that you are turning into a fine young woman."

Daddy grinned like Sophie had just won the Super Bowl all by herself.

When the Round Table meeting was over, Miss Imes and Mrs. Clayton handed Mama and Daddy Sophie's latest papers—the 95 and the A+.

"Okay, Soph," Daddy said. "Looks like you've earned back that video camera."

Miss Imes stopped on her way to the door and nudged Mr. Stires. "Video camera?" she said.

"My friends and I make movies," Sophie said.

"From original scripts," Mama put in.

"We were making one about medieval maidens, but then I got busted."

"Be sure that there is no more 'busting,'" Miss Imes said, her mouth twitching. "Mr. Stires and I have been talking about starting a film club. It sounds like you need to be in it—you and those other little imps you hang around with."

"Family meeting tonight," Daddy said before he and Mama left.

"With GOOD news," Mama said.

The prospect of something that didn't involve Sophie on the hot seat sang through her. But as Sophie floated off to class, Aurora suddenly appeared—

*She gave a deep, sweeping bow that dipped her sleeves to the ground. "It is time for me to release you, maiden," she said, "so that you can become Cecilia B. DeMovie, great twenty-first-century film director."*

Sophie could already picture herself with a black beret covering her spiky hair, sitting in a canvas chair, shouting, "Cut!"

But Aurora whispered once more in her ear, *"Don't forget what we failed to remember in our mission together. What King Arthur discovered he had put aside, why the Round Table crumbled—"*

"I know," Sophie whispered back.

She stopped at the railing and closed her eyes. "I love you," she whispered to Jesus. "And I'll always remember."

# Glossary

**abyss** [a-BISS] a hole or space so deep and scary that when you look into it you can't see the bottom

**accustomed** [a-KUS-tuhmed] when things are done in a way that you're used to

**ammunition** [am-yu-NI-shun] something embarrassing that can be fired back at you like bullets

**assurance** [a-SHUR-ance] a promise that puts your mind at ease

**beckoning** [BEH-kun-ing] a way of signaling someone to come closer without words

**bevy** [BEHV-ee] a large group

**blaggards** [BLAG-ghards] an Irish pronunciation of "black-guards," which are very rude and offensive people

**brandishing** [BRAN-dish-ing] waving something around in a threatening way

**bronchial spasms** [BRON-key-al SPA-zims] literally, when the tubes in your lungs go out of control from laughter, which could only mean something is incredibly funny

**chivalry** [SHI-val-ree] a code of honesty, kindness, and thinking of others before yourself; something usually associated with knights or thoughtful boyfriends

**cowering** [COW-er-ing] becoming very shy and wanting to run and hide when something scary comes

**discouraged** [dis-CUR-aged] how you feel when you lose confidence in yourself

**duress** [der-RES] extremely stressed to the point you just want to hide from the world

**eejit** [eeg-it] the way someone from Ireland might say "idiot"

**enthusiastic** [in-thew-zee-AST-ick] really excited and happy about something

**executioner** [eck-sa-KEW-shun-er] a person who is paid to put criminals to death

**feistiest** [FIE-stee-ist] very energetic and spirited compared to other people; a person who doesn't give up

**gnaw** [nawd] chewing on something over and over again

**heinous** [HEY-nus] unbelievably mean and cruel

**icily** [I-sill-ee] looking at someone in a very cruel way so it seems like icicles are shooting from your eyes

**impediment** [im-PE-di-ment] an obstacle that keeps something from happening, or at least slows it down

**javelin** [jahv-lin] a long pointy stick; it can be used for sport—to see how far it can be thrown into a field—or as a weapon

**jousting tournament** [JOWST-ing tur-na-ment] a type of entertainment in the Middle Ages when two armored knights would mount horses and charge at each other with long wooden poles, trying to knock each other off horseback

**loathe** [lowth] really, really hating something

**maiden** [MAY-den] a young unmarried woman

**make a bags of** [mayk a baygs of] do a poor job at, or screw things up

**medieval** [me-DEE-vul] something or someone from the Middle Ages, which lasted from the fifth century to the fifteenth century; this wasn't a fun time to live in, but it is now remembered for castles, knights, and fair maidens

**ponder** [POHN-der] to think really hard about something

**puppeteer** [puh-peh-TEER] someone who controls puppets on a stage

**round table** [ROWND taybull] according to stories about King Arthur, there was a special circular table where all the bravest knights in the kingdom met to discuss their good deeds

**sarcastic** [sar-CAS-tik] comments that are meant to hurt people

**sheath** [sheeth] a protective cover for a really sharp sword; it's sometimes carried on a person's hip

**smugly** [SMUG-lee] looking at someone in a proud "look what I did" way

**slagging** [slag-ging] mocking or making fun of someone

**squabbling** [SKWAH-bling] arguing wildly over something
**surveillance** [ser-VAY-lence] secretly watching someone in an attempt to gather proof they're doing something wrong

**swaggering** [SWAG-gur-ing] walking around in a way that is supposed to make people think you're important, but usually ends up making you look silly

**vexed** [veckst] completely confused and upset because of something that happened

**villain** [vil-an] a person who is basically evil, constantly trying to do bad things

**virile** [VEAR-il] the definition of manly; muscular, strong, and really hunky. Think cute movie star meets not-so-icky body builder

**vixen** [VICK-sin] a female villain; also means a woman or young girl who is mean

**wench** [whench] in medieval times, this was a servant girl, or the lowest class there was; it's also a mean insult

**whacked-out** [WHAKT-owt] crazy, out of your mind

**wistfully** [WHIST-ful-ee] longingly, wishing you could be part of something again

# Sophie and the New Girl

# One

"First we'll go to the cheerleaders' booth," said Sophie LaCroix's best friend, Fiona Bunting. The breeze loosened a strand of her golden-brown hair, and she tucked it behind her ear. "They've got corn dogs. And then we'll hit the Film Club—they're selling flan over there. And then we can stop off at the Round Table booth for kabobs—"

Sophie squinted at Fiona from behind her glasses while Fiona sucked in a breath. She hadn't taken one for a while.

"We're supposed to be filming the booths." Sophie nodded at the video camera in their friend Darbie O'Grady's hand. "Not pigging out at them."

Fiona grabbed a handful of candy corn from the chorus booth. "Who says we can't film and eat at the same time?"

Darbie O'Grady grinned, dark eyes dancing beneath her fringe of reddish bangs. "You're foostering about," she said. Although Darbie had lived in the United States long enough for her Irish accent to fade some, she still used her Northern Ireland expressions. So did Sophie.

"I guess I don't blame you for foostering," Sophie said. "Documentaries are boring."

"It's all about facts," Fiona said, her mouth stuffed.

"Facts aren't very creative." Sophie pushed her glasses upward on her nose. "I wish we were working on a *real* movie again."

"Uh-oh," Darbie said to Fiona. "She's got that look in her eye."

"You know it," Fiona said. Her own gray eyes were shining.

Sophie didn't need to see her brown ones to know what "look" they meant. She could feel it from the inside: that dreamy thing that happened when her mind started to wrap itself around a new character. If she still had her long hair, she would this very minute pull a strand of it under her nose like a mustache. That always helped her sort her thoughts. But it was impossible now that her hair was two inches high in fuzziness—although it was *long* compared to two months ago when she'd first shaved it off.

Sophie ran her hand over her fuzzy head. Closing her eyes, she saw herself as the tall, statuesque (that was one of Fiona's many impressive words) *Liberty Lawhead, swinging her briefcase as she marched briskly up the courthouse steps, heels clicking on the marble—*

"Hel-lo-o, So-o-phie." Darbie tugged playfully at Sophie's earlobe. "Miss Imes will eat the heads off us if we don't get *this* film done for Film Club."

"*Then* we'll tell her how we really want to do movies," Fiona said. "Corn Flakes Production–style."

Sophie nodded as she followed Fiona and Darbie and the smell of corn dogs across the field to the cheerleaders' booth. There Willoughby Wiley was practically doing a handspring waiting for them. "The Corn Flakes" was what the four of them, plus Maggie LaQuita and Kitty Munford, had called themselves ever since the Corn Pops, the popular girls in sixth grade last year, had told them they were "flakes."

*That means we aren't afraid to be just who we are*, the Corn Flakes had decided. So it only made sense that the movies they created from their amazingly intense daydreams were called Corn Flakes Productions.

But making a documentary about Great Marsh Middle School's Fall Festival for the new Film Club wasn't anything like making their own "flicks," as Darbie called them. Sophie sighed as she caught up to Darbie, who was already setting up the shot, and Fiona, who was already munching on a corn dog.

Willoughby's short mane of wavy, almost-dark hair trembled as she let out a shriek that always sounded to Sophie like a poodle yipping.

"Where have y'all been?" Willoughby said. "I've been waiting all day!" She waved her arms in what Sophie figured was a new cheerleading routine. She'd been to enough Corn Flake sleepovers to know Willoughby did cheers in her sleep.

"Be still, Willoughby," Darbie said. "Sophie has to interview you."

As Darbie started filming, Willoughby snatched up a corn dog in each hand and shook them like pom-poms. Two other cheerleaders posed beside her.

"What's the cheerleading booth up to?" Sophie said.

"We're selling corn dogs!" they all shouted together.

"Why?" Sophie said.

"Because they're good!" Willoughby said.

"No, eejit," Darbie said—using her Irish word for "idiot." "What are you going to use the money for?"

*It's a good thing Mr. Stires has editing equipment back at school*, Sophie thought. "To go to cheerleading camp this summer!" they all screamed.

"Thanks, girls," Fiona said, voice dry. "We'll call you if we can use you."

"Okay!" the squad cried out.

*Willoughby's going to be great in our Liberty Lawhead film,* Sophie thought. *She can lead the crowds of protesters in yelling … while the majestic Liberty Lawhead goes into battle for people whose rights are being tromped on. That was what made her a civil rights leader—*

"Beam yourself back down, Soph," Fiona said. "Let's hit the Film Club booth before all Senora's flan is gone."

Sophie pulled herself out of the 1960s, where she'd spent a lot of dream-time ever since they'd started studying the Civil Rights Movement in English/History block. When she got to the booth, Fiona was drooling over Senora LaQuita's shiny squares of sweet flan.

"I save you some, Fiona," the senora said. Maggie's mom was from Cuba, and Sophie loved her special way of speaking English.

Fiona pulled the plastic spoon out between her lips and closed her eyes. "It is *muy bueno,*" she said.

"That means 'very good,'" Maggie informed them. Maggie's words always fell like thuds, as if each one were a fact you couldn't argue with. With her steady dark eyes and solid squareness, the Corn Flakes usually *didn't* argue with her.

Right now Maggie nodded toward the camera, her black bob splashing against her cheeks. "Are you going to interview me?" she said. "I wish Kitty was here. She's better at this than me."

Kitty was the sixth Corn Flake, and Maggie's best friend. She had leukemia and was in the hospital in another town getting more chemotherapy, which, among other hard things, made her hair fall out. Sophie had shaved her head at the beginning of middle school so Kitty wouldn't be the only bald girl.

"I'm rolling," Darbie said.

"Tell us what the Film Club's up to here at the festival, Mags," Sophie said.

Maggie looked stiffly into the camera. "We're selling flan."

"What's flan?" Sophie said.

"It's like pudding."

There was a long pause. Fiona poked Sophie in the side.

"Have you sold a lot to make money for Film Club supplies?" Sophie said.

"We *did*," Maggie frowned, "until Colton Messik told everybody it was phlegm, not flan."

"What's 'phlegm'?" Sophie whispered to Fiona.

"Stuff you cough up when you have a cold," Fiona said.

*"EWWWW!"*

Darbie focused the camera on Miss Imes and their other sponsor, Mr. Stires. Miss Imes, their math teacher, pointed her dark arrow-eyebrows toward her short, almost-white hair. "Ready," Darbie said.

"Senora LaQuita has made some luscious *flan* for us," Miss Imes said into the camera. She didn't miss much, especially if it was some kid doing something wrong.

Sophie turned to their science teacher, Mr. Stires, who stood next to Miss Imes. He was short, bald, and cheerful, and his mustache stuck out like a toothbrush.

"Tell us about the equipment we're going to buy with the flan money," Sophie said.

Sophie heard Fiona groan as Mr. Stires launched into a lecture about DVD recorders.

"Oops, battery running low!" Darbie said after two very long minutes. "I'll get the extra one." She darted off.

"We could have been there for decades," Fiona said as she and Sophie followed. "Let's go for the kabobs."

Fiona took off for the Round Table booth on legs longer by several inches than tiny Sophie's, and Sophie hurried to keep up. Since Film Club had turned out to be pretty boring, being on the Round Table was Sophie's favorite school activity.

It was a special council of teachers and a few handpicked students who had set up an Honor Code for the school. They were responsible for deciding consequences for people who broke it, things that would help them learn to be better people instead of just punishing them.

No cases had been brought before them yet, and Sophie was anxious for one. It would be a great opportunity to be like Liberty Lawhead ...

*Who entered the room with her jaw set, looking down from her impressive height into the eyes of a heinous offender who had stomped on the rights of an innocent person. He looked back at her, his face set with stubborn heinous-ness, but she met his gaze firmly, without wavering. He finally dropped his eyes. He had obviously seen the honor in her face, honor he could never hope to match—*

"What are *you* looking at?"

Sophie found herself blinking into an unfamiliar face. Hazel eyes, set close to a straight, very-there nose, blinked back at her. The girl shook sandy-blonde bangs away from her eyebrows and pulled back her upper lip. Sophie wasn't sure it was a smile, but she couldn't take her eyes off the gap between the girl's two front teeth.

"I said, what are you looking at?" the girl said.

"Nothing!" Sophie's high-pitched voice went into an extra-squeaky zone.

"You were looking at something if you were looking at me," the girl said. Sophie was sure she smiled then, although mostly it looked like she smelled something funny.

Fiona and Darbie joined them, Fiona giving Sophie a we-thought-you-were-right-behind-us look. "You're Phoebe, huh?" she said to the girl.

"Yeah. Phoebe Karnes. I just transferred into your PE class." Phoebe tossed her bangs out of her eyes again and licked her full lips. "I was in all the wrong classes — it was all messed up. What are y'all's names?"

As Fiona introduced everybody, Sophie studied Phoebe. She had a look Sophie hadn't seen on many girls in well-off Poquoson, Virginia: faded jeans a little tight and a little short, graying tennis shoes with untied laces, and a long-sleeved T-shirt with ANGEL printed on it in fading glitter. Earrings with rhinestones sparkling down the length of them dangled from her ears.

*She's definitely not a Corn Pop*, Sophie thought.

"So, if you're interviewing people, interview me," Phoebe said. She lifted her lip at the camera before Sophie could even think up a question. "Hi — I'm Phoebe! My opinion of the festival? It's hilarious. For instance, let me direct your attention to the arm-wrestling booth."

Phoebe pointed to several tables set against a display of neon-colored stuffed animals. Members of the GMMS eighth-grade football team were arm-wrestling kids for chartreuse elephants and hot-pink teddy bears.

"There goes another one down," Phoebe said to the camera. "Flop — right to the table like a wet noodle."

Sophie saw she was right. One after another, kids gripped a football player's hand and pushed until their faces turned purple and their arms slapped to the table.

"Get this one on film, Darbie," Fiona said.

Sophie felt a smile wisp across her face. Eddie Wornom, a more-than-just-chubby member of the heinous group of boys

141

the Corn Flakes called Fruit Loops, was sitting down across from a fullback almost the size of Sophie's father.

Eddie glanced at B.J. Schneider, the Corn Pop standing behind him with her thumbs hooked into her hip-hugger pants. Behind her stood the other three Pops, all in ponchos that obviously didn't come from Wal-Mart, all with lip gloss shining.

"You better win this time, Eddie," Sophie heard B.J. say. Her pudgy cheeks were red, either from the crisp October air or because she was getting impatient with Eddie. He pushed so hard against the fullback's hand the veins in his neck bulged like ropes.

"If anybody can beat that football player, it's that bull Eddie," Darbie said from behind the camera.

"Nah, that's all blubber," Phoebe said. "See—there he goes!"

The eighth grader eased Eddie's arm to the table like he was knocking over one of the teddy bears.

"Eddie, you loser!" B.J. rolled her eyes with the rest of the Corn Pops.

"He cheated!" Eddie cried. "That—"

Sophie covered her ears so she wouldn't hear what came out of Eddie's mouth. It was usually gross.

"Hey, Jimmy! I bet you could win me a stuffed animal."

The Corn Flakes and Phoebe turned toward Julia Cummings, the tall leader of the Corn Pops. She was tilting her head at blond seventh grader Jimmy Wythe, so that her own dark auburn hair fell just so across her face. Jimmy looked as if he'd rather drown at the dunking booth than have Julia look at him that way.

"She should give up," Darbie whispered. "Sophie's the one he likes."

"He doesn't *like* me like me," Sophie said, voice squeaking. "*Eww.*"

It wasn't that Jimmy was at all heinous like a Fruit Loop. In fact, the Corn Flakes usually referred to him and his friends as Lucky Charms because they didn't make disgusting noises with their armpits or make fun of people until they withered. But Sophie just couldn't see wearing tons of makeup for one of them the way the Corn Pops did. Life was complicated enough.

"He's gonna do it!" Phoebe said.

Sophie stared as Jimmy shrugged and sat down across from the fullback.

"I give it fifteen seconds max," Phoebe said.

But Fiona shook her head. "Jimmy wins at, like, all these gymnastics competitions. That football player *wishes* he had Jimmy's arm muscles."

Darbie held the camera up just as Jimmy and the other guy linked hands. Immediately, both their faces turned red. The eighth grader got a concerned look in his eyes and grunted.

"He's fakin' it," Phoebe said.

But Jimmy didn't make a sound as he slowly pushed Mr. Fullback's arm flat onto the table.

"Dude," Phoebe said.

"I told you," Fiona said.

"I want the lime green one, Jimmy!" Julia said.

"We don't want *that* on film," Sophie said.

"That Eddie kid's about to explode." Phoebe's full lips spread into a smile. "I think it's funny."

"You stay and watch it, then," Fiona said. "Where to next, Soph?"

"Dunking booth," Sophie said.

She wanted to see Coach Nanini, the boys' coach she always thought of as Coach Virile because he actually *was* bigger than Sophie's dad. Besides, *virile* was such a masculine word. He was Sophie's favorite GMMS teacher.

143

"I'm taking you down, Coach!" Gill Cooper was yelling when they got there. Gill was one of the athletic girls the Corn Flakes referred to as Wheaties. She was about to pitch a softball at a target that, if she hit it, would dump Coach Nanini right into a huge vat of water.

"You couldn't hit the broad side of a barn!" Coach yelled back in his high-for-a-guy voice. To Sophie he looked like a big happy gorilla with no hair.

"Wanna bet?" Gill hurled the ball, and Coach Nanini went down with a splash that soaked everybody standing within two yards.

"Did you get it, Darbie?" Fiona said.

"In more ways than one," Darbie said. She rubbed the camera dry against her sweatshirt.

Suddenly a whole chorus of "Fight! Fight!" broke out, and it seemed like the entire festival crowd surged toward the snow-cone booth next to the dunking tank. Before she could turn around, Sophie was swept up by the mob, feet not even touching the ground. "Take him down, Eddie!" the kid directly next to her screamed. It was Colton Messik, the Fruit Loop with the stick-out ears.

Sophie swung her elbows around and got herself down onto the ground. Squeezing her eyes shut and digging her fingers in, she started to crawl.

"Hey, somebody get that girl out of the way!"

Sophie raised her head to see what girl they were talking about, but something came down hard on her back. She was flattened to the dirt.

144

# Two

All right, break it up!" Coach Nanini's voice cut through the roar of the crowd, and whoever was on top of Sophie rolled off. She gasped for air.

"Good grief—are you all right, LaCroix?" Coach Yates, the girls' PE teacher, was suddenly beside her. Sophie couldn't mistake that voice either. It had yelled her name enough times in class.

But now Coach Yates was saying gently, "Let's make sure you're okay before you get up. Anything hurt so bad you can't move it?"

Sophie shook her head, cheek still in the dirt.

"I didn't even get to see who was goin' at it," some kid whined from the crowd.

"Eddie Wornom," somebody answered him. "He fell on that little seventh-grader chick."

"All right, everybody move on," Coach Nanini said. "Nothing to see here."

Sophie kept her head down until everybody shuffled away. If Eddie Wornom had been on her, she didn't want anybody seeing who she was. *Ewww.*

"He was fighting that gymnastics dude," the same kid said.

*Gymnastics dude?* Sophie thought. *Not Jimmy!*

Coach Yates told Sophie to try to sit up.

"Was it really Jimmy Wythe?" Sophie said as she struggled to get upright.

"Yes," Coach Yates said, "but he doesn't look as bad as you do."

"I'm okay."

"Except for the blood dripping from your nostrils and the scrape across your forehead."

Sophie rubbed her hand under her nose. Her fingers came away red.

By then the rest of the Corn Flakes had squatted around her. From the looks on their faces, Sophie was sure she was disfigured for life.

"No broken bones, though, I don't think," Coach Yates said. She shook her head, stirring the too-tight, graying ponytail that stuck out through the opening in the back of her GMMS ball cap. "You always end up at the wrong place at the wrong time, don't you, LaCroix?"

"Wherever Eddie Wornom is *is* the wrong place," Fiona muttered.

Sophie didn't remind her that it was against the Corn Flake Code to put people down, even when those same people took *them* down. She looked at her bloody fingers again. Literally took them down.

"Well, Sophie," said a voice behind them.

Sophie tilted her head back to look up at Mrs. Clayton, the head of the Round Table. She stood over them, frowning beneath her faded-blonde helmet of hair.

"Looks like we have our first case," she said. "Are you hurt?"

Sophie was suddenly tired of answering questions. She was starting to shake.

"Could somebody find my dad?" she said. "I want to go home."

Daddy was brought over from the pony rides, with Sophie's six-year-old brother, Zeke, screaming that he didn't get to ride long enough. After asking Sophie the same questions everybody else had, Daddy tucked her into the front seat of the pickup beside him, and they listened to Zeke wail all the way home.

"We didn't get to go to the bonfire! I didn't get to have a corn dog!"

"You ate two cotton candies and a taco." Daddy gave Sophie a sideways grin. "Your mother is going to be mad enough at me as it is."

"I wanna go to the bonfire!"

Only Daddy promising they would have their own fire in the backyard shut him up, which was good, since Sophie's head was starting to sting.

"Now, remember, Z-Boy," Daddy said as they pulled into the driveway, "don't upset Mama. I want you to chill."

*Right,* Sophie thought as Zeke ran to the house, still screaming about corn dogs. *Zeke doesn't know how to chill anymore.*

But Mama "chilled" him as nobody else could. With her arms around Sophie, she told Sophie's fourteen-year-old sister, Lacie, to get some hot dogs out of the freezer and dig out the cooking skewers. Then she described the wiener roast they'd have so well that Sophie could almost taste it. Zeke went happily outside with Daddy to pile on the wood.

"Now, Dream Girl," Mama said, turning Sophie around so she could inspect her face. "Where had you drifted off to when this happened?"

Mama smiled the wispy smile that Sophie knew matched her own. Everybody said she and Mama looked just alike, except that Mama actually *had* hair, and it was curly and highlighted; she claimed it covered the gray that three kids had given her. And right now, Mama was puffier than usual. She was going to have a baby.

"I wasn't daydreaming this time," Sophie said. "Two boys were fighting, and I got caught in the crowd. Then Eddie Wornom fell on me—"

Mama's eyes got stormy. "They were fighting at the festival?"

"It was heinous," Sophie said.

"Let's get you cleaned up—come on."

Sophie sat in the chair by the window in her parents' upstairs bedroom while Mama cleaned the scrape on her forehead. Even though the hydrogen peroxide stung when Mama dabbed it on with a cotton ball, Sophie loved her alone time with her mom. It was a rare thing these days. When Mama wasn't resting, Zeke got most of her attention, acting out like he was practicing to be a Fruit Loop. Even now, Sophie could hear him hollering down in the yard.

"What's his deal?" Sophie said. "It's like he's Terrible Two all over again."

"He was never this bad when he was two." Mama blew softly on Sophie's forehead. "I hope this is just some phase he's going through. You girls never went through it."

"Girls are so much better than boys," Sophie said. "Do you hope our new baby is a girl?"

"I hope our new baby is healthy." Mama patted her tummy. "How do you feel about having a little brother or sister? We haven't had a chance to talk about it much."

Sophie hadn't had a chance to think about it much, either. Ever since the family meeting when Mama and Daddy had announced that there was going to be another LaCroix, Sophie had been wrapped up in Round Table and Film Club and Corn Flakes and Bible study with Dr. Peter and keeping her grades up so she could still have her video camera, according to her deal with Daddy. Besides, the new baby didn't seem real yet. Mostly it was just about Mama needing a lot of rest and Mama not getting upset and Mama taking vitamins the size of checkers.

Lacie came in then. She had a Daddy-look on her face, which wasn't hard because she, like Zeke, had his dark hair, his intense eyes, and his way of having everything figured out. "I hope you're almost done," she said, tossing her ponytail, "because Zeke is going to jump *into* the fire if we don't start cooking hot dogs in the next seven seconds." She grinned. "Which doesn't sound like a bad idea, actually."

"Lacie!" Mama said.

"Kidding—just kidding."

But as they followed Mama downstairs, Lacie looked at Sophie with a gleam in her eyes that clearly said, *"Which one of us is going to flush the kid down the toilet first?"*

The bonfire didn't go well.

At first, as Sophie smiled into the steam of her apple cider, she decided this was better than the bonfire at the festival. There were no Corn Pops or Fruit Loops doing stuff that would land them at the Round Table, where Liberty Lawhead would look at them solemnly and say...

*"What were you thinking? Were you thinking that these innocents who are not as hot as you are, not as rich—do not have rights too? The right to walk down a hallway without being teased? The right to be exactly who they are without being told they are lame and weird?"* She leaned across the table, pointing her pencil in their direction—

"Sophie," Daddy said, "I think that one's done enough."

"Oh, go all the way and burn it to a crisp, Soph," Lacie said.

Sophie looked at her black, shriveled hot dog.

Zeke, of course, wanted his charbroiled like that. When Daddy wouldn't let him, he pitched a fit that knocked his chair over into Mama's and sent them both tumbling to the ground.

Daddy yelled about Sophie not paying attention to what she was doing and Zeke and Mama almost falling into the fire, all the while dousing the flames with water as Zeke screamed. As Lacie and Sophie headed for the house with the skewers and the unopened bag of marshmallows, Lacie pointed out that they had been miles from getting burned.

"I thought it was the pregnant mother who was supposed to get cranky," Lacie said. "Not the pregnant father."

Behind them, Mama was saying, "I'm fine, honey," while Zeke howled about corn dogs and pony rides and everything else that had been denied him. Daddy was just howling—at everybody.

Sophie couldn't get to her room fast enough. She didn't even stop to examine the bandage on her forehead or the condition of the rest of her face. She just crawled under her pink comforter, within the sheer curtains Mama had hung around her bed, and pulled a purple pillow over her head.

"I hope you're there, Jesus," she whispered, "because I need to talk to you!"

That was what Dr. Peter—once her therapist and now her Bible study teacher—had taught her to do: to imagine Jesus and tell him anything she wanted and ask him anything she wanted. Since, according to the Corn Flakes, she was the best ever at imagining, she could see in her mind right now Jesus' kind eyes understanding absolutely everything.

*This has been like the most confusing day*, she said deep inside. *First that Phoebe girl hung out with us—and Jimmy Wythe got into a fight and I don't know how that's going to work out because he's on the Round Table Council and now he has to go* in front *of it—and I got trampled—and Mama asked how I felt about the new baby and I don't even know—then Zeke acted out like no other time—and then the worst: Daddy got all mad and yelled at everybody, even though it was only Zeke who was being evil. What's that about?*

She didn't expect an answer right then. Dr. Peter said that imagining Jesus talking back to her would be like putting words in his mouth. But she knew from experience that he *would* answer somehow, if she kept asking and kept waiting and kept looking in unexpected places.

Since that was the case, she made sure she was asking him exactly the thing she needed.

"Will you please help me find a way to make things more fair?" she whispered.

Then she added that she'd like for Zeke to please hush up so she could go to sleep—and then she did.

# Three

❋ ⌂ ✸

By the time Sophie got to her locker before school on Monday, she'd heard three different rumors about what was going to happen that day.

"Eddie Wornom broke Jimmy Wythe's nose, and he's gonna get suspended by that Table thing."

"Jimmy Wythe knocked Eddie Wornom unconscious, and they're just gonna expel him, period."

"They broke Sophie LaCroix's back, and they're both being put in juvenile detention."

The fact that Sophie was standing right there, obviously in one piece, didn't change their minds.

"It's like there's nothing else to talk about," Darbie said to Sophie and Fiona at the lockers.

Fiona nodded toward the chattering knot of Corn Pops a few lockers down.

"I *know* Eddie didn't start it," B.J. was saying, cheeks already three shades of red. "He knows he can't play basketball if he gets in trouble."

Sophie knew what Fiona wanted to say: that Eddie was getting way too honkin' huge to run down a basketball court.

"That is just *wrong*, B.J.," Julia said. She raked her hand dramatically through her thick hair. "Jimmy obviously didn't start it. He's a lover, not a fighter."

*Ewww*, Sophie thought.

"I'll tell you one thing for sure," silky-blonde-haired Anne-Stuart said, sniffing juicily. The skinniest Corn Pop, she always seemed to have a sinus problem. "If that Round Table thing tries to suspend Eddie, the office won't let them. He's too valuable to the school."

"Do straighten them out, Sophie," Darbie said.

The four Corn Pops swiveled their heads at the same time and, as usual, looked at the Corn Flakes as if they had been invisible until then. Sophie had figured out that was the only way the Pops could express their attitude toward the Flakes—ever since the Flakes had exposed them and gotten them kicked off the cheerleading squad. The Pops would get suspended from school again if they did anything more than just pretend the Corn Flakes weren't there.

"Straighten us out on what?" said Cassie, the newest Corn Pop. Her more-blonde-than-red hair trailed in strings down her back, and her mouthful of blue braces were a perfect match for the Limited Too top hugging her ribs.

"Sophie knows about the Round Table," Fiona said. "She's on it."

Julia gave Sophie a bored look. "So?"

"So," Sophie said, straightening her tiny shoulders, "it's our job to sort out who did what and then help them behave better. We don't do punishments."

"Of course you don't." Anne-Stuart gave a particularly gooey sniff. "You can't. Like I said, Eddie's popular, and his father gives the school, like, a ton of money."

"It doesn't matter," Sophie said. "We just go by the Honor Code, no matter who the person is."

"Sounds lame to me," Cassie said.

B.J. gave her buttery-blonde bob an impatient shake. "You dis us all the time," she said to Sophie. "So how can you be fair to Eddie? You just better—"

"Shut up, B.J.," Julia said.

"Excuse me, girls." A wiry man with a tool belt was standing behind Darbie. His voice was sandpaper scratchy. "I need to work on that locker right there."

"Oh, sorry," Darbie said as she and Fiona and Sophie scooted out of his way.

The Corn Pops moved aside without looking at him.

*I guess the janitor's invisible too*, Sophie thought.

"What's wrong with it?" Fiona said.

"It's broken," B.J. said. "Duh."

"It's broken, all right," the janitor said. He ran his hand over his no-color hair that was so thin red scalp showed between the waves. "And it didn't happen by accident, far as I can tell."

Sophie liked his sandpaper voice. It was kind of grandfather-y, even though he didn't look as old, even, as Fiona's Boppa.

"That's Eddie's locker," B.J. said.

Julia looked into her until B.J.'s cheeks went pale.

"Well, it looks like Eddie was doing pull-ups on it," Mr. Janitor Man said, pulling a huge screwdriver out of the tool belt. "There are bars down in the gym for that. This wasn't made for it." He glanced over his shoulder without really looking at B.J. "You tell your friend Eddie that, would you?"

Sophie and the Corn Flakes escaped before Julia could stare B.J. into a dead faint.

When they got to their two-hour English/History block, Mrs. Clayton called Sophie to her desk right away. Her usually dry-looking face was almost glowing.

"Round Table will meet after school today with our two little warriors," she said. "Try not to listen to any of the scuttle-butt that's going around school between now and then."

Sophie was pretty sure "scuttlebutt" meant rumors.

Mrs. Clayton was nodding her blonde helmet of hair. "This will be our first opportunity to change some attitudes around here," she said. "Remember, it's not about taking sides. It's about making this a safe place for people to learn."

"What about Jimmy?" Sophie said. "Will he get kicked off the Round Table?"

"That's what we're going to decide," Mrs. Clayton said.

*Liberty Lawhead walked solemnly to her desk in the Civil Rights for All office, feeling the weight of important work on her shoulders. As she slid into her chair, she saw the downtrodden she was about to save huddled in the waiting room. They looked so weary, so disappointed, and her heart ached for them. I will make change happen for them, she vowed. She doubled her fist and pounded it on the desktop—*

"Did somebody knock?" Ms. Hess said.

Sophie swallowed as their other block teacher hurried her trim little self toward the door, gold hoop earrings bouncing. Oops.

Fiona cleared her throat then, the signal she used when Sophie drifted too far into a Sophie-World and lost track of what was going on in class. Sophie nodded at her and turned to the "I Have a Dream" speech she was supposed to be reading.

*It's definitely time to start working on a Liberty Lawhead movie,* she thought. *Before I get in trouble and lose the camera.* With the way Daddy was yelling again, it could happen even without her making less than a B.

The "scuttlebutt" had reached record heights by the time Sophie, Darbie, and Fiona met Maggie and Willoughby in the locker room for third-period PE.

Willoughby's eyes were practically the size of Frisbees as she pulled her GMMS T-shirt over her head. "Everybody says Jimmy started the fight," she said. "But he's so nice!"

"Whether he started it or not, I think he won," Fiona said. "He doesn't even look as banged-up as you do, Soph."

Sophie realized she hadn't even looked at Jimmy during first and second periods, or thought about the scrape across her very-exposed forehead. She'd been too caught up in Liberty Lawhead.

"Eddie has a bruise on his arm," Maggie said as she tied a neat knot in her shoelace and straightened up. "We better get out there, or we'll be late for roll call."

Maggie, Sophie thought as she followed her outside, had never been late for anything in her life. If there was a rule, Maggie would follow it. Gill gave Sophie a soft punch on the arm as they lined up. "Hey, Sophie," she said, "is that Round Table like a court where you decide who's guilty and stuff?"

Before Sophie could answer, another voice poked itself in.

"I already know who's guilty," said Phoebe. "I saw the whole thing."

"Of course you did," Fiona said. She grinned at Sophie.

"So what happened?" Gill said.

She and her friend Harley, and the twin Wheaties, Nikki and Vette, gathered with the Corn Flakes around Phoebe, whose eyes took on a sharp gleam. She gave everybody that sort-of-a-smile Sophie remembered from the festival. Sophie zeroed in once again on the gap between Phoebe's front teeth. Big teeth, Sophie noted.

"The chubby kid couldn't stand it when Gymnastics Boy won that retarded stuffed animal for Little Miss Don't You

Think I'm Cute," Phoebe said. "So he follows him around, working himself into a sweat."

Phoebe pushed up her sweatshirt sleeves and lowered her head like a bull. Her nostrils were actually flaring. Willoughby gave her poodle shriek.

"Finally," Phoebe went on with the group around her watching, mouths open, "Chubbo can't stand it any longer, and he goes up to Gymnastics Boy. He doesn't even say anything, he just shoves him — "

Phoebe stepped forward with her hands outstretched and shoved Maggie backward at the shoulders. A shrill whistle shattered the moment, and Coach Yates was suddenly on them.

"What's this about?" she yelled.

"I was demonstrating," Phoebe said. Her eyes were still on Maggie.

"If demonstrating means you have to put your hands on somebody, Karnes, you can't do it. Period." Before Sophie could get her hands over her ears, Coach Yates put her whistle to her lips and gave it an extra-long blow. "All right, let's hit the volleyball court!"

The Wheaties took off. Phoebe motioned the Corn Flakes toward her. "Since she interrupted, let me just cut to the chase," she said. "Gymnastics Boy defended himself, but he should have taken Chubbo out totally, in my opinion." She looked straight at Maggie. "I bet you thought the same thing."

Maggie blinked. "I wasn't even there."

"Well, I'm just saying. You people like a good fight, right?"

"Who wants detention over here?" Coach Yates yelled.

Everybody scattered for the court, except for Fiona, who held on to Sophie's sweatshirt as they ran. "What did she mean, 'you people'? Not us!"

"I don't know," Sophie said. "Mrs. Clayton told me I'm not supposed to be listening to rumors anyway."

"Then we better stay away from that Phoebe girl," Fiona said. She put her hand up. "I know, I know, we still have to be decent to her. Corn Flake Code. But decent doesn't mean we have to be her best friend."

"I'm *fine* with that," Sophie said. Because Phoebe Karnes made her feel more than a little bit squirmy inside.

During lunch that day, the Corn Flakes met in Mr. Stires' science lab to edit the Fall Festival film. Since only two people could use the equipment at the same time, Fiona and Maggie took that over while Darbie filmed Sophie doing an introduction. Willoughby "directed," which meant she stood behind Darbie doing cheer motions. Sophie was starting her introduction over for the third time when Fiona let out a "*Score!*"

"You guys have to see this!" she said. "Come here—quick!"

All of them, including Mr. Stires, hurried over to her and Maggie.

"Whatcha got?" Mr. Stires said.

"*Only* the proof of who started the fight." Fiona shoved the stubborn strand of hair behind her ear and pointed to the screen. "Look."

"Coach Nanini getting dunked," Darbie said.

"No, look behind him, at the snow-cone booth." Fiona ran the film back and played it in slow motion. "Watch what's happening."

Sophie squinted through her glasses. "Hey!" she said. "That's Eddie—shoving Jimmy!"

"Just like that one girl told us," Willoughby said. "He *did* start it!" She punctuated her words with a poodle shriek.

Sophie watched, smile spreading. In the background of the dunking footage, Jimmy took a step backward, shaking his head. Eddie kept moving toward him. Just as Eddie threw the first punch and Jimmy ducked, there was a splash of water, and the film stopped.

"It looks like you just made Sophie's work at the Round Table a piece of cake, girls," Mr. Stires said. Even his bald head was shining. "Let's polish this up for prime-time viewing."

"Ladies and Gentlemen of the Round Table Council," Sophie said that afternoon in her best Liberty Lawhead voice, "I have not shown you this film to prove who is guilty, but to show who needs help. I have a dream that we can change Eddie Wornom's attitude, and the attitude of every other student who needs it. Thank you."

There was a murmur of agreement as Sophie took her seat. Jimmy gave Sophie a shaky smile. Across the table, Mrs. Clayton nodded. Sophie was pretty sure she hadn't missed the "I Have a Dream" part.

*But I was being sincere,* Sophie thought. After all, Liberty Lawhead never used the words of people like Dr. Martin Luther King Jr. simply to impress people.

*Liberty folded her hands neatly on the table. She didn't have to try to impress people. She merely did her job and did it well. At this very moment, she was about to change the life of the angry young man who couldn't keep his fists to himself. She tilted her face toward the head of Civil Rights for All, Mr. Virile—*

"I suggest," Coach Nanini was saying, "that we use our Campus Commission program with Eddie."

The eighth-grade girl on the council, a serious brunette named Hannah who wore contact lenses that made her blink a lot, raised her hand. "Is that like community service, only they do it at school?"

"Yard duty," said the eighth-grade boy with the two pimples on his chin.

"He'll have work to do on campus during lunch and after school," Coach Nanini said, "but I'm going to use that time to work on anger management with him."

Pimple Boy grinned, showing the rubber bands on his braces. "So he'll think he's picking up trash, but he's really getting therapy."

"Thank you, Oliver," Mrs. Clayton said drily. "We can always count on you to sum things up for us."

News that the Film Club's footage had brought Eddie down spread like a rash of poison ivy the next day. No matter how many times Sophie explained that bringing people down wasn't the Round Table's goal, nobody believed it. Least of all Eddie.

During announcements first period, Miss Imes got on the intercom in the office and said that Film Club was meeting during lunch, and new members were welcome to join. When the Corn Flakes got to third-period PE, Willoughby's eyes were once more Frisbee-size.

"Before Miss Imes even got done with the announcement," she said, "Eddie goes, 'Film Club is a bunch of losers. All they do is try to get stuff on people and turn 'em in.'"

"Well," Fiona said cheerfully, "at least we don't have to worry about Eddie joining Film Club."

Sophie sighed. "I don't think *anybody* will want to join Film Club unless we make it more exciting."

But somebody else did want to join. When the Corn Flakes showed up in Mr. Stires' room that day at lunch, there sat Phoebe. Gap-toothed smile and all.

# Four

❋ 🐦 ❋

W elcome to Film Club," Miss Imes said to Phoebe. "And you are?"

"Phoebe Karnes, and I have a *ton* of acting experience."

Miss Imes twitched an arrow-eyebrow. "We aren't so much about acting as we are about the art of film, the technical side."

Fiona raised her hand. "Uh, Miss Imes?"

"Yes, Fiona," Miss Imes said in her pointy-sharp voice.

Fiona gave Sophie a poke.

"We wanted to talk to you about that," Sophie said. "We really want to act in our films. We can show you what we mean."

"Do you have the films, Mags?" Darbie said.

Maggie, of course, produced the Corn Flakes Productions' Treasure Book and opened it to the back, where all their DVDs were neatly tucked into plastic sleeves.

"These are some of the movies we've made," Sophie said.

Miss Imes' other eyebrow went up, and Mr. Stires stroked his mustache. It didn't look good.

"So pop one in." Phoebe shook her bangs out of her eyes. "Let's see what ya got."

Maggie slipped a DVD into the player, and the title *Medieval Maidens* glowed on the screen in the gold letters Kitty had designed before she left for the hospital. The sight of them made Sophie sad.

But it was hard to stay that way watching herself and the other Corn Flakes cavort across the screen in the flowing gowns and pointy hats, and at times shiny armor, which Senora LaQuita and Maggie had made. It *was* hard to hear what their characters were saying, though, because Phoebe talked through the entire thing.

"Costumes aren't bad," she said.

"Dude—who taught you guys swordplay?"

"Oops, somebody dropped a line there—nice save, though."

"Yeah, get them with that speech, Sophie Baby. That's the best piece of acting in the whole thing. You're cookin'—you're hot."

Sophie didn't know whether to tell Phoebe to shush or keep it up. She was giving Corn Flakes Productions great reviews—sort of.

When Kitty's THE END appeared, both Mr. Stires and Miss Imes clapped. Phoebe whistled through her teeth. Sophie wondered if that space between them helped her do that.

"All right, I see the potential," Miss Imes said. "Go ahead and introduce drama. But we still expect you to continue to improve your technical skills."

"I don't know about technical stuff," Phoebe said, shrugging. "But trust me, I can act."

"I don't doubt it for a moment," Miss Imes said.

Fiona watched Phoebe exit, leaving a trail of acting credits behind her. "I said we'd be decent to her, but I didn't know we'd have to work with her."

"Maybe it won't be that hard." Willoughby's bubbly voice flattened. "You think?"

Darbie fiddled with her bangs. "She's different—and we're all about accepting people being different—"

Her voice trailed off. There was a big question mark in the air. They all looked at Sophie.

"She's just not different the way we're different," Sophie said. "She's like, way bossy—"

"She thinks she's ready for Hollywood," Fiona said.

Willoughby's little eyebrows knitted together. "It's like, she could be mean if she didn't like somebody."

"She doesn't like *me*," Maggie said. Her words fell harder than usual.

"Really, Mags?" Darbie said. "You mean, because she pushed you when she was talking about the fight?"

"She said she was just demonstrating," Willoughby said.

So far, Sophie couldn't see anything in Maggie's face.

"I'm just saying she doesn't like me," Maggie said.

"Which means it won't be that much fun for you," Fiona said. "I say we—"

"We can't 'say' anything," Sophie said. "This isn't Corn Flakes Productions, it's the Film Club. We don't get to say who can and can't be in it."

Willoughby seemed to wilt. "Then what do we do? Quit?"

"No way!" Fiona said.

"Then what, Sophie?" Darbie said.

Sophie nodded slowly. "The only thing we *can* do. We talk to Dr. Peter."

Fortunately, there was no Film Club meeting the next afternoon, the day they always met Dr. Peter at the church for Bible study. It was a good thing his class was based on the problems they brought in, because they hauled in a big one that day.

Dr. Peter was waiting for them with an eye-twinkly smile on his face. Their different-colored beanbag chairs and matching Bible covers formed a circle.

Sophie loved Dr. Peter more than any grown-up outside her own family. He was the one who had taught her to make films from her daydreams instead of escaping into them and missing what was going on in real life. Now that he led their Bible study, he taught cool things like that to the whole group. That included all the Corn Flakes except Willoughby, who had cheerleading practice after school, plus two of the Wheaties, Harley and Gill.

"You girls look like you're ready to pop open like a soda can." Dr. Peter grinned at them in that way that made his short, gelled curls seem to perk right up. It was impossible not to feel like everything could be okay with Dr. Peter around. "Let the fizzing begin," he said.

"Well, there's this girl," Fiona said.

She plunged into the story of Phoebe, with Darbie and Sophie adding details. The Wheaties put in a few of their own.

"I didn't like the way she pushed Maggie," Gill said.

"Did that bother *you*, Maggie?" Dr. Peter's eyes looked concerned.

Maggie shrugged. "She was just telling a story, I guess."

"She needs to lighten up," Gill said. "Only we're not supposed to put her down, are we?"

"We're just supposed to try to help people be better, right?" Sophie said.

Dr. Peter grinned at them again. "What do you need me for? You already know the answers."

"But what if I don't like those answers?" Fiona said. "This isn't very Christian, but I don't especially want to help her. She's just sort of—"

"Okay, tell you what," Dr. Peter said. "Let's dig into a Bible story and see if we can't figure this out."

"That's class, Dr. Peter," Darbie said.

Sophie liked it when Darbie said that, especially about Dr. Peter. He *was* great.

He had them turn to the Gospel of Luke, chapter 15, verse 1. They were all getting pretty good at finding their way around in the Bible, and everybody found it in the New Testament right away. Sophie prepared to go into imagination mode. "I want you to picture yourself as one of the 'bad guys' this time," Dr. Peter said.

"I don't want to be a bad guy," Maggie said.

"Nobody does," Dr. Peter said.

Fiona grunted. "I know some people that do. Oops, sorry, Dr. P. Go on."

"Trust me, you'll understand it better if you put yourself in the place of one of the teachers of the law."

"Those blackguards who were always blathering to Jesus about following the rules?" Darbie said.

She pronounced "blackguards" like "blaggards," one of Sophie's favorite Darbie-words. Sophie pressed her lips into a tight line and made her body stiff, so she'd feel more like a blackguard who couldn't even smile because having fun was against the rules.

"Now imagine that you are there," Dr. Peter said in his soft about-to-read voice. "And Jesus is talking to you."

Sophie pictured an outside hallway with columns, like she'd seen in Bible story books. With imaginary sandals on her feet and the taste of Israel dust on her tongue, she was ready.

"'Now the tax collectors and "sinners" were all gathering around to hear him,'" Dr. Peter read. "'But the Pharisees and the teachers of the law—'" He paused. "That's you."

"Got it," Fiona said.

" 'The teachers of the law muttered, "This man welcomes sinners and eats with them." ' "

Sophie pinched her Pharisee face tighter. *How wretched,* Sophie/the Pharisee thought. *Those slime.*

" 'Then Jesus told them this parable—' "

"What's a parable?" Maggie said.

Sometimes it was hard to stay in character with Maggie there. She wasn't the Corn Flake with the most imagination.

"A parable is a story that's told to teach a lesson," Dr. Peter said. Sophie could hear the grin in his voice. "Like this one is about to do, any minute now."

Sophie tightened back into her Pharisee self.

"This is Jesus talking now. 'Suppose one of you has a hundred sheep and loses one of them. Does he not leave the ninety-nine in the open country and go after the lost sheep until he finds it?' "

*Of course,* Sophie/the Pharisee thought. *It doesn't take a brain surgeon to figure that out.* She knew they didn't have brain surgeons in Bible times, but it was the best sarcastic thing she could think of on short notice.

" 'And when he finds it, ' " Dr. Peter read on in his Jesus-voice, " 'he joyfully puts it on his shoulders and goes home. Then he calls his friends and neighbors together and says, "Rejoice with me; I have found my lost sheep. " *Get to the point, man,* Sophie/the Pharisee thought. *I'm an important person. I can't stand around here all day listening to stories.* She/he *tugged impatiently at his long beard.*

" 'I tell you that in the same way there will be more rejoicing in heaven over one sinner who repents than over ninety-nine righteous persons who do not need to repent.' "

Maggie said, "What does 'repent' mean exactly?"

So much for imagining. Sophie wasn't enjoying being a bad guy to Jesus anyway.

"'Repent' means you admit that you've messed up," Dr. Peter said, "and you accept the forgiveness of God that's always there for you. Then you change your life."

Fiona leaned back in her purple seat, crackling the beans. "No offense," she said, "but what's this got to do with Phoebe? Are we supposed to try to save her, like, get her to be—what was that—'righteous,' instead of a sinner?"

"God is the only one who can save her," Dr. Peter said. "Matter of fact, he's the only one who can change her at all."

"So what do we do?" Maggie held a gel pen, like she was ready to write down his answer.

Dr. Peter pushed his glasses up by wrinkling his nose. "For starters, you can pray for her and appreciate her, the way Jesus does a lost sheep. Do that instead of putting her down. Jesus will go after her. God loves her just as much as he loves you." He rubbed his hands together. "There's more to this story, but let's just concentrate on that for right now."

"That sounds pretty easy," Fiona said. "We can do that, right?"

Everybody nodded, although Maggie didn't look all that enthusiastic to Sophie. "I'm staying away from her," Maggie said.

"Don't quit the Film Club, Mags!" Darbie said.

"I won't," Maggie said. "I'll just stay away from her."

"As long as you're praying, Maggie," Dr. Peter said. "Just remember that we all get lost now and then."

Sophie rested her chin on the edge of the Bible. Phoebe was lost? She didn't act that lost. She acted like she knew everything.

*But if the great civil rights leader Dr. Barton Gunther Prince Jr. says we must pray for her, then we must, Liberty Lawhead thought.*

*But as a civil rights leader herself, she must do more than pray for this actress, Diva Dramatica. If only she knew what.*

"Sophie-Lophie-Loodle."

Sophie's eyes popped open to see Dr. Peter's eyes twinkling at her.

"Your dad's here to pick you up," he said. "Who were you?"

"Liberty Lawhead, civil rights leader," Sophie said.

"A noble profession." Dr. Peter's eyes twinkled some more. "I can't wait to see this film."

Daddy was in the truck waiting for her, and Lacie was with him.

"I wanted to talk to both of you without Zeke around," he said as Sophie climbed into the backseat of the crew cab.

Lacie gave a grunt. "It was either take a ride in the truck or lock the kid in the closet."

In the rearview mirror, Sophie saw a trace of a smile go through Daddy's eyes.

But by the time they got home, Sophie wasn't smiling, and Lacie looked like she wanted to smack somebody.

Because Daddy announced that he'd be out of town the next week, and they needed to help Mama with Zeke after school. Even their protests that they had stuff to *do* after school didn't sway him. The "game plan," as Daddy put it, was that Lacie had Zeke duty Monday and Wednesday, and Sophie had it Tuesday and Thursday.

"With a new baby coming, we'll all have to take a hit for the team," Daddy said. "Just keep him out of your mother's hair for a couple of hours while she fixes dinner and gets some rest. No big deal."

*Uh-huh*, Sophie thought as she nodded at him. The former Zeke was no big deal. The little Act-Out King he'd become was the biggest deal in family history. And what about her busy schedule? Especially her making-a-film-about-Liberty-Lawhead time?

That night, Sophie imagined Jesus the minute she crawled under the covers. His kind eyes were there as she asked him first to deliver her from this evil, and then she gave in and asked him to help her want to do this for Mama. As she drifted off to sleep, she half dreamed of Jesus running after Zeke—but it was tough to imagine her screaming little brother as a lost lamb.

# Five

When Sophie got to first period the next morning, Ms. Hess was writing on the board: CIVIL RIGHTS GROUP PROJECT.

Everything in Sophie snapped to attention. She was sure even her spiky hair stood up straighter. *Project* was one of her favorite words. So was *group*, if that meant the Corn Flakes could work together. And, of course, she was all about *civil rights* now. Could this *get* any more perfect?

It could, and it did.

"Divide into groups of your own choosing," Ms. Hess said when class started. Her lips pronounced each word precisely, which Sophie wished she could do. It would make her sound more like Liberty Lawhead.

"Your groups may include people from the other section," Ms. Hess went on, "since you will do the work for this project outside of class."

Sophie covered her mouth so she wouldn't squeal out loud. From two rows over, Fiona was mouthing all the Corn Flakes' names to her.

Mrs. Clayton put her palm up to stop the buzz. "We want your group to ponder this question: How did the Civil Rights

Movement of the 1960s affect the way people have respected the rights of minorities since then?"

Julia's hand shot up, and she smiled syrupy-sweetly at Ms. Hess. Sophie knew that was part of the Pops' plan to get back on Ms. Hess's good side, since she was the cheerleading adviser who had kicked them off the squad.

"I thought," Julia said, dripping a smile, "that after the law changed, everybody was equal and civil rights wasn't a thing anymore."

"It most certainly is still a 'thing,'" Mrs. Clayton said. "Racial prejudice has always been present in American society, and it continues to be." She drew two long, wavy lines on the board. "The idea that all people are equal is the main flow that has shaped our country and how we live." Mrs. Clayton drew some hard, straight lines moving in the opposite direction from the flowing ones. "As long as there are people who think some races are inferior to others, that will run against what this nation stands for, and some people won't get fair treatment in jobs, things like that." She tilted her helmet head toward them. "Your task is to take one of the research areas from the list Ms. Hess is handing out and decide whether what the great civil rights leaders of the 1960s did has actually helped in that area to stop this current of prejudice." She pointed to the hard lines.

"How long does our report have to be?" Anne-Stuart said.

"No written reports," Mrs. Clayton said. "We want you to make a creative presentation to the combined two classes to show what you find out."

All through PE Darbie, Sophie, and Fiona told Maggie and Willoughby about the project assignment. They decided that whatever topic they picked, they'd do a film—and maybe it could be their next Film Club movie too. Mr. Stires had such awesome equipment.

"Pinky promise," Darbie said when they were closing up their gym lockers. "We're going to make the most class film ever."

Each girl hooked her little fingers and linked them with the Corn Flake's on each side of her until they were connected in a circle.

"What's going on?" said someone outside the circle.

Sophie felt Fiona's pinky tighten on hers. "Hi, Phoebe," Sophie said. "We're just—um—doing our friend thing."

"Cool." Phoebe shook her bangs out of her eyes. "That would make a good bit in one of our movies. See y'all at lunch."

"She's eating with us?" Willoughby said after Phoebe left.

"We have Film Club at lunch," Maggie said, words thudding.

Sophie felt another *uh-oh* coming on.

Phoebe wasn't the only other person who showed up for Film Club after fourth period. Jimmy Wythe and two of his friends, Nathan and Vincent, were there too. At least, Sophie thought, they were all Lucky Charms. If a Fruit Loop or a Corn Pop had shown up, she might have given up film directing forever.

"How's this gonna work for our project with all these people?" Fiona whispered to Sophie.

"Fiona," Miss Imes said, pointing her eyebrows, "do you want to share with the whole group?"

Fiona stuck out her bag of sour cream and onion chips. "Anybody want some?"

"Me," Phoebe said, and took the whole bag.

"That isn't what I was referring to," Miss Imes said.

All the Corn Flakes looked at Sophie, and Miss Imes tucked in her chin. "Is there a problem?"

The Corn Flakes looked at Sophie again.

"What?" Phoebe said.

"I think they want you to speak for them, Sophie," Mr. Stires said with a chuckle.

Trying to pronounce carefully the way Ms. Hess did, Sophie explained about the project. "The problem is," she said, even more carefully, "not everybody in the club is in our project group."

"We could be, since we're in the block too." Jimmy's bright blue eyes seemed shy as he glanced at Sophie. "I figure since you helped me prove I didn't start that fight, we could—y'know—sorta help you."

Nathan nodded his curly head. Vincent just watched everybody out of his very thin face. He always looked very scientific to Sophie, like somebody on a *Star Trek* rerun.

"We're gonna need guys," Phoebe said. "I can play a boy—I can play anything—but why waste me on that when we can get actual males?" She poked her finger toward Vincent. "Can you act?"

"Yeah." Vincent looked at her poking finger like it was a fascinating insect. "We all can."

Nathan turned scarlet all the way up to the tips of his ears. He didn't usually say much, Sophie remembered. He just communicated by the shade of red on his face.

By now, Fiona was clearing her throat so hard Sophie thought she was going to cough up a hair ball.

"Do you have a problem with that, Fiona?" Miss Imes said.

"Phoebe's not in either one of the English/History blocks," Fiona said.

Miss Imes' eyebrows almost disappeared into her hair. "And your point is?"

"I get it," Phoebe said.

Sophie squirmed and held her breath.

"You guys think if I don't have to do the movie for a class I might, like, drop out or something and you'd end up getting a bad grade. I'd think that too if I was you—but y'all don't know me." Phoebe gave her bangs a dramatic toss. "When it comes to acting, I am, like, obsessed. I wouldn't walk out on a play or something if I was *dying*. You'll get an even better grade on this project because I'm in it—trust me."

"You certainly don't have any confidence issues," Miss Imes said.

Mr. Stires chuckled, but Sophie didn't see anything funny. Phoebe had just pushed herself into the Corn Flakes' special project, and the teachers had let her.

Nathan and Vincent looked at Jimmy, who scratched his blond head and shrugged his big-for-a-seventh-grader's shoulders.

"Works for me," he said.

Sophie could see *It doesn't work for us!* in every one of the Corn Flakes' eyes, except for Maggie. Her eyes had no more expression than a pair of pebbles.

"What wouldn't work for us," Miss Imes said, "is your using Film Club time and equipment to work on a class project that can't include everyone in the club. I'll go talk to Ms. Hess and Mrs. Clayton right now to make sure Phoebe can be involved. Otherwise, no deal."

After she left the room, Mr. Stires said, "I think it will work out. Go ahead and pick your topic, and I'll be right over here." Then he escaped into the lab.

"Sweet!" Phoebe said. "This is going to be cool. What are our choices? Let's see that sheet."

She snatched Darbie's list out of her hand.

Darbie snatched it back. "I'll read it out loud," she said.

Sophie groaned inside. How were they supposed to pray for this bossy girl, much less "appreciate" her? "*God loves her just as much as he loves you,*" Dr. Peter had said. Sophie was glad *God* did—

Darbie read the list, but nothing on it seemed to shout, "Take me! Take me!" Sophie tried to think what Liberty Lawhead would want to get into.

"'Discrimination against Latinos,'" Darbie read. She looked up. "What's a Latino?"

Phoebe poked the usual finger toward Maggie. "Like her. Mexican."

"I'm Cuban," Maggie said.

"Same thing. You all speak Spanish." Phoebe tapped Darbie's sheet. "Go on."

"Wait a minute," Vincent said. A big, loose grin filled up most of his face. "We could do that one—y'know, since Maggie's a Latino person."

Sophie looked nervously at Maggie. She was sitting very still.

"Do you care if we do that, Mags?" Fiona said.

Maggie shrugged.

"We did a film about me being Irish," Darbie said. "The Corn—well, people stopped teasing me after that."

"Nobody teases Maggie about being Cuban, though," Sophie said.

Willoughby gave a half-shriek. "I never even knew she *was* Cuban until I met her mom."

"Her mom's cool," Jimmy said.

"She made that phlegm stuff," Vincent said.

*"Flan!"* the Corn Flakes said in unison.

Vincent blinked. "It was good. Anyway, if Maggie's okay with it—"

"Would everybody stop talking about me like I'm not here?"

Sophie glanced at Maggie. Her dark eyes finally had expression. They were flashing.

"Sorry, Mags," Fiona said. "Just tell us if you want to do it, yes or no."

"I vote no," Phoebe said.

"Is your name 'Mags'?" Fiona said. Sophie could tell Fiona was gritting her molars.

"Just listen," Phoebe said.

*Do we have a choice?* Sophie thought.

"I don't see how we're going to do a movie about Cubans getting their civil rights violated if we only have one Cuban in the group." She panned the circle with her eyes. "I'm sure not gonna play a Cuban."

"You have the wrong color hair anyway," Willoughby said. She gave a random shriek.

"Some Cubans have light hair," Maggie said.

"I never saw one." Phoebe pushed her finger into the gap between her teeth.

"How would you know?" Vincent said in his scientific voice. "You thought she was a Mexican."

"I want to do it."

Sophie stared at Maggie.

"You sure, Mags?" Darbie said.

"We don't have to," Fiona said. "There's other stuff on the list."

Willoughby flung an arm around Maggie's neck. "We know you don't like to be the main character—"

"What, are all of you her mother or something?" Phoebe pointed her finger yet again at Maggie. "Do you want to do it or not?"

"I said I do," Maggie said. "And they aren't my mother. They're my friends."

Phoebe shrugged. "That's cool. Okay—I'll play somebody who stages a protest march or something. I'm good in parts where I get in people's faces and yell."

"We don't even know if there's going to be a part like that," Fiona said. Sophie could tell her teeth were practically cemented together by now. "We do the research first. That's usually my job."

"I'll help you," Vincent said.

"Then we work out the script by playing with scenes. Maggie writes it down—"

"I can put it on my computer," Nathan said. They were the first words he'd uttered the whole time. His face was the shade of a tomato.

"Then we cast the roles," Fiona went on. "And the only one we know right now is Sophie's."

"Liberty Lawhead," Sophie said. "Civil rights leader."

"Don't we get to audition for that?" Phoebe said.

"No!" everybody said. Including Jimmy and Vincent.

Phoebe's eyes went round. "Okay," she said. "Don't have a heart attack. But just so you know: that's not the way it's done professionally."

"That's the way it's done here," Fiona said.

There was a stiff silence. Sophie tried not to take big mad-breaths that everybody would hear.

"Works for me," Jimmy said finally.

If he hadn't been a boy, Sophie would have hugged him.

# Six

Miss Imes came back to tell them that Ms. Hess and Mrs. Clayton said Phoebe could be involved in the project.

"As long as the rest of you do all the research," she said. "I personally think Phoebe will add a great deal to the film."

Sophie felt prickles on the back of her neck.

Phoebe threw out both skinny arms. "Fabulous! I'm gonna make you look so good. Are we meeting after school?"

"*We'll* meet to do research." Fiona was barely opening her mouth. "You don't have to be there."

"You know she'll come," Darbie whispered to Sophie when the bell rang. "The whole bloomin' football team couldn't keep her away."

Darbie was right. After school that day, when the Flakes and Charms were all in the library finding books and websites for Fiona, Phoebe flitted from one to the other, reading over their shoulders and talking nonstop.

"The Cubans that escaped from Cuba and went to Miami in the 1960s didn't even get discriminated against like the blacks did," she said. "People thought they were heroes because they left that loser Castro to come here." She tossed her bangs. "They just set up their Little Havana and lived it up."

"That's not what it says," Fiona said without looking at her.

Phoebe moved to stand behind Vincent at the next computer. "Yes, it does. Right there, it basically says the Cubans that left Communist Cuba were rich and all the Americans accepted them because they kept to themselves." She looked at Maggie. "Are you rich?"

"No," Maggie said.

"Didn't think so." Phoebe stuck her tongue thoughtfully into her tooth-gap. "So how come you're not?"

Willoughby nudged Sophie. "Do we have to let her be rude?" she whispered.

Sophie almost squirmed right out of her chair. *Jesus*, she squeezed out, *help Phoebe know when to shut up.* This was definitely the hardest thing Dr. Peter had ever asked them to do.

Jimmy looked up from the book he was poring over across the table from Sophie.

"Hey, Maggie, when did you come to the United States?" he said.

"I was born here." Maggie's words thudded harder than usual. "My mom came in 1980. She was twelve."

"Our same age!" Sophie said. A character for Maggie began to form in her head. A character Liberty Lawhead could protect…

*The little senora—or was it senorita?—blinked her dark, Cuban eyes up at Liberty. They begged silently for acceptance. "I know you aren't rich," Liberty said, "but you will find no discrimination here."*

Sophie propped her chin in her hand. That was the problem, though. They could show that the Civil Rights Movement had worked for the Cubans, but that wouldn't make a very hot movie.

"Did you say 1980?" Nathan was at the computer farthest away from the table. His ears went radish-colored immediately as everyone looked at him.

"That's what she said." Phoebe bounced in sideways steps to get behind him. The tops of his ears got even redder as she got closer. "Did you find something good?"

"No," he said.

Sophie saw his fingers swarm over the keys like bees. But Phoebe grabbed one of his hands and stared, mouth hanging open, at the computer screen.

"'Marielitos,'" Phoebe read. "'Fidel Castro, Cuban dictator, allowed 125,000 people to leave the port of Mariel, Cuba, for Miami between April and October 1980. Most were unskilled and uneducated. Many were prisoners and patients from mental institutions.'" She looked like she wanted to lick her chops. "Now *that's* what I'm talkin' about."

"Maggie's mom probably wasn't like that," Jimmy said quickly.

"Hello!" Sophie said. "She was twelve years old!"

Vincent, who had been clacking away at his keyboard ever since Phoebe uttered the word *Marielitos*, said, "Dude, this *could* be good movie stuff. It says here the people in Miami didn't accept them like they did the Cubans that came in the 1960s. Even the Cubans that were already there didn't want them. They were lowlifes."

Phoebe curled one of her smiles at Maggie. "Oh," she said.

"Excuse me," Darbie said, "but Senora LaQuita is not a 'lowlife.'"

"And since we're doing a movie about her and Maggie," Fiona put in, "this Marielito thing won't work anyway."

Maggie stared at the stack of books she had just put on the table. The nothingness on her face made the back of Sophie's neck feel like it was being stuck with tacks.

"So keep looking, you guys," Sophie said.

Phoebe grabbed her hoodie, the one that said BRAT on the back. "I give you brain children one more day to find something juicy for our movie," she said. "But personally, I think this is it. See ya."

"I'm telling you, Sophie," Fiona said when Phoebe was gone, "I don't see how I'm going to hold up the Code much longer."

Sophie ran her hand over her hair-spikes. "Dr. Peter said to pray for her and not judge her," she said. "And whatever that other thing was."

"When is it supposed to start working?" Darbie said.

Maggie didn't say anything. Her silence was like a thud of its own.

"She's probably wrong about this being a good movie for our project anyway," Vincent said, still squinting at the computer screen. "Technically, the way the people in Miami treated the Marielitos isn't discrimination." He cocked his head like he was studying a math problem. "Who would want a bunch of crooks and crazies—"

"Vincent," Fiona said. She kept her eyes on Maggie.

"Yeah?"

"Stop talking."

Maggie backed away from the table, her own dark eyes so blank it was scary. "You got it messed up," she said.

"No," Vincent said, "it's right here on the Net."

"Would you hush?" Sophie turned to Maggie. "Your mom wasn't a Marielito, so it doesn't matter. We *aren't* doing the film on that—"

"It *does* matter," Maggie said. Sophie had never heard Maggie's words fall so hard. "The Internet doesn't even know—"

And then she turned with a squeal of her sneaker and was gone.

"That went well," Vincent said.

"Shut *up*!" they all said to him.

There was no time to go after Maggie because the late bus would be there any minute. Besides, Sophie reminded the Corn Flakes, when Maggie had hurt feelings, she usually needed time to simmer before people got in her face.

"I wasn't even gonna let that Phoebe girl see the website," Nathan said as they left the library. He put on the Redskins cap he always wore when he wasn't in class. It covered the ears that now looked like the inside of a watermelon.

"Let her?" Fiona said with a flare of her nostrils. "She practically took your hand off!"

"She's pushy, that one," Darbie said.

Sophie didn't remind them about the Code again. She was having a little trouble upholding it herself.

*But I personally must follow the directions of Dr. Barton Gunther Prince Jr., Liberty Lawhead told herself as she left the Civil Rights for All building. Even if it doesn't feel like Diva Dramatica is truly worthy of our support.*

*Liberty drew herself up to her statuesque height and headed for her limousine. She must remember that Diva needed prayer—and whatever else the great doctor had said. Swinging her briefcase briskly at her side, she—*

"Watch it, freak!"

Sophie pulled her backpack against herself just before it smacked into Eddie Wornom's knees. He stood between her and the late bus, eyes bugging out.

"Sorry." Sophie's voice squeaked. She made a mental note to sound more like Liberty Lawhead, or at least like Ms. Hess.

"You oughta be sorry," Eddie said, and he moved a step closer.

*He smells like one big armpit*, Sophie thought, holding her breath.

"It's 'cause of you I hadda hang out with Coach Nanini," Eddie said. "I coulda used that time to get in shape for basketball tryouts."

Sophie choked back the words. *There isn't that much time left in the world.*

"I'm gettin' my dad to come down here and get me off this stupid Campus Concentration thing."

"Campus Commission," Sophie said.

"Shut up! It's stupid, because *you* thought it up!"

"Eddie, Eddie, Eddie," said a familiar voice behind Sophie. "Why are you making a holy show of yourself in front of everybody?"

"Huh?" Eddie said to Darbie.

Fiona pulled Sophie back so Darbie could wedge herself between Sophie and Eddie.

"Everybody's starin' at you," Darbie said into his baffled face. "You want them to think you're an eejit?"

"What's an eejit?" Eddie said, then he lowered his head like a bull and practically snorted. "I don't care what it is, I ain't that."

Then with an *actual* snort, he stomped away.

"Did he say something heinous to you before we got here, Soph?" Fiona's gray eyes were like thunderclouds.

"He just blames me because he got caught being heinous," Sophie said.

Darbie shook her head. "You know what, Sophie? Even you couldn't dream up somebody who was that much of an ee—"

"Corn Flake Code," Fiona and Sophie droned together.

*Eddie can blame me all he wants*, Sophie thought as she boarded the bus. *But I'm gonna help make this a safe place for everybody to go to school.* That was what Liberty Lawhead would do.

And right now, that seemed to include Maggie. They *weren't* going to do a movie about the evil Marielitos, but there was still something about them even talking about it that had done more than make Maggie nervous. Sophie knew

183

her fellow Corn Flake. When Maggie shut down, she was feeling extra bad inside.

That night, Sophie talked to Jesus about that. And about keeping her from smacking Zeke because he'd drawn Spider-Man webs all over her math homework while she was downstairs doing her English on the computer. And about the possibility of Eddie Wornom being miraculously turned into a Lucky Charm by Coach Virile.

She talked to Jesus about everything she could think of so she wouldn't have to talk to him about Phoebe. But finally, with Jesus' kind eyes waiting patiently, she prayed to him, *I know you love her just like you do us because she's a lost sheep and all that. I just hope you find her soon—because she's trying to take over everything like she's the boss of the world.*

She tried to leave it at that, but his eyes were still waiting.

*Okay*, she thought to him, *then please help me remember what that other thing was that Dr. Peter said we're supposed to do. Because it's getting way hard not to judge her.*

Sophie fell asleep praying that Jesus would make her more like Liberty Lawhead. That, she decided, was the only way this was going to work.

The Corn Flakes didn't see Maggie before school the next day, and she was late for PE, so they couldn't talk to her in the locker room, either. Willoughby said she'd been called to the office at the end of second period and left without a word. Evidently Maggie was still simmering, and Sophie was beyond squirmy. It didn't help that Phoebe pestered the Corn Flakes all during PE.

"So, did you come up with anything really delicious for our movie? It has to be something totally dramatic, you know, like someone gets thrown in jail or somebody gets murdered. We should have taken the Puerto Ricans in New York for this project. They get knifed all the time, and I know how to fake a stabbing and make phony blood that looks totally real—"

"I'll go mental if I have to listen to that girl for one more minute," Darbie said on the way to fourth period.

"We have to remember that she's lost," Sophie said without much enthusiasm.

"Not lost enough, if you ask me," Fiona said.

Sophie could hardly concentrate in math class, and when Miss Imes announced that Film Club was having an urgent meeting during lunch, Sophie gave up completely.

*I bet Maggie told her we were accusing her mom of being a criminal or something,* Sophie thought. *Maggie wouldn't even listen to us . . .*

*Liberty Lawhead shook her head. It was so difficult to fight for a person's civil rights when that person went off angry and didn't get all the necessary information. "Ignorance is the root of prejudice," Liberty Lawhead always said. Well, she wasn't the first one to say it, but she lived by it as no other civil rights leader did in these evil times. She would simply have to find a way to make the young senorita listen to her. First she would have to find out where she was hiding—*

"Soph, look who's here."

Sophie shook herself back to Fiona, who stood next to her desk, nudging her with a pencil.

"Did you find Maggie?" Sophie said.

"What? No—*look.*"

Sophie turned her gaze toward the door. Miss Imes stood in the doorway. With her was Maggie's mother.

"That can't be good," Sophie said.

"You know it," Fiona said.

# Seven

When the lunch bell rang, the rest of the Film Club arrived in curious bunches and sat in the front-row seats. Sophie didn't take her eyes off Maggie's mom.

Sitting in a chair at the front of the room, Senora LaQuita wasn't wearing her usual smooth expression. Her coffee-with-milk-colored forehead was in folds, her lips pressed together in a line. Sophie had seen her angry look before, and this wasn't it.

*She doesn't look like she wants to hug all of us, either,* Sophie thought as she slid into a desk. She probably hadn't brought them any flan.

Sophie looked at Maggie, who sat a little apart from the rest of the group, eyes on her mom, face still showing nothing. Sophie felt squirmier than ever.

*Liberty Lawhead folded her hands neatly on the desk and collected her thoughts. It was obvious that the Cuban senora was here to accuse them, the most conscientious civil rights workers on the planet, of discriminating against her and her daughter. I will simply tell her that we do not believe the information we have collected is about her, Liberty decided. Surely with her low, cool voice she would be able to soothe the senora into listening.*

"Why is the cleaning lady here?" Phoebe muttered, landing in the desk next to Sophie.

Sophie glared at Phoebe. "That's Maggie's mom," she whispered.

"Oh." Phoebe leaned close to Sophie's ear. "I see a Mexican woman around here, I figure she must be on the janitor's staff."

"She's *Cuban.*" Sophie's whisper-voice squeaked out of hearing range.

Miss Imes leaned against the front of her desk, and all whispers shushed. "We understand that you've uncovered some information in your research," she said, "but that there are some holes in your facts."

"I must be outta the loop," Phoebe said. "I don't know what you're talking about."

"You're about to find out," Mr. Stires said without his usual chuckle.

"Maggie?" Miss Imes said. "Why don't you start?"

This time, Sophie squirmed for Maggie. She knew that talking in front of people was *not* one of Maggie's favorite activities.

Maggie's face still didn't change as she turned her eyes on the club members and dropped her words like clumps of wet cement.

"My mom was a Marielito," she said. "But they weren't all criminals and crazy people like everybody thought."

Fiona opened her mouth, but Miss Imes said, "Just listen. Senora LaQuita has agreed to tell you what it was like for her when she left Cuba. Then there can be no mistake."

The way Senora LaQuita was pulling herself up to her full height reminded Sophie of Liberty Lawhead. It riveted Sophie's attention.

"*Gracias.* Thank you." The senora lifted her chin. "My English is no very good, but I will try to explain."

Even though Senora LaQuita pronounced "ex" like "es," Sophie wanted to cry out, *Your English is beautiful.* Beside her, Phoebe grunted.

"My father," the senora began, "he did no like Fidel Castro. Our life in Cuba—"

She pronounced it "Cooba," Sophie noticed. "It was very hard. We could no go to the church. I could no get good education because—" She frowned and said something in Spanish. "We were no like Castro. When he say anybody can go to America, my father, he build a boat for us."

Sophie suddenly felt as if she'd never really seen Senora LaQuita before. This senora was a hero, the kind movies were made about. As she told her story, the scenes unfolded in Sophie's mind.

A scene where a twelve-year-old girl and her mother and carpenter father boarded a leaky, lopsided raft held together by tires. Her face was all shiny with hope for a life in America where she could go to any church she wanted.

A scene where the boat sank with Miami in sight—and where the girl woke up in a hospital, surrounded by people who babbled in a language she couldn't understand.

A scene where she and her mother sat in a city of tents and mourned her father, drowned just a few feet from the Florida shore.

A scene where her mother tried to find work, but even Cuban Americans didn't trust her because she had arrived with the Marielitos. They were angry with *her* because other people from her country had been in Castro's prisons.

And a scene where the frightened twelve-year-old Cuban girl learned her first English word. "Scum," said the American officer as he jerked his thumb toward her and her mother. She only had to see the man's face to know what it meant.

The room was silent when Senora LaQuita finished talking. Sophie could hear her own heartbeat pounding in her ears.

"I think you've found your story of discrimination," Miss Imes said to the group. "Thank you — *gracias*, Senora LaQuita, for sharing your story with us."

Before anyone else could speak, Phoebe said, "Yeah, thanks. That story'll make a great movie. When do we start?"

*Did somebody die and leave you in charge?* Sophie thought. The back of her neck was alive with prickles.

The Film Club agreed to meet the next day, Saturday, at Darbie's. But the Corn Flakes spent Friday night there to paint each other's toenails and write letters to Kitty and make sure their Maggie didn't think they were heinous.

"I wasn't mad at you," Maggie said while Willoughby applied an exact replica of Sponge Bob to each of Maggie's two big toenails. "I just couldn't explain it like my mom did."

"She was so beautiful," Sophie said.

"Your mom has great nails," Willoughby said.

Darbie snickered. "I don't think that's what Sophie meant, Willoughby."

Willoughby blinked her almost-Frisbee-size eyes, and the Corn Flakes sent up a chorus of giggling snorts. Then they linked pinkies just because.

The next day, Sophie was glad they'd done that, because working on the movie definitely didn't feel like Corn Flakes Productions. Not with so many other people involved.

Actually — not with Phoebe involved.

Phoebe wanted to do every scene six times until it was perfect, even though they were just playing with them to get ideas written down.

She said things like, "I want to try it again, only with Cuban Girl here."

"Her name is Maggie," the Corn Flakes told her nine times. By the tenth time, they all shouted it together, with the boys joining in—even Nathan.

A smelling-something-funny smile spread across Phoebe's face.

"That was good. You guys should all be off-camera yelling during the scene where I get in Cuban Girl's—Maggie's—face in the Food Stamp Office."

"Yelling what?" Darbie said.

"You know, stuff like 'Get a job or go back where you came from, moocher.'" Phoebe looked at Willoughby. "You're a Rah-Rah Girl. You know how to yell."

Willoughby gave a nervous half-yip. "I don't think I can yell *that*."

"It's acting," Phoebe said. "Okay, I'll do the scene, and when I wave my hand, you just yell stuff like you agree with me."

"You know," Fiona's pink bow of a mouth twisted into a knot even as she spoke, "Sophie is usually the director."

Sophie folded her arms. "Yeah, if you don't mind—"

"Just let me show you," Phoebe said. "You—" She looked at Maggie. "Sit in this chair. I'm behind the desk, and you just came in asking for food stamps."

She half pushed Maggie into a dining room chair. Maggie looked down at the table. Once again, all expression disappeared.

"We'll work on your part later. Let's just do mine." Phoebe leaned back in the chair and narrowed her eyes until Sophie was sure they would cross. "I am so sick of you people," she said.

Willoughby yipped. Darbie put a hand on her arm. "She's acting," she said.

"Miami isn't even an American city anymore," the Phoebe character said. "Once you people started running out the whites, that was the end of anything American." She crawled

190

her forearms halfway across the table. "I bet somebody's payin' you under the table so you don't have to pay taxes, and here you are trying to get money from *our* taxpayers. The *real* Americans."

Phoebe waved her hand, but nobody said anything. Sophie didn't even know what she was talking about. Besides, she was frozen by the hatred Phoebe was acting out.

"Nobody wants to live near you people," the Phoebe character said, her voice rising. "All the whites are running from you aliens. That's what you are, you know, trying to make us all speak Spanish and running for office so you can turn Miami into another Cuba. No!"

Phoebe banged her fist on the table and made Darbie's aunt Emily's crystal vase jitter in place.

"*Some* people might help you, but I intend to remain civilized! Otherwise, they're gonna let anybody in here. Any scum, do you hear me?"

"*What in the world?*"

Sophie jittered like the crystal vase. Aunt Emily crossed the dining room with one manicured hand over her mouth. She was what Mama called a true Southern lady, and right now she looked like she was about to faint like one.

"Why am I hearing this kind of talk?" she said in her very-proper Virginia accent.

"Phoebe was just acting a part for our flick, Aunt Em," Darbie said.

"Cool," Phoebe said. "I had you convinced." She turned to Darbie. "Did you get any of that on film?"

"I'm not so sure I like this movie," Aunt Emily said.

"You're not actually supposed to like it." Vincent's voice cracked. "It's supposed to educate you and make you think."

"Or make you mad," Fiona said.

Aunt Emily tapped a finger against her lips. "I think it will."

As hard as it was, Sophie had to agree with her. Phoebe was an amazing actor. She might *know* it like no other, but she was good.

Even Fiona nodded her approval as Aunt Emily left the room.

"You should be in real movies," Willoughby said.

"I will be someday," Phoebe said. "Wait 'til you see what I do in the tent-city scene." She looked at Fiona. "That's at your house tomorrow?"

"We have to switch to plan B," Fiona said. "My dad said he doesn't want us putting up a bunch of tents in the yard and messing up the lawn."

"No problem," Phoebe said. "We'll do it at my house. My dad could care less about the lawn." She curled her lip into that smile. "You guys really think I'm good?"

"Hello!" Willoughby said. "Look—I chewed off two fingernails!"

There was smiling. Something, Sophie thought, had kind of changed. Still, she felt squirmy.

After Sunday school the next day, the Corn Flakes talked nonstop about Phoebe.

"We have to admit she's an incredible actress," Fiona said. "Even though I hate to because she thinks she's better than the rest of us."

Willoughby tilted her head. "I think she started being nicer after we gave her all those compliments."

"She did?" Darbie said.

"She invited us to her house," Sophie said. "That might be Phoebe being nice."

"What's 'nice' for Phoebe is, like, almost heinous for one of us." Fiona put up her hand. "That's not against the Code. I'm just agreeing."

Sophie felt the shiver of an idea, something Liberty Lawhead herself might come up with. "You know what?" she said. "I just remembered that other thing Dr. Peter said. We're supposed to appreciate her for her good stuff."

"Like tell her she's all that as an actress?" Willoughby said.

"Yeah," Sophie said. "'Cause like you just said, she was a little nicer when we did that."

Fiona pulled back and frowned. "Dr. Peter said we shouldn't try to change her."

"Maybe that's not changing her," Darbie said. "I acted like an eejit when I first met all of you — worse than Phoebe — but I wasn't really like that inside. I just did it because I was all angry and afraid." Sophie thought Darbie's eyes got a little misty. "But then you accepted me, and now I'm — "

"Fabulous!" Willoughby said. She gave her happy-poodle yip.

Sophie didn't get to find out if anybody else agreed. Daddy appeared and sent her to the primary room to sit with Zeke because he was having a meltdown. His third one that day.

Sophie had to feed him an entire roll of Smarties she'd been saving, even her favorite green ones, just to get him calmed down from the fit he was having because somebody else was playing with the Noah's ark set. She tried not to think about what Tuesday afternoon was going to be like.

It was easy to forget about that the minute Fiona's grandfather, Boppa, pulled up to Phoebe's house that afternoon in the SUV loaded with the Corn Flakes and their tents.

"I see why Phoebe's father doesn't care about his lawn," Fiona said. "He doesn't have one."

Sophie couldn't actually tell if there was any grass around the house with the peely green paint. There was something on every square inch of the ground—old lawn mowers and gas cans and something that might have been a car once.

"Where are we going to put up tents?" Darbie said.

"Someplace safe, I hope." Boppa's caterpillar eyebrows almost met in the middle. "I think I'll stick around and watch the rehearsal."

"That would be fabulous, Boppa," Sophie said. Something about Phoebe's yard was making her want to stay in the car.

Phoebe bolted out the front door wearing a faded poncho that looked like somebody had worn it the last time ponchos were in style. Nathan, Vincent, and Jimmy trailed out after her. Nathan's face was so red, Sophie couldn't tell where it stopped and his Redskins cap started.

"I thought you'd never get here," Phoebe said. "The call was for two o'clock and it's five after."

"The call?" Fiona said, lips already bunching up.

"That's theater talk," Phoebe said. "I can give you a lesson on that later."

"I thought you said she was getting nicer," Darbie whispered to Sophie as they followed Phoebe to the backyard.

Fiona grunted. Maggie didn't say anything. She hadn't said anything since they'd pulled in.

"We have to keep giving her compliments," Sophie whispered back.

"Great space for the tent scene," Vincent said.

There wasn't as much stuff in the backyard. Just one rusty wheelbarrow and a chicken coop minus the chickens.

"They all died," Phoebe told them.

It took a few minutes for the girls to get their tents up near where the boys had already pitched theirs. Boppa stood on the back porch until the door creaked open. A man almost as stick-skinny as Vincent came out.

"Ned Bunting." Boppa stuck out his hand.

"Buck Karnes." The man shook Boppa's hand absently as he squinted at the kids. Sophie was amazed how much Phoebe looked like him. The only thing missing was a gap between his two front teeth.

"Don't be touchin' none of my stuff, Phoebe," he said.

Okay, so the gap wasn't missing. But there was something—in his eyes—that Phoebe didn't have in hers.

"We aren't gonna touch any of your precious stuff," Phoebe said without looking at him.

"I'd be afraid to," Fiona murmured to Sophie.

Sophie knelt to check her tent spikes. Jimmy was suddenly there beside her. "Phoebe must be really poor," he whispered. "I kinda feel sorry for her." His blue eyes looked sad.

Sophie decided she liked that about him. "We're all trying to tell her she's fabulous and all that," she whispered back. "She seems nicer when we do that."

Jimmy nodded his blond head toward the back porch. "I don't think that'll work on her dad. He's pretty mean. You shoulda heard him yelling at her before you came."

Even now, Mr. Karnes' voice was way louder than it needed to be for Boppa, who was standing right next to him.

"This is some thing they picked to do a movie about," he said. "Cubans. I told Phoebe all they're good at is highjackin' planes."

He grinned like he'd just delivered a hilarious punch line. His lip even curled back like Phoebe's. Boppa didn't smile with him.

"I remember back in '80 when Castro let all his rejects go," Mr. Karnes went on. "It was all over the news, them washin' up right on those fancy beaches in Miami and spongin' off

Americans the minute they got here." He spat off the side of the porch. "I heard any white person wants to stay livin' down there has to have bars on their windows."

"I don't think so," Boppa said.

"Oh, yeah. Crime's worse down there than in New York City. Cubans are dealing drugs and counterfeiting money and robbing tourists."

"Excuse me," Fiona said.

Sophie sucked in her breath. Fiona was marching toward the porch.

# Eight

In case you haven't noticed," Fiona said before she even reached Phoebe's father, "our friend Maggie is Cuban. I'm sure she doesn't appreciate you saying things like that."

"Who's a Cuban?" Mr. Karnes' eyes darted across the yard like he was looking for a rattlesnake.

Darbie stepped in front of Maggie. Jimmy was right beside her. Sophie was stuck between wanting to cover Maggie's ears and wishing she could escape into Liberty Lawhead on the spot.

"Fiona," Boppa said, "let me handle this."

"You better do it quick," Fiona said. "Before I—"

"Fiona," Boppa said.

Their beloved Boppa didn't raise his voice that often. When he did, everybody shifted into obedience mode. Fiona backed down from the porch.

"You kids get to work," Boppa said. He looked at Mr. Karnes. "Could we talk privately? Inside?"

Mr. Karnes shrugged, and they disappeared inside the house. Nobody said anything for a minute. Even Phoebe was quiet as she stared at the door.

"I wondered where you got that big speech yesterday," Vincent finally said to Phoebe. "Now I know."

"You sounded just like your father," Darbie said.

Fiona snorted. "Go figure."

Phoebe took a bow. "Thank you," she said. "I get my material wherever I can."

"Do you believe him?"

Sophie jumped. It was the first thing Maggie had said since they'd arrived. And Maggie's face wasn't blank anymore. Her eyes were hard and shiny, like wet stones.

Phoebe looked as startled as Sophie felt, but only for a few seconds. Then something hard came into her eyes too. That final piece made her look identical to her father.

"My dad's a jerk," she said. "I never even listen to him except when I need an example for a character. When I told him what we were doing our movie on, he just came out with this whole monologue—"

"Then you don't believe him," Sophie said quickly. She could practically feel Maggie growing stiffer by the second.

"Who cares?" Phoebe said. "It's all about the part for me."

"*We* care if Maggie gets her feelings hurt." Fiona's nostrils were flared so wide, Sophie was sure she herself could have crawled in. "Your father needs to apologize to her."

"Right," Phoebe said. "Like I can make him."

"You probably can't," Vincent said. He sounded like he was talking about a math problem. "On the meanness scale, he's about a—"

"So, do you guys want to do this scene or what?" Jimmy said.

Sophie decided she liked him for that too. But as they set up the "scum word" scene, Sophie couldn't help wondering—

Was Phoebe really that good an actor? Had she really just played her father yesterday when she yelled at Maggie?

Or did she believe what she was saying?

*She can't even remember Maggie's name half the time,* Sophie thought. *And she just automatically assumed Senora LaQuita was the cleaning lady.*

Not only that, but Phoebe pushed Maggie around like she was her servant or something. Even now, she was saying, "You—get behind Fiona since she's your mom and act like you're scared. Do something besides just stare."

"You know what, Phoebe?" Fiona said. "Why don't you just worry about your own acting and let Maggie do her thing?"

"Works for me," Vincent said.

"I'm just trying to make this thing sensational," Phoebe said. "You guys could learn so much from me."

*Liberty Lawhead drew in a deep breath. This was the hardest case she had ever come up against. It was so much easier when the bad guys were totally bad and there was no mistaking their heinous-ness. But when someone was sometimes right, but was so hard to listen to, and when that same someone didn't come right out and say she, well, hated Cubans, what was she to do?*

"*I must remember what Dr. Barton Gunther Prince Jr. told us,*" Liberty said out loud so she would be sure to hear herself. "*We must pray and not judge. God will make it clear to us when we need to speak out.*"

"How does that fit into this scene?" Phoebe said.

*I think it fits into every scene,* Sophie thought.

She looked at Maggie and wished the hardness would disappear from her friend's eyes.

But that look stayed with Maggie over the next several days.

They practiced at Sophie's after school Tuesday because of Zeke. When Sophie set him up on the back patio with his Spider-Man toys, he swept them all off the table with one arm and wailed that he wanted to be in the movie.

Phoebe said Maggie should watch him because wasn't that what "you people are good at?" It didn't sound like a compliment to Sophie, and it obviously didn't to Maggie, either. She looked so hard at Phoebe, Jimmy jumped in to sling Zeke over his shoulder and carried him around through the whole rehearsal. Sophie *really* liked that about him.

But Zeke was so wired after everybody left, he grabbed the plates off the dinner table and flung two of them like Frisbees before Sophie could stop him.

"I'm staging a protest!" he said.

No more rehearsals at their house, Mama said.

Wednesday, Phoebe complained because the rest of the girls went to Bible study instead of meeting to practice.

"So come with us," Sophie said.

Three different Corn Flakes poked her in the back.

"Me go to church?" Phoebe said. "Nah. Religion is a bunch of hooey." She looked at Maggie. "Do you go to this Bible study thing too?"

"Yes," Maggie said woodenly.

"Why wouldn't she?" Fiona said.

Fiona's voice got colder every time she spoke to Phoebe. Pretty soon, she was going to frost Phoebe's eyebrows.

"I thought the Cubans did, like, weird rituals and stuff. I read it in some of that stuff Vincent printed out."

Sophie made a mental note to tell Vincent to stop with the Internet, already.

"I'm a Christian," Maggie said, staring at Phoebe.

Phoebe shrugged. "Okay. Don't have a seizure."

During Bible study that day, Dr. Peter had a fall feast for them, with grapes and bread and apples and pumpkin squares. There was a lot of giggling and grape peeling, but they didn't have time to discuss their problems like they usually did.

That was okay with Sophie. She wanted to talk to Dr. Peter alone about it, and she hung back after everybody else left. She especially didn't want Maggie to hear—just in case Maggie wasn't catching all the little remarks Phoebe muttered under her breath. It would be okay after she told Dr. Peter everything, she just knew it.

"We really, really tried to appreciate her and not judge her and stuff," Sophie told Dr. Peter after she'd brought him up to speed, "and I've been sort of praying for her. She's nicer to the rest of us now, but not to Maggie." She wrinkled her nose to push her glasses up, the way Dr. Peter always did. "Maybe she's just naturally mean that way, you know, like her father."

Dr. Peter wrinkled his nose too. "I don't think any kid is just naturally mean," he said. "Usually a girl acts mean because she's angry or scared."

"But we don't have to keep trying if what we're doing isn't working, do we?" Sophie could hear her voice squeaking up hopefully. "It isn't fair to Maggie."

"Just because it doesn't look like it's working doesn't mean it isn't," Dr. Peter said. "I'm not saying you have to make Phoebe a member of the Corn Flakes, but you've made a commitment to work with her on this project."

Sophie squirmed.

"And I'm not saying you should let her get away with being mean to Maggie. I'm concerned about that part. If Maggie is having trouble with it, you need to bring in some grown-ups. That isn't busting people, you know."

"Maggie keeps saying she's fine." Sophie ran her hand over her fuzzy do. "But she doesn't really know how bad it is. And I don't want her to find out."

Dr. Peter leaned back in his beanbag and put his hands behind his head. "Basically, Sophie-Lophie-Loodle, you want me to give you permission to cut this girl loose."

Sophie didn't say anything. The back of her neck prickled. This wasn't going at *all* the way she wanted it to.

"That's your decision," Dr. Peter said. "You can try to protect Maggie from experiencing prejudice, and that's a very nice thing to want to do. Or —" He rubbed his hands together. "You can do what Jesus did and help Maggie stand up for herself and help Phoebe understand that what she's doing is — what's that word you like?"

"Heinous," Sophie said.

"And you can do it the way the Corn Flakes always do — with honesty and respect — all that good Code stuff."

The prickling on Sophie's neck was going out of control. "I told you it isn't working," she said.

Dr. Peter squinted a little behind his glasses. "Keep doing what you're doing, Loodle. And do two more things."

"I don't want to do two more things, Dr. Peter!" Sophie said. "I just want you to tell me it's okay to dump her!"

"I can always count on you to be honest, can't I?" He shook his head. "But I have to be honest too. That isn't the right thing to do. It would make you a Pharisee."

"Me?" Sophie said.

"Maggie isn't a lost sheep. She has a Shepherd to show her who she is. But your Phoebe is one. Most people who need that much attention are acting out their lostness. And most people who exhibit prejudice are afraid." He leaned toward Sophie. "I wouldn't say this to most kids your age, but you're special this way, Soph. You get it. Think of Phoebe as a lost lamb instead of a bossy girl who doesn't like Cuban people. Isn't that what Jesus was trying to tell the Pharisees in that story?"

"But I'm not like them!" Sophie said.

"No, you're not," Dr. Peter said. "But sometimes a little Pharisee-itis can sneak in."

The back of Sophie's neck felt like it had a cactus stuck to it.

"I have to go." For the first time ever, Sophie was glad to leave Dr. Peter. She'd never imagined it could happen, but Dr. Peter just didn't understand.

And he wasn't the only one. That night while Lacie did double duty with Zeke and told Sophie she owed her big-time, Mama came into Sophie's room for a talk. Sophie saw a tiny line between Mama's eyebrows, and she knew whatever her mom had to say wouldn't make her any happier.

Still, Sophie shared the only package of Smarties she'd kept out of Zeke's clutches and even gave Mama the green ones, just in case it might sweeten things up some.

But Mama delivered bad news anyway: there were to be no more rehearsals for the Cuban movie project at *any* of the Corn Flakes' houses.

"I know the movie is important," Mama said before Sophie could protest, "but it has some pretty rough scenes. None of us Corn Flake parents feel like we can supervise so many of you. You know, the boys. And your new friend."

"But we could still rehearse at Phoebe's," Sophie said. "Her dad didn't care—"

She trailed off as Mama stopped with the last green Smartie almost to her mouth. "Absolutely not," she said. "Boppa was very concerned about that situation. You girls are wonderful about bringing out the best in people, but we think that should be done where you have better adult supervision."

The way Mama said it made Sophie wonder if all the parents had memorized the same speech and were right now delivering it to their own Corn Flakes. At least Daddy wasn't here, putting in a bunch of sports stuff she never understood.

Suddenly, Sophie felt like she was being pulled in two directions like a Gumby doll.

In one direction was the hope that her parents would say she couldn't be around Phoebe ever again. Then she wouldn't have to do all the stuff Dr. Peter told her to do.

But in the other direction was their project. *This is all Phoebe's fault!* she thought.

"How are we going to practice then?" Sophie said. Her voice entered a whole new squeak-zone.

"We talked to the school. You have permission to practice on the school grounds after classes. They'll have an adult there." Mama smiled her wispy smile. "You can even take your camera if you keep it in Mr. Stires' room when you aren't using it."

Sophie wondered if Mama had checked with Daddy about that one. Taking the camera to school was *huge*. But even that didn't help. Sophie choked the Smarties package closed with a twist. This was getting less and less like a Corn Flakes Production every single second.

"Dream Girl," Mama patted the pillow next to her, "join me for a minute."

Sophie flopped back against the cushions.

"Are you feeling a little bit like everything's upside down right now?" Mama said.

*I'm feeling a lot that way*, Sophie opened her mouth to say.

But then she stopped. Daddy said they were supposed to keep Mama from getting upset, not give her more stuff to worry about.

So instead, she said, "Want some more Smarties?"

There was a scream from the direction of the bathroom.

"Mo-om!" Lacie yelled. "I can't be responsible for what I'm going to do to that kid when you get me out of here!"

Sophie could hear Zeke taking the steps down two at a time.

"You want Lacie or Zeke?" Mama said.

Sophie took Lacie. Once she'd climbed up on a chair to get the bathroom door key off the ledge and released a froth-ing Lacie from Spider-Man's prison, she retreated to her room again.

*Liberty Lawhead curled up in the corner of her jail cell. I must remain strong, she told herself. Even though the powerful people who don't understand keep squeezing me in, tighter and tighter. I must continue to reveal the truth about such things as Diva Dramatica's prejudice —*

"And about Dr. Peter being wrong," Sophie said into the pillow over her head. "And all the parents being wrong."

She tried to imagine Jesus, but all she could see was a strange progression of people who might supervise their next rehearsal. Miss Imes. Coach Yates. Mr. Janitor Man.

"This is just heinous," Fiona said after school Friday as the Corn Flakes trailed with the camera out toward the field hockey practice area.

It was a bright, crisp November day, perfect for filming, but Sophie nodded at Fiona. This situation gave heinous a whole new meaning.

"I just hope there aren't a lot of kids out there watching us," Darbie said.

Willoughby nodded grimly. "It would be just like the Corn Pops to spy on us and steal our ideas."

As they stepped onto the edge of the field, the Lucky Charms joined them.

"That's the least of our worries," Vincent said.

He pointed toward a small set of bleachers, and Sophie groaned out loud. There was Eddie Wornom, doing something to a bleacher seat with a screwdriver big enough to be seen across the field.

"What's he doing here?" Jimmy said. Sophie thought he suddenly looked all protective. "I thought he had Campus Commission."

Sophie said, "He does, only where's Coach Nanini?"

"I'm not a coach today," said a high-for-a-guy voice behind them. "I'm a Hollywood producer."

Sophie turned to see him wiggling his one big eyebrow and peering at them over the tops of his sunglasses.

"Who's in charge of this production?" he said. "You, Little Bit?"

Sophie grinned. She wished Phoebe'd heard that. This was the first decent thing that had happened all day. "Are you babysitting us?" said another voice.

Phoebe trotted up, her own pink-glittered plastic sunglasses riding on top of her head.

"I'm supervising," Coach Nanini said.

Phoebe shook her bangs out of her eyes. "We don't really need supervising," she said. "What we need are some extras."

"Extra what?" Fiona said.

Her voice could have freeze-dried Phoebe's lips. Sophie rubbed the back of her neck.

"Extra people," Phoebe said. "I need to teach you some vocabulary. Anyway, I just don't see how we can stage a riot scene with just us." She tossed her head dramatically. "These working conditions!"

"I can create the illusion with the camera," Vincent said. "So it'll look like we have, like, a cast of thousands."

"We want real," Phoebe said. "Not a delusion."

"Illusion," Fiona said. "I need to teach you some vocab—"

"We should get started!" Sophie said, although she would have loved to let Fiona finish that sentence and more. Her neck was on fire with prickles.

"We still need at least one other person to play another cop." Phoebe pointed toward the bleachers. "What about Chubbo?"

"You mean Mr. Wornom?" Coach Nanini said.

All of the Corn Flakes and the Lucky Charms shook their heads, but Coach slowly nodded his.

"Mr. Wornom!" he shouted. "We need you over here."

Eddie turned, then stuck the tool he'd been using into his back pocket and lumbered toward them.

"He'll do," Phoebe said.

"We're putting Eddie in our movie?" Willoughby whispered to Sophie.

Sophie didn't answer.

# Nine

How about no!" Fiona said through clenched teeth as Eddie approached.

"So much for a totally class flick," Darbie said through hers.

Willoughby just stifled a shriek. Maggie didn't say anything. Neither did her face. Sophie chomped down on her own tongue.

Phoebe pranced at Eddie's side before he even got to them. "Have you had any acting experience?" she said.

"He only knows one way to act," Nathan muttered.

Eddie looked Phoebe up and down like she was a space alien. "I ain't no actor," he said.

"You've got the perfect look for the part, though," Phoebe said.

"Oh, yes," Darbie whispered to Sophie. "He'll fit right into a scene about a shower of savages."

Eddie opened his mouth, and Sophie covered her ears. But to her surprise, he looked at Coach Nanini and said, "Do I gotta?"

*Say no!* Sophie wanted to blurt out.

Coach Nanini adjusted his sunglasses and folded his ham-like arms. "You don't have to, but it would sure prove to me that you're getting this whole help-and-cooperate thing."

Eddie glared at Sophie as if she alone were responsible for this torture. "Will it get me off earlier?" he said.

"The only thing that will get me out of your life, Mr. Wornom," Coach Nanini said, "is for you to show me a genuine change in your attitude."

*Now we'll see if he can act,* Sophie thought.

"Come on, you'll be a natural," Phoebe said. "You get to yell at them."

She pointed to the Corn Flakes. Eddie's face lit up. "And you can spit over your shoulder," Phoebe told him. "I saw cops do that when they came to our house because people complained about our chickens."

"Just confine your spitting to the ground, Mr. Wornom," Coach Nanini said. "If a loogie hits skin, you go back ten steps."

A slow grin scrunched up Eddie's cheeks. Sophie felt her eyes bulging almost to her glasses as he said, "Okay. I'll do it. Do I get a gun?"

While Phoebe explained to him that, unfortunately, there would be no weapons involved, Coach Nanini motioned Sophie over to him.

"It's still up to you whether you let him in, Little Bit," he said. "I won't let him mess up your movie. But having him help is what the Round Table program is all about, right?"

Sophie didn't remember anybody on the council ever saying *that*. She just felt squirmy and squeezed and prickly at the same time. *But Liberty Lawhead raised up her chin. If she had to think of the lowest of the low as people with rights, who should be called "Mr." instead of "Scum," then she would. That was the price one paid in being a leader.*

"Places for the riot scene, everyone," Sophie said. "The role of the policeman will be played by Eddie Wornom."

"Good choice, Little Bit," Coach Nanini said as the group scattered to set up. "You're on the top shelf looking down."

Jimmy produced a box he'd brought for Sophie to stand on so Liberty Lawhead could be seen. Maggie/Senorita stood on the ground beside her, head still as high as Sophie's, and Nathan and Eddie parked behind them as the two police officers. The crowd gathered in front of them, with Phoebe right in the middle, already warming up to shout protests in the middle of Liberty's speech. Vincent stood apart with the camera. It was his turn to film, and he'd been dying for the chance.

Sophie took a deep breath while Phoebe gave the Corn Flakes some final pointers. All the things the grown-ups had said squeezed her again.

*How am I supposed to not judge them and bring out the best in them*, Sophie thought, *with Eddie Wornom standing there hating me and Maggie looking like she would rather be having a heart transplant—*

"What's the matter?" Phoebe said to her. "You got gas?"

Eddie sputtered out a loud, nasty laugh.

"Okay, action," Sophie said.

"Hey, by the way," Vincent said. "Nice camera, Sophie." Then he gave her a thumbs-up that he was shooting.

"It is dangerous to deny rights to individuals," Sophie/Liberty cried out to the crowd in her best Ms. Hess voice, "by lumping them into a group and judging each by the guilt of a few. Only one percent of the Marielitos are actual criminals, and this girl and her mother are certainly not among them."

She put her hand on Maggie/Senorita's shoulder. The words were still pulsing through her as if they had been real.

"They're all guilty!" Phoebe shouted from the crowd. "They all carry guns! Frisk her—they're probably using her to smuggle in weapons!"

Phoebe charged toward Maggie, dragging a reluctant Willoughby with her. Right on cue, Nathan stepped forward and said, "That's far enough. Get back."

"Everybody start rioting," Phoebe said under her breath to Jimmy and the Flakes.

They rushed toward Liberty/Sophie and Maggie/Senorita just like they were supposed to, with the two "cops" pushing them back with their hands. Officer Eddie, Sophie noticed, seemed to be enjoying grabbing Phoebe by the arm and flinging her skinny body from side to side. Just as Sophie/Liberty put her arms around a very stiff Maggie/Senorita to protect her, Phoebe's voice swelled above it all.

"Keep your hands off me, pig!" her character screamed into Officer Eddie's face. "I know my rights!"

Eddie's eyes squinted until they were mere poke holes in his face.

"Who you callin' a pig?" he said.

"You!" Phoebe's character shouted. "We're the ones you should protect, not them, you fat excuse for law enforcement!"

"Shut up!" Eddie shouted back.

In the instant that he reached for his back pocket, Sophie knew Eddie wasn't acting, and that he didn't know Phoebe was.

"Go ahead, hit me!" Phoebe's character cried. "I'll sue you for police brutality."

Eddie's face went purple. He yanked the giant screwdriver out of his pocket, fist clenched around the handle, and drew his arm back.

"Phoebe, look out!" Sophie screamed.

Suddenly things seemed to shift into slow motion. Phoebe threw up her arms and shouted, "Cut!" Coach Nanini ran for Eddie, but before he could get there, Eddie flung the screwdriver, and it tumbled end over end through the air, landing just inches from Maggie's foot. Eddie dived for it, landing on his belly with a grunt.

Everyone else froze. All except Phoebe, who went after Eddie, teeth bared like tiger fangs. Coach Nanini hauled Eddie out of the way and lifted him to his feet, but Phoebe kept coming at him, clawing the air with her fingernails.

"Guys," Coach Nanini said, "this is one time when you can grab a girl."

Nathan and Jimmy got hold of Phoebe from behind and pulled her back, dodging her heels as she kicked at them.

"What are you, some kind of crazy method actor?" Phoebe screamed at Eddie. "You coulda hit me!"

"I was *tryin'* to hit you!" Eddie screamed back. "You called me a pig!"

"I don't think anger management is working too well," Fiona muttered to Sophie.

Sophie shook her head. *And Mama thought we'd be safer here.*

Coach Nanini got Eddie calmed down enough to send him off to the locker room to be dealt with later, but it wasn't that easy to handle Phoebe. She carried on for a good two minutes before Nathan and Jimmy could let her go without her trying to take them out. When they did set her free at Coach Nanini's command, she shot off like a missile toward the gym building.

"She'll go right into the boys' locker room, that one," Darbie murmured.

"I'd kind of like to see that, actually," Fiona said.

Willoughby let out a yip-giggle, and then she couldn't seem to stop. Darbie snorted, and Fiona just collapsed on the ground.

"What's the deal?" Jimmy said to Coach Nanini.

"Son, don't ask me to explain women," Coach said, "because I won't even try."

As he jogged off toward the locker room, Sophie felt a relief giggle coming up in her own throat, until she looked at Maggie.

Maggie wasn't laughing, but her face finally had something in it. Something that made her eyes swim and made her hug her arms around herself. Something that made her look afraid.

"Stop, you guys," Sophie said.

The Corn Flakes cut off their laughter in mid-giggle.

Sophie held out her hand to Vincent for the camera. "We're through rehearsing for the day. See you guys tomorrow."

"You don't want to see the footage?" Vincent said as he handed it to her. "I got some great stuff—"

"Come on," Jimmy said. "I think this is some kind of girl thing."

After Jimmy herded Vincent away, with Nathan several red-eared yards ahead of them, the Flakes huddled around their Maggie. Attempts at comfort flew out of every mouth.

"She was only acting—"

"When she got really mad, it was about Eddie—"

"You almost can't blame her—he threw a big ol' screwdriver thing at her!"

"Don't be shook over her, Mags—"

"You've got us."

But Maggie stopped it all with just one sentence. "She hates me like that too."

For a long moment, nobody said it wasn't true. And when Willoughby tried, things began to fire out of Maggie—not in thuds, but in flaming cannonballs she'd obviously been storing up for a long time.

213

"When you aren't looking she gives me hate stares," Maggie said. "And when you can't hear her, like when she gets me off away from you and tries to tell me how to act, she says other stuff too, like why do I always smell like beans and does my mother have a gun in our house and is my father in prison." She took a breath. "And when she gets all in my face when we're practicing and everybody says she's such a good actor, that's not acting. She means it. Just like she meant it when Eddie threw that thing at her. And now I'm scared because I know how bad she can hate. And I don't even want to be in this movie, even if I have to take an F."

Maggie sucked in another big gulp of air. Sophie knew that was a lot for her to say.

"Okay, that's it," Fiona said. "We are so not putting up with this anymore. I say we go to Miss Imes right now and tell her Phoebe has to go."

"No," Maggie said.

"We have to," Sophie said. "Mags, this is so unfair." She found herself shaking, and she knew even Liberty Lawhead would do the same. This was scarier than anything.

Dr. Peter had said that when Maggie started having trouble with it, it was time for a grown-up.

But Maggie was shaking her head so hard, her hair was slapping against her cheeks.

"When you try to stop people like her, they just treat you worse," she said. "My mother said so. That's why she left Miami when I was a baby and came here." Maggie's voice trembled. "I just want to stay away from that Phoebe girl."

"But you can't take an F, Mags," Fiona said.

"Why can't we just keep Maggie away from her?" Darbie said. "All the scenes she's in with Mags are done. We can do the rest on the sly."

"That's sneaking," Maggie said. "It's against the Corn Flake Code."

"It's the only way to protect you if you won't go to Miss Imes or somebody." Fiona put her hands on Maggie's shoulders. "You have to make a choice."

"Come on, Mags." Willoughby sounded like she was about to cry. "We're the Corn Flakes."

Whatever that meant to Maggie seemed to settle over her, and she nodded slowly. "Okay," she said. "I'll finish the movie. Just keep her away from me."

Pinkies came out for a solemn promise.

*Finally*, Sophie thought. *We can just get away from Phoebe and not feel bad about it.*

But even as they linked fingers, Sophie felt something that wasn't a squirm or a prickle or a squeeze. It was just a deep feeling that something was wrong somehow.

That feeling faded a little as they sat on the bleachers and made a plan for keeping Maggie safe from Phoebe. The only thing Maggie insisted on was that Sophie be with her all the time.

Darbie gave a soft snort. "Do you really think Sophie is the person to have with you if Phoebe starts scratching your face with her fingernails like she tried with Eddie?"

"I can keep her from hurting me outside by myself," Maggie said. "But Sophie can keep her from hurting me inside." She turned her frightened eyes on Sophie. "Stay with me all the time."

Sophie nodded until she could get some words out. "I won't leave your side at school when we're not in class, Mags," she said.

*As Liberty Lawhead followed her Civil Rights for All team toward their building, with the terrified senorita at her side, she tried to raise her chin and straighten her shoulders and draw up to her statuesque height.*

*But there was a deep feeling. Something she had never felt tugging at her insides before. If she hadn't known herself so well, she would have thought it was doubt.*

Willoughby gave Sophie a tiny push toward the open bus door.

"Where's Maggie?" Sophie said.

"Boppa's giving her a ride home," Darbie said. "She'll be safe."

*Liberty Lawhead sighed as she stepped into the backseat of her limo. She must get her confidence back. They had made a decision, and they must follow through—*

But as Sophie turned her face to the bus window, she saw herself reflected there, not Liberty Lawhead. Her own brown eyes were as frightened as Maggie's.

She closed them and tried to get Liberty back. But there were only the kind eyes there.

"I think we better talk when I get home," she whispered to Jesus. "Or there's gonna be big trouble."

# Ten

Sophie decided to go straight to her room when she got home and imagine Jesus. She was way too confused to do anything else.

But when she walked into the kitchen, Daddy was home, and he had that face on that Lacie always said was like the coach's at halftime when the team was losing bad.

And Zeke was the player he was blaming.

Zeke sat on the snack bar, legs swinging and eyes lowered. Daddy leaned over him so that their faces almost touched. Lacie stood just inside the open pantry closet like she was looking for the perfect snack to go with watching their little brother get busted. But Sophie had a feeling she was just trying to stay out of sight.

Sophie joined her.

"Now, buddy," Daddy said. "Mama tells me you didn't behave like a big guy while I was gone."

"Ya think?" Lacie whispered to Sophie.

"You want to tell me what you did?" Daddy said.

"I did some stuff," Zeke said. Sophie could tell he was hardly opening his mouth. "I don't remember all of it, though."

"Did you write all over Sophie's math paper?"

"No. Spider-Man drew webs on it."

"Did you lock Lacie in the bathroom?"

"No," Zeke said again. "Spider-Man locked his *main enemy* in jail."

"Did you flush the ultrasound picture of the baby down the toilet?"

Sophie and Lacie stared at each other. Lacie looked as surprised by that one as Sophie felt.

"Spider-Man did that too," Zeke said. "He had to."

"Why?" Daddy said.

"I don't want to talk about that," Zeke said.

"Does Spider-Man want to talk about it?" Daddy said. "Because Spider-Man's dad does."

Sophie was even more surprised by that.

Daddy's voice got softer. "So what's the problem, superhero?"

Zeke launched into a long explanation of Spider-Man's latest attempt to save somebody from something. Lacie nudged Sophie with a bag of pretzels.

"He gets that from you," she whispered. "You used to blame everything you did wrong on your imaginary characters."

"Only Daddy never believed me," Sophie whispered back.

"Well, go figure," Lacie said.

"Why are we in here whispering anyway?" Sophie said.

"Because I've already figured out why Z-Boy's been behaving like the Tasmanian Devil, and if Dad starts to punish him, I'm stepping in."

The only sound coming from the direction of the snack bar now was the thump of Zeke's tennis shoes as he swung his legs.

"Let me ask you this, Spider-Man," Daddy said. "Do you think there's a new invader coming in? Somebody that people might listen to more than they do you?"

"There you go, Dad," Lacie murmured.

"There *is* gonna be one," Zeke said. "And I don't want it 'cause everybody's already forgetting about me."

The tears in his voice made Sophie want to cry too.

"Then I think Spider-Man's mom and dad need to make sure he knows he'll never be replaced," Daddy said. "What do you say we go upstairs and get to work on that?"

"Is Spider-Man gonna get a punishment?"

"Not if I have anything to do with it," Lacie muttered.

"I'm with ya," Sophie muttered back.

"You two mother hens in the pantry can relax," Daddy said as his voice and Zeke's faded out of the kitchen. "Spider-Man's safe with me."

Lacie grinned. "You rock, Dad," she called to him.

When Sophie got up to her room, she pulled the gauzy curtains closed around her bed and settled against the pillows. As soon as she shut her eyes, she could imagine Jesus. But it was Dr. Peter's voice she heard.

*"I don't think any kid is just naturally mean,"* he'd said. *"Usually a girl acts mean because she's angry or scared. "*

Sophie's eyes came open. Wasn't that what Daddy had just figured out about Zeke? That he was acting like the Terminator because he was afraid everybody would pay more attention to the new baby than him?

So was Phoebe afraid of something? Or somebody?

*I'd be afraid of Mr. Karnes if he was my dad*, Sophie thought.

But it still didn't make sense that Phoebe would take it out on Maggie.

What else had Dr. Peter said?

Sophie stopped a minute to remember that she was supposed to be mad at Dr. Peter. But she snorted right out loud.

When had he ever told her the wrong thing? She closed her eyes and remembered.

*"If Maggie is having trouble with it, you need to bring in some grown-ups."*

"We have to," Sophie said out loud. "No matter what we said the plan was before."

In fact, it seemed like every part of their plan was just like Dr. Peter had said: not the right thing to do. They weren't helping Maggie stand up for herself. They were just protecting her, and they weren't even doing it the way Dr. Peter expected—the way the Corn Flakes always do—with honesty and respect and all that good Code stuff. Not when they planned to sneak rehearsals without Phoebe.

And they sure weren't helping Phoebe understand that some of the things she did were heinous. They were just shutting her out.

Down the hall, Zeke giggled in that insane little-boy way. Sophie didn't see how anybody could laugh that hard and not barf.

*I guess they convinced him he isn't being replaced by New Baby*, Sophie thought.

Sophie tried to get a picture in her mind of Phoebe's skinny, gap-toothed father explaining something to her the way Daddy had talked to Zeke that day, but even she couldn't imagine that. All she could imagine him saying was that all Cubans were good for was hijacking planes and mooching off people.

*"Think of Phoebe as a lost lamb instead of a bossy girl who doesn't like Cuban people. Isn't that what Jesus was trying to tell the Pharisees in that story?"*

Sophie grabbed her Bible off the night table where it rested in the light of her princess lamp. Luke 15—

With the bed curtains draped around her like a learned man's robe, Sophie sank herself in. As she read, she saw the kind eyes and heard the voice in the verses.

*"Suppose one of you has a hundred sheep and loses one of them."*

"I'd leave the rest and go look for it and bring it back," Sophie/the Pharisee said.

That was just what the man named Jesus was saying. *"Then he calls his friends and neighbors together and says, 'Rejoice with me.'"*

*I would do that*, Sophie/the Pharisee thought. She closed the Bible on her finger. *What I wouldn't do is decide the lamb was just heinous and say, "Serves you right for being so evil."*

Especially if the lost sheep just did it to get attention because it was scared.

*"But sometimes a little Pharisee-itis can sneak in—"*

"Then it can just sneak right back out," Sophie said out loud. "Right along with our plan."

She scrambled off the bed and headed for the phone in the kitchen, already planning what to say to each of the Corn Flakes. What she *didn't* plan was how to answer Fiona's arguing, Willoughby's skittish little yip, and Darbie's stubborn Irish silence. She finally said they all had a case of Pharisee-itis. Nobody seemed to get it.

Maggie was the hardest one of all.

"I'll just take an F on the project then," she said.

"You don't have to," Sophie said. "We just have to come up with a different plan."

"What if she's still mean to me? I don't want to do this anymore."

Sophie wished Dr. Peter were there to help Maggie get it. She wished she really was Liberty Lawhead so the right words would fall from her lips like silk.

But she knew none of that would happen. The only thing making her try to convince Maggie were the kind eyes—

"Mags?" Sophie said suddenly.

"Yeah."

"Have you talked to Jesus about this, the way Dr. Peter says to?"

"It didn't work. Phoebe's still mean."

Sophie would have made Dr. Peter king of the Corn Flakes if he'd been there, just for giving her the silken words she'd been wishing for.

"Just because it doesn't look like it's working doesn't mean it isn't," she said. "We're not gonna, like, make Phoebe a member of the Corn Flakes. But we did say we'd work with her on this project."

"I didn't know it would be this bad." Maggie's words thudded right through the phone.

"It doesn't have to be." Sophie closed her eyes as she said the rest, just to be sure Jesus' eyes were still there. "We have a Good Shepherd, Mags. We're not lost. We'll be okay after this. But Phoebe doesn't have one."

"I thought only God could save her."

"But we can at least show her that we're not Pharisees."

There was a silence so long Sophie was afraid Maggie had put down the phone and walked off. But finally, some words plunked down.

"I hope Jesus gives you a different plan before Monday," Maggie said.

*I hope he does too*, Sophie thought as she hung up the phone.

And then she did more than hope. She prayed—long and hard, with her chin in her hands on the snack bar and her eyes squeezed tight. When she opened them, Mama and Daddy were standing there.

"That was some pretty serious daydreaming," Daddy said, roughing up her fuzz with his hand.

"I was praying," Sophie said. "And it was serious. I've got a major problem."

The minute it was out of her mouth, Sophie shook her head. "I'm sorry. I'm not supposed to get you upset, Mama."

"Stop right there." Mama tried to get up on the stool next to Sophie's, and Daddy gave her a boost. "I'm pregnant, but that doesn't make me a piece of glass everybody has to tiptoe around. I want to know what's going on with you."

"And we always will," Daddy said. "No matter how many kids we have."

Sophie looked into their eyes that were almost as kind as the ones she'd seen in her mind. Suddenly, she wanted to cry.

"Okay, dish, Soph," Daddy said. "Are you worried about this baby taking over too?"

Sophie swallowed down a guilty lump. "I haven't even hardly thought about the baby!" she said. "I've been too busy being a Pharisee!"

Daddy pulled up a third stool. "I think I'll sit down for this one."

Sophie told them everything, including the Corn Flakes' plan and how she needed a new one.

"You've come to the right place," Daddy said. "Your mother and I are in planning mode. We just came up with a killer one for dealing with Z-Boy."

"Let us help you," Mama said.

So Sophie did. And when they were done, she felt like Liberty Lawhead herself, chin raised, shoulders straightened—

Except that Liberty Lawhead didn't have a mom who sat with her on the couch and let her feel her tummy until the baby inside fluttered against her hand.

"That's your little sister," Mama said. "We found out today."

"A girl?" Sophie said.

"A little Corn Flake," Mama said.

And for the first time, that tiny flutter of a baby seemed real.

Part of the plan Mama and Daddy helped Sophie form was for her simply to hang with the family over the weekend and let the other Corn Flakes talk to God themselves. They watched movies and took turns feeling for baby moves and played endless games of Chutes and Ladders with Zeke. Since he didn't stuff any of the game pieces up his nose or scream that the whole world was cheating, Sophie actually got into it.

But on Sunday at church, Sophie wasn't sure any of the Corn Flakes had spoken even the first word to God. Willoughby wouldn't look at her. Darbie and Fiona chattered about everything except what they really needed to talk about. Maggie didn't say anything.

"I have a plan," Sophie said.

"So did we," Fiona said. "And I personally think we should stay with it."

"At least let her tell us what it is," Darbie said.

Fiona grunted and gave Sophie a jerky nod.

Sophie told them what she and Mama and Daddy had come up with. "It's way more like a Corn Flake thing than our other plan," she said at the end.

"What if Phoebe just wants to get revenge then?" Willoughby said.

"It could make things worse," Darbie said.

"I hate when we have to do it the right way," Fiona said. "My rotten selfish way is always so much easier."

Darbie sighed. "All right, let's stop foostering about. Pinkie promise."

They locked pinkies. All except Maggie. She left to go to the bathroom.

Sophie tried not to think about that the next morning before school, when Phase One of the Plan went into motion. She went to Mrs. Clayton and told her all about Phoebe and how she thought she needed Round Table help.

As soon as Mrs. Clayton heard Phoebe's name, she shuffled through some file folders on her desk. "Phoebe Karnes," she said. "That's interesting, because she's already on our schedule. Coach Nanini said she has some anger issues he thinks we should work with."

Sophie tried to stay businesslike and not grin too big. Now that Coach Virile was with them, it was hard not to giggle right out loud.

Phase Two was getting through PE with Phoebe. Although they still claimed Sophie was nuts, the Corn Flakes agreed to think of Phoebe as a lost sheep.

"Did you get busted for going after Eddie last Friday?" Fiona asked Phoebe when they were in line for roll call.

Sophie bulged her eyes at Fiona.

"That's Fiona being interested," Darbie whispered.

"Not yet," Phoebe said. "I'm supposed to talk to Mr. Unibrow this period, though. I figure he'll just give me a lecture."

Coach did call Phoebe aside. That meant the Flakes wouldn't do anything until Phase Three, their lunchtime filming session. They were ready for that.

According to the Plan, they met on the school steps, the closest thing they had to a courthouse. Sophie and Maggie went to Mr. Stires' room to get the camera. Mr. Stires was still puttering around with test tubes when they arrived.

"Are you coming out to the filming?" Sophie said.

He chuckled. "Wouldn't miss it. I was just waiting for you girls."

"I don't think we're gonna be filming today," Maggie said from the storage room doorway.

"Why not?" Sophie said. "Mags, don't give up now—"

"No," Maggie said. "Your camera's gone."

# Eleven

"What do you mean it's gone?" Sophie said. Her voice squeaked beyond itself.

"I mean it's not there," Maggie said. "I looked everywhere."

If Maggie said it wasn't there, it wasn't there, but Sophie had to double-check anyway. She could almost hear Daddy lecturing her as she stared at the empty place on the shelf.

"Nobody else came and got it?" Sophie said to Mr. Stires.

He shook his bald head. His usually happy mustache drooped. "I don't let anybody check it in and out but you."

"Hel-lo-o," Phoebe said from the doorway. "What's taking so long?"

Fiona ran into the back of her. "I told her we were supposed to wait for you out there," she said to Sophie, "but no-o-o, she had to — "

"The camera's gone," Maggie said.

Fiona stared. So did the rest of the group who were now clumped in the doorway.

"You mean, like, stolen?" Willoughby said.

"Let's not jump to conclusions," Mr. Stires said.

But Sophie could see by the faces of the Charms and Flakes that they had already made that leap. Fiona had obviously

227

made another one too, because she was driving her eyes into Phoebe. Phoebe herself was fingering her tooth-gap and staring at Maggie.

"All right, folks." Mr. Stires brushed his fingers back and forth across his mustache about six times. "Let's fan out and look and make sure it didn't just get moved."

"Yeah," Phoebe muttered, "moved to somebody's locker."

They searched Mr. Stires' classroom and storage area until the end of lunch period, but there was no trace of the camera. Vincent even got a magnifying glass out of his backpack and looked for a stray hair they could use for a DNA sample. Jimmy told him he watched too much TV.

When Miss Imes arrived and got the news, her eyebrows shot almost into her scalp. Sophie had to admit Phoebe was probably right. Somebody had stolen her camera.

Jimmy folded his arms and looked shyly at Sophie. "I'm really sorry this happened," he said.

"Yeah, bummer," Nathan said.

Willoughby ran her hand up and down Sophie's back. "Why would somebody do this?"

"Because they're heinous," Fiona said.

"Because they're eejits," Darbie said.

Miss Imes shot silence through them with her eyebrows. "Here's how we'll handle this," she said. "Next period I'm going to make an intercom announcement that the camera has gone missing. I'll ask that it be returned to its original place, no questions asked."

"Then we can check it for fingerprints," Vincent said. "I know how to do that."

"Of course you do," Miss Imes said, "but 'no questions asked' means exactly that. We'll give our thief a chance to reconsider and make this right."

"Not gonna happen," Phoebe said. She gave Maggie one last long look before she exited with a wave of her hand.

*She thinks Maggie took it,* Sophie thought. *She so does!*

The back of her neck started to prickle—but she closed her eyes and recited the phases in her head.

1. *Tell a grown-up.*
2. *Remember that Phoebe is a scared lost lamb without a shepherd.*
3. *Help Maggie stand up for herself with all the good Corn Flake stuff.*

That second one was harder than ever at the moment, but Sophie made herself pray for Phoebe like the Flakes had all promised to do. That phase of the Plan was supposed to go on all day.

When the bell for fifth period rang and she opened her eyes, there was a note on her desk, folded Fiona-fashion, like a bird.

*What about the Plan now?* she'd written.

Before Sophie could get her gel pen out to answer, the speaker box squawked. Miss Imes made her announcement, and the class immediately buzzed like a hive.

"I can tell you exactly who did it," Julia said.

"Who?" Colton said. His stick-out ears suddenly reminded Sophie of antennae.

Julia cupped her hands around her mouth. Both Colton and Tod leaned so far into the aisle, Sophie was sure they'd end up in Julia's lap. Sophie had to force herself not to lean too, because she couldn't see what Julia was mouthing.

"Who's Fee-Bee?" Colton said, stretching his lips across his teeth.

"That girl who buys her clothes at Kmart," Anne-Stuart said with the usual sniff. "You know—" She put her finger up to her two front teeth.

Tod's face came to a point at his nose. "You mean that chick that tried to slash Eddie's face with her fingernails?"

Sophie felt her eyes widen, and she turned to Fiona, who was already nodding.

The minute Mr. Stires told the class to pick up their materials for the lab, Sophie got to Fiona with the words already on her lips. "You think Phoebe—"

"I *know* she did—"

"That doesn't make sense!" Sophie said. "All she wants to *do* is this movie. Why would she take the—"

"So she can blame it on Maggie," Fiona said. "Didn't you see the way she looked at her?"

Sophie had; she couldn't deny that.

"*Or*—and you don't know this yet—" Fiona took two test tubes from the tray and pulled Sophie toward their lab station, glancing warily over her shoulder. "When we were all out on the steps waiting for you and Maggie to show up with the camera?"

"Yeah?"

"Phoebe said Coach Nanini told her that she was going to Round Table tomorrow. She said if she got detention and couldn't work on the movie, somebody was going to pay." Fiona grabbed two vials of liquid from the tray Gill was passing by with and lowered her voice. "I'm thinking that somebody is you."

"I still don't get it—"

"If we don't have the camera, we can't keep working on the film without her."

230

Sophie began to nod. "This film or any other film. We have to tell Miss Imes what we suspect."

Fiona wiggled her eyebrows. "Unless we can prove it ourselves—"

"Un-uh," Sophie said. "We have to do it the right way, or we're just—"

"Yeah, yeah, Pharisees." Fiona flipped open the lab workbook and cut her eyes toward Sophie. "You think she did it, though; I can tell."

Sophie didn't answer, but Fiona kept looking at her.

"Okay," Sophie said finally. "But we have to let the Round Table handle it. And we can't tell Phoebe we think she's guilty."

Fiona bunched up her lips. "I'm gonna have to put duct tape on my mouth."

"After you tell everybody else in the group to keep quiet about it," Sophie said. "Right after class, I'm going to Coach Nanini."

At the end of the period, Sophie raced to Life Skills for a pass from Coach Yates. "Just don't make a career out of it, LaCroix," she said. "I want you back here in fifteen."

Sophie shifted into high gear as she raced down the hall, but at the corner, bony fingers wrapped themselves around her arm. Phoebe hauled her into the girls' restroom.

"I don't have time for this!" Sophie said. "I have to—"

The door slapped closed behind them. Phoebe's mouth came so close to Sophie's face, Sophie thought she might fall right into the gap between her teeth. Phoebe took a step forward, and Sophie backed into a sink.

"Everybody thinks I stole your camera," Phoebe said.

"Who's 'everybody'?" Sophie managed to say. Her voice couldn't have sounded less like Ms. Hess or Liberty Lawhead or anybody else who wasn't squeaking off the scale.

"Those rich chicks with the manicures," Phoebe said. "I heard them running their mouths about me in the hall between fifth and sixth. I get to sixth period and everybody's looking at me like I'm a serial killer or something."

Sophie could only stare. It always amazed her how fast the Corn Pops worked.

"So I gotta ask you something." Phoebe raked her bangs out of her eyes with her fingers. "Do *you* think I did it?"

Sophie opened her mouth, but a tangle of words caught in her throat, and nothing came out.

Phoebe's eyes searched Sophie's face. "You do," she said. "You don't even have to say it—I can see."

Phoebe's lip curled, but not into a smile. She took two steps backward before she turned and headed straight for the door. When she got there, she stopped and looked over her shoulder at Sophie through her fence of bangs.

"I just thought you were better than most people." She made a dramatic exit. But Sophie knew that, for once, Phoebe wasn't acting.

Sophie wasn't sure how long she stood there, arms wrapped around herself, remembering the look on Phoebe's face and feeling the cold of the sink through her parachute pants. Two things were for sure. She now knew what a lost lamb looked like. And she knew what a Pharisee felt like.

Sophie stuffed Coach Yates' pass into the pocket of her hoodie and headed for the door. She'd probably used up ten of her fifteen minutes, but now she had to see Coach Virile more than ever.

He was in the gym, watching lines of eighth-grade boys dribble basketballs up and down the court. The squeal of sneakers was deafening. There were so many long arms and legs dangling between her and Coach Virile, Sophie didn't see who stood next to him until she was almost on them.

It was Phoebe.

Sophie's own sneakers squealed as she stopped dead. But Coach Virile's eyes met hers, and he said something to Phoebe that sent her out onto the court, picking up balls. Coach blew his whistle, and the boys bounded to the bleachers and ran up them, two rows at a time. Coach motioned Sophie toward himself, but now she wasn't sure she wanted to go. There was no guessing what Phoebe had told him. The worst would be if she had told him the truth.

"Hey, Little Bit," he said. "You look like a whupped puppy."

She could hardly hear him over the pounding of feet, but at least she didn't see disappointment in his eyes.

*Tell a grown-up*, she could hear herself saying to the Flakes.

So she did—all their suspicions and their reasons and her feeling at that moment like a finger-pointing tattletale.

"I had to tell a grown-up that she was being mean to Maggie and scaring her," Sophie said. "And I guess she just wanted to get back at me." She swallowed hard. "Only, how come I feel like maybe she didn't do it?"

"Because maybe she didn't."

He nodded his shiny head toward the court, where Phoebe dragged a bag of basketballs twice her size toward a storage closet. She was bent over like an old woman walking in the wind. Sophie felt a pang inside.

"You don't think she did?" Sophie said.

"She was with me all third period. She's in my fourth-period Life Skills class, and we were talking until the last bell rang for lunch. I'm not a detective, but I don't see where she ever had the chance." He looked down at Sophie, his one big eyebrow hooding his eyes like a visor. "Proving her innocence isn't what's hard for Phoebe right now," he said. "It's dealing with the fact that you automatically assumed she was guilty."

"She automatically assumed Maggie was guilty!"

As soon as she said it, Sophie looked at the floor. "That doesn't make it right, does it?" she said. "I feel like a heinous Pharisee."

"Little Bit."

Sophie looked up. His eyes were kind.

"Why don't you just tell her that?" he said. A smile twitched at his lips. "Only I don't think she knows what a Pharisee is. You might want to change that part."

Sophie felt Phoebe getting closer. When she stopped next to Coach Virile, he pointed to the bottom row of bleachers. They both sat. Coach Virile climbed up to the row behind them and leaned back, arms stretched out.

"I'm here if you need me," he said.

*Need you?* Sophie wanted to cry. *Do this* for *me!*

Phoebe struck a pose like the victims of kidnapping Sophie had seen on the news, all shaken and brave. Phoebe's eyes watered, and as her lips headed toward a curl, they trembled. Suddenly, it hurt to see her.

"I'm sorry!" Sophie blurted out. "We shouldn't have suspected you right away—I should have thought about you being a lost sheep—only we were mad at you for being prejudiced against Maggie—only we should have done something sooner—only I was being a Pharisee, and I know you don't know what that means, but it's like so heinous and even being nice to you didn't change the way you treated Maggie—and I know we didn't try that hard—"

"Little Bit," Coach Virile said, "take a breath."

Sophie tried, but it was hard. Her chest was squeezing in.

"I didn't steal the camera," Phoebe said.

"I know," Sophie said.

Phoebe looked at Coach Virile. "Then are we done?"

"Are we?" Coach Virile said.

For a second, Sophie was confused as Phoebe shook her head and shoved her bangs back. And then Phoebe said, "I don't know why I act like that to Cuban Girl—"

"Excuse me?" Coach Virile said.

"Maggie," Phoebe said. Her bangs fell in her eyes again, and this time she hid behind them. "She just makes me feel scared. It's like, she's not like regular people, and that freaks me out." Her eyes filled up again. "I don't know why. But he—" She jerked her head toward Coach Nanini. "He's gonna help me figure it out—him and that Round Table thing."

Finally, she looked at Sophie, cringing as if Sophie might slug her.

"I know you hate me," she said, "but don't let them give me detention, okay? I want to do this movie really bad—and I don't want you guys to get a bad grade—and my dad will—"

It was as if her voice caught on something in her throat, and the words stuck. Sophie wasn't sure she could stand to hear them anyway. Not if they matched the fear on Phoebe's face.

The bell rang, sounding far away, as if it belonged to some other school. But with a start, Sophie remembered Coach Yates.

"I was supposed to be back to class in fifteen minutes!" she said.

"I've got your back." Coach Nanini turned to Phoebe. "You have something you want to say to your film buddies?"

Phoebe looked like she would rather have climbed into the bag with the basketballs, but she nodded. Then there was a silence, the kind where no one knows what to say.

*Liberty Lawhead would know exactly what to do right now,* Sophie thought.

It was the first time she'd thought about Liberty all day. But come to think of it, she, her Sophie-self, did know what to do.

"I'll walk with you," she said to Phoebe.

Coach Nanini made a soft sound in his throat.

"You don't have to," Phoebe said.

"I know," Sophie said.

Phoebe shrugged, slung her backpack over her shoulder, and looked at Coach Nanini with questions in her eyes.

"Come see me when you're done," he said.

Sophie started across the gym, and Phoebe caught up. "I have to go to my locker first," she said.

"I'll go with you," Sophie said.

They dodged the after-school crowd in silence until they were almost to the lockers. Then Phoebe said, "What did you mean when you said I was a lost sheep?" She curled up a smile. "I've been called a lot of things before, but never that."

Sophie stopped beside the locker as Phoebe twirled the combination lock. The Corn Flakes hadn't planned this part. She closed her eyes for a second.

"Hello, what's the deal? Why won't you open?" Phoebe tugged at her locker door. "I hate these things." She started dialing again. "Are you going to tell me why I'm a sheep or not?"

"It's from the Bible," Sophie said.

"I'm in the Bible?" Phoebe said, frowning at her lock. "Go figure."

"We all are," Sophie said.

"You're a sheep too?" Phoebe said.

"Yeah. Only I'm not lost. You know, because of Jesus."

"Is that what you talk about in that class you go to?" Phoebe gave the locker door a yank, and it flew open, knocking her back a step. She stared into the locker. Sophie stared with her.

Because there, inside, was Sophie's camera.

# Twelve

I don't know how it got there, I swear!" Phoebe said.

Her face went as white as teeth. Sophie could feel the color draining out of hers too. All she could do was gape at her camera, displayed like a museum piece on top of Phoebe's books.

"Here she is!" she heard Willoughby say behind her.

Those were the last clear words Sophie understood for a while. The rest was all gasps and people coming and going in scenes.

Miss Imes appeared and took Phoebe to the office with the camera.

Mrs. Clayton came and said there would be a Round Table meeting the next day at lunch.

The Corn Pops arrived in a bunch and told each other out of the sides of their glossy mouths that they always knew Phoebe was nothing but trash. Fruit Loops stuck in words like "Dude!" and "Sweet" and "Score," none of which seemed to fit at all.

Several teachers finally herded the gathering crowd outside to get on their buses.

Through it all, Sophie's thoughts circled in her brain.

*I was almost sure she didn't do it. But my camera was in her locker.*

*Coach Virile says she couldn't have done it.*

*But how did it get in her locker if she didn't put it there?*

"She's just a lost lamb with a mean father," Sophie said out loud. "Right?"

She blinked. Fiona, Maggie, and Darbie stood on the sidewalk, staring at her.

"That doesn't make it okay for her to commit grand larceny," Fiona said.

Sophie shook her head. "She didn't."

"Sophie," Darbie said, "the bloomin' camera was sitting right in her locker."

"Somebody else must have put it there," Sophie said.

"Why are you defending her?" Fiona glanced over at Maggie. "After all the stuff she's done."

"But she didn't do *this*," Sophie said. And then she told them what Coach Virile had said, and how Phoebe had looked, and how that had felt. By the time she was finished, her bus had pulled up and kids were boarding.

Fiona groaned. "I guess you're not going to let us off and leave it to the Round Table to handle this, are you?" she said.

"No," Sophie said. "Somebody planted my camera in her locker, and we have to prove it before the Round Table meets."

"Tell me again why we're going to all this trouble for that little blackguard?" Darbie said.

"Because she doesn't have anybody else to do it for her," Sophie said. "We all have each other—and we have Dr. Peter—and we have Jesus. Phoebe's just—lost."

Nobody shook her head or groaned or whined. Fiona just said, "I hate it when you're right."

"Hurry, she's closing the door," Darbie said, pushing Sophie gently up the bus steps.

Sophie stopped at the top and looked back at Maggie, who hadn't said a word. "Are you going to help, Mags?" Sophie said.

Maggie didn't answer. Sophie sagged.

"In or out, missy?" the bus driver said.

Sophie stepped inside and watched through the closed doors as Maggie turned away and went to her own bus. Sophie flopped into a seat and leaned against her lump of a backpack, now softer without her camera inside. Everything seemed to sink.

What was Daddy going to say when she told him? And how were they going to find out who planted the camera by lunchtime tomorrow?

And what about Maggie? How was she going to deal with all this?

*Liberty Lawhead leaned across the backseat of the limo and brought her face close. "The same way you always do. A great civil rights leader listens to the counsel of her advisers — especially to the greatest leader, who lives in her heart and bestows his kind eyes on her. Then she waits, and she knows, and she follows. She isn't lost, because she knows her Shepherd."*

Sophie opened her eyes and rubbed the crop of fuzz on her head. *I never heard Liberty Lawhead talk like that,* she thought. *I didn't know she knew that much about Jesus.*

And then she smiled at herself in the glass. Of course. Liberty Lawhead knew, because *she* knew.

But that didn't mean everything was easy after that.

When Sophie told Mama and Daddy about the camera, Daddy got his halftime-in-the-locker-room face on. It took Sophie half an hour to convince him that Phoebe wasn't guilty. Then Mama got her somebody's-going-to-get-hurt-on-the-field look on, and it took Sophie another thirty minutes to assure her that the Flakes and the Charms wouldn't be in danger looking for the real culprit. She had to promise to tell Mama and Daddy and a grown-up from the Round Table what they planned to do before they started.

The next hardest thing was coordinating the Flakes and the Charms. Sophie received so many e-mails that night, Daddy finally turned the computer completely over to her. In her final Instant Message exchange with Fiona, it was decided that the Charms would find out all the ways somebody could get into someone else's locker and investigate.

WordGirl:     Vincent is all over that.

DreamGirl:    Ya think?

WordGirl:     LOL

WordGirl:     Willoughby will check out
              the rumor situation and do
              squelching duty.

DreamGirl:    U and Darbie work on Mags.

WordGirl:     Thanks for giving us the
              hardest job.

DreamGirl:    I have the hardest job.

WordGirl:     Phoebe?

DreamGirl:    You know it.

As she lay in bed imagining Jesus, though, Sophie knew how she'd handle Phoebe. The only way there was to handle a lost sheep.

But it still didn't get easier after that. The only Round Table adult they could find to tell about their investigation plans before school was Mrs. Clayton. She tapped her blonde helmet with a red pen and looked at them with her blue-bullet eyes.

"I appreciate your trying to help this girl," she said. "That is, after all, what the Round Table is about. But the evidence is fairly clear. Today's meeting is more about helping Phoebe change than determining her guilt or innocence."

"So she won't actually get in trouble?" Fiona said.

Mrs. Clayton bulleted her eyes again. "There will be consequences for the theft. That's a serious thing."

"Not as serious as what her father's going to do to her," Sophie said when they were out in the hall.

"Then we better get started," Jimmy said.

But Phoebe wasn't in third-period PE class, and Coach Yates wasn't in the mood for answering questions. It was all she could do to break up the gossip groups just so she could take roll. Maggie was there, but she stayed away from the Flakes. Willoughby reported that she hadn't said a word all through first and second periods. The same was definitely *not* true of the two Corn Pops in her classes, B.J. and Cassie.

"All they could talk about," Willoughby said, "was how Phoebe is white trash, and she's gonna be put in Juvie Hall, and the Round Table is gonna be broken up because it isn't doing any good — "

"No way." Fiona parked a ball on her hip.

"It isn't working on Eddie." Willoughby gave a nervous poodle-yip, and her eyes went wide. "He was all talking about how Phoebe was like this criminal because she attacked him—and he was bragging about how if Coach Nanini hadn't been there, he would have taken Phoebe out."

"I'm impressed," Darbie said in a dry voice. "Big blaggard like that taking out a skinny little thing like Phoebe."

"Yeah," Willoughby said, yipping more happily. "What a man."

"Speaking of men—" Fiona pointed at Nathan, who was jogging toward them from across the gym.

Sophie could tell by the neon pink of his ears that he was going to talk to them.

But instead, he tripped a few feet away. In the process of untangling his legs, he pulled a piece of paper out of his sneaker and kicked it toward Sophie. She picked it up as he flailed away.

Sophie stared at the writing scrawled across the paper. "Listen. 'CSI has detected suspicious markings on alleged thief's locker, indicating forced entry with a metal object. Fresh shavings indicate this was recent activity. We have a digital photo. Investigation continues to identify said object.'"

"*What?*" Willoughby said. "Why can't he speak English?"

"Somebody opened Phoebe's locker with something metal!" Fiona said.

"Hi, Mags!" Darbie said.

Sophie turned around to see Maggie standing just a few feet from her. But before she could say a word, Maggie's eyes flashed, and she hurried away.

A blast from Coach Yates' whistle bounced off the gym walls. "Let's go, people! I'm in the mood to give detentions!"

The Corn Flakes latched onto each other and sprinted for the drill line. Sophie looked over her shoulder, but she couldn't find Maggie.

"She's our job," Darbie said.

"Yours is to find Phoebe and tell her there's hope," Fiona said.

Sophie liked hearing the tone in Fiona's voice, as if she were really pulling for Phoebe. But she wasn't sure how much hope she could give the lost lamb.

She crumpled the note and stuck it in the waistband of her track pants. *This doesn't really prove anything,* she thought. *Not unless somebody was seen doing it.*

And even if somebody had, the chances of him coming forward got slimmer by the minute. The gym, the locker room, the halls between classes throbbed with talk of Phoebe the Thief. It seemed like the entire student body of GMMS was ready to hang her from the flagpole.

If they could only find her.

Fourth period was almost over, and Sophie still hadn't had a chance to talk to her. When the bell rang for lunch, she practically ran to the Round Table meeting room. Maybe the office had been keeping her, Sophie thought, and they would bring her in before the meeting started.

But the only person there was Jimmy, holding out a digital camera to Sophie. His shy face told her their ongoing investigation had turned up nothing.

"The pictures of the locker are on here," he said.

"Thanks," Sophie said. "But I don't think they'll do any good."

"It'll create reasonable doubt." Jimmy shrugged his gymnast-shoulders. "I think I watch too much TV too."

"Is that like, if there's any doubt at all, they can't say she stole it?" Sophie said.

"Yeah," Jimmy said.

Sophie watched as the eighth graders trailed in whispering to each other, and Mrs. Clayton talked into Coach Nanini's ear just inside the doorway.

"I don't know," Sophie said to Jimmy. "It's like everybody's already made up their minds, just because she's poor or something."

"It's discrimination," Jimmy said.

Sophie felt her mouth falling open. "It *is*, huh?"

"It's like Phoebe's a Marielito now—"

"And everybody thinks she'd steal just because she looks like people who do!" Sophie lowered her voice. "Do you think I can convince them?"

"Are you serious?" Jimmy whispered back. "I don't think there's anybody else who could."

Sophie decided that was the thing she liked about him best, best, *best* of all.

But she was still shaky inside when Mrs. Clayton called the meeting to order and explained Phoebe's case.

"So why are we here?" Hannah the eighth grader said, blinking away at her contact lenses.

Oliver slouched down in his chair, gesturing with one hand. "She should just go to Juvie for this. If she's already heisting people's stuff, how are we supposed to change her?"

"We can't change people," Sophie said. "We just have to see who they really are."

"She showed us who she is," Oliver said.

But Coach Nanini put up his hand and nodded at Mrs. Clayton, who slipped out of the room. Sophie's heart sank. Mrs. Clayton was one of the people who needed to hear this.

"Go ahead, Little Bit," Coach Nanini said.

*Liberty Lawhead lifted her chin. She had to say what she had to say, whether anyone believed her or not—*

And then Sophie LaCroix lifted *her* chin and said, "Phoebe didn't have a chance to steal the camera. Coach Nanini can testify to that. And she wouldn't have anyway, because with-

244

out the camera we can't make the movie, and she *lives* to make movies because she has such an awful home life. And I don't know what she'd do with it because all she wants to do is act — she doesn't even know how to turn the camera on."

"Then how did it get in her locker?" Oliver said.

Sophie looked at Jimmy, who produced the digital camera. "We have evidence that somebody might have gotten Phoebe's locker open with some kind of metal thing."

"Let's see," Hannah said.

Jimmy handed the camera to her. Oliver craned his neck to see.

"Still doesn't prove somebody framed her," he said.

"But it gives—" Sophie groped for the words.

"Reasonable doubt," Jimmy said.

Hannah looked up from the camera. "I don't see why we should give her the benefit of the doubt. She attacked Eddie Wornom right in front of Coach Nanini. And I don't mean to be snotty or anything, but she isn't exactly an honor student—"

"Phoebe," Coach Nanini said, "do you have anything to say to that?"

Sophie jerked around to see Phoebe standing near the door with Mrs. Clayton. Her eyes were red-rimmed and swimming.

"I didn't do it," Phoebe said.

Mrs. Clayton nudged Phoebe toward a seat, and Coach Nanini said, "Let's give Phoebe a chance to speak for herself."

"Do you know of anybody who'd want to get you in trouble?" Oliver said.

"Is anybody mad at you?" Hannah said.

Phoebe curled her lip. "Who isn't?"

"I'm not," Sophie said.

"See, I don't get that," Hannah said, eyes blinking double-time. "If it were my camera that got stolen, I'd be so ticked off—"

"Let's stick to the facts," Mrs. Clayton said. "Bottom line: all the evidence points to you, Phoebe. Yes, you'll have to take responsibility for that, but we just want to help you so you won't do something like this again."

"I didn't do it in the first place!" Phoebe said.

There was a knock on the door, and Miss Imes got up. Sophie closed her eyes. The whole conversation was like a wheel spinning and not getting anywhere.

"Just stop," Sophie said.

The room got quiet.

"Go ahead, Little Bit," Coach Nanini said.

"Okay," Sophie said, "Phoebe has an awful father, and she doesn't have any friends, and she acts because she's scared, and I don't know of what, but she is." She took a breath. "Why can't we help her with that and forget about the camera?"

"I wish we could, Sophie," Mrs. Clayton said. "But we can't just let it go." She turned to Phoebe. "It would be so much better for you if you would just admit that you took—"

"I might as well," Phoebe said, lips quivering. "You've already made up your minds—"

"No!" Sophie said.

"Wait," somebody else said.

Miss Imes opened the door wider, and Mr. Janitor Man stepped in. Right behind him was Maggie.

"What's up with that?" Jimmy whispered to Sophie.

The only other person in the room who looked as shocked as Sophie felt was Phoebe. And then Phoebe's whole body began to shake.

"Don't believe anything she says against me!" Phoebe cried out, pointing at Maggie. "You want to know who's mad at me and wants me to get in trouble? It's her! I treated her like dirt, and now she wants to nail me—"

"Hold on," Miss Imes said. "It's nothing like that." She stood behind Maggie and put her hands on Maggie's shoulders. Sophie could see Mags stiffening, and her eyes went straight to Sophie. Then they darted away, as if she were ashamed of something.

*NO!* Sophie wanted to cry out to her. *Don't tell them you did it. I don't care about the camera—we'll help you. We're all Corn Flakes—*

But Miss Imes was already saying, "Tell them what you know, Maggie," and Maggie was opening her mouth.

Sophie clung to the arm of the chair. Why had Maggie done it? They were getting ready to help her stand up to Phoebe. Why hadn't she trusted the Corn Flakes?

"I have a confession," Maggie said. Her voice was heavy. "I wasn't going to tell anybody because I kind of wanted her to take the blame."

"I told you," Phoebe said.

Mrs. Clayton told her to shush.

"I saw somebody throw a big screwdriver in the trash can by the lockers yesterday," Maggie went on. "Right next to Phoebe's locker."

*A big screwdriver—*

"And he was looking all around like he didn't want anybody to see him do it, so I hid—"

*He?*

"And he met this girl in the hall and she said, 'Did you get it in there?' and he went—" Maggie turned a thumb upward.

"Maybe he used the screwdriver to get Phoebe's locker open," Jimmy said.

"Who?" Hannah and Oliver said together.

But Sophie knew, even before Maggie said, "Eddie Wornom."
The room came alive.

"Wait a minute now, before we get all excited," Coach Nanini said. "Eddie was using that screwdriver to help me with the bleachers, but I sent him to return it."

Mr. Janitor Man raised a finger. "Never got it," he said in his sandpapery voice. "Me and her"—he glanced at Maggie—"just went through yesterday's trash bags. Found it."

He reached into his tool belt and pulled out the same screwdriver Eddie had thrown at Phoebe.

"Maybe we can get prints," Jimmy muttered to Sophie.

Coach Virile stormed out of the room like a bull charging a fence. Mrs. Clayton was still watching Maggie.

"Who was the girl?" she said.

"B.J. Schneider," Maggie said.

"Do you know her?" Mrs. Clayton said to Phoebe.

Phoebe shook her head, but Sophie was nodding hers.

"B.J. was there the day he"—Sophie nodded toward Mr. Janitor Man—"was fixing Eddie's locker. She saw him get the door open with a screwdriver."

"Mr. Fenwick?" Mrs. Clayton said to the janitor.

He grunted. "I remember. One of them told me that was 'Eddie's locker' like it was King Tut's tomb."

"That actually does sound like B.J.," Mrs. Clayton said. She looked around the room. "But I want all of you to understand that this doesn't prove Eddie planted the camera—"

"Don't need to." Coach Virile stepped into the room and pulled Eddie in after him, lunch ketchup still at the corners of his mouth. "Eddie's going to prove it himself. Let's go, Mr. Wornom."

Eddie turned his radish-red face toward Phoebe. "You're trash," he said. "If I hadn't of gotten caught, they woulda kept thinking you did it."

Beneath the voices that all rose at once, Jimmy's made its way to Sophie. "I guess he proved it," he said.

There was a lot to sort out before the Round Table adjourned that day. Maggie apologized to Phoebe for not coming forward right away. Phoebe apologized to Maggie for being hateful—at least as much as Phoebe could, Sophie decided. Phoebe got Campus Commission with Coach Nanini for attacking Eddie—which brought on a gap-toothed smile. Eddie was taken out of their hands by Mr. Bentley, the principal.

Although it was almost time for fifth period when they left Round Table, the rest of the Corn Flakes and the Lucky Charms were waiting for them in the hall.

"They talked me into telling," Maggie said.

"We saw her with Vincent's note that must have fallen out of your track pants, Soph," Fiona said.

"And she was all bummed out," Willoughby put in.

"So we interrogated her," Fiona said.

"But we were nice," Darbie said. "Corn Flake style."

Fiona grinned. "Just doing our job."

"And we did ours," Vincent said. He pulled a Q-Tip out of his pocket. "If Wornom hadn't confessed, I was ready to get his DNA."

"I guess I'm the only one who didn't do my job," Sophie said. "I never even got to talk to Phoebe."

"She's right there," Fiona said, nodding down the hall.

Phoebe was indeed lounging by the water fountain.

"I don't think she's standing there because she's thirsty, Soph," Darbie said.

Sophie tilted her chin and walked toward the victim of discrimination whose rights she had just stood up for.

*I can't change her,* she thought in an inner voice that sounded very much like Liberty Lawhead's. *But I can help her see who she really is. Well,* she added as she dodged the last person between her and the Diva at the water fountain, *Jesus and me, that is.*

# Glossary

**blackguards** (bLAK gards) very rude and offensive people

**civil rights** (siv-il rites) laws and ideas that are supposed to make sure everyone is treated equally. Civil rights movements try to bring attention to people who need these rights.

**delusion** (di-LOO-shun) believing something is there when it's not, and thinking it's still there no matter what anyone tells you

**Dr. Martin Luther King Jr.** (Doktor Mar-tin Loo-thur King Joon-yur) a very important man in the 1960s. He used nonviolence to help make African Americans equal in the United States. He was shot and killed on April 4, 1968.

**flan** (flahn) a really thick and wiggly custard dessert that is popular in some Hispanic cultures

**foostering about** (FOO-stur-ing a-bout) an Irish way of saying "stop wasting time"

**heinous** (HEY-nus) unbelievably mean and cruel

**illusion** (eh-LOO-shun) when something looks incredibly real, but it isn't

**Latino** (lah-TEE-no) a person whose family was originally from Latin America (Central and South America), but who now lives in the United States

**Marielitos** (mar-e-el-EE-toes) people who left Cuba by boat to Key West to be free from the Cuban government. They lived in tents on an Air Force base until the U.S. government could find places for them to live, and some people treated them badly afterward because they believed the Marielitos were all criminals.

**monologue** (MAW-nol-og) a long speech given by one person who doesn't allow anyone else to talk

**phlegm** (flem) thick, icky stuff in your throat that usually appears when you're sick

**scuttlebutt** (skuh-tell-but) juicy rumors and gossip

**statuesque** (stah-chew-ESK) tall and graceful, and looking a lot like a really impressive statue

**swordplay** (sord-play) showing you can use a sword very well, and could defend yourself if necessary

**virile** (VEAR-uhl) the definition of manly; muscular, strong, and really hunky. Think cute movie star meets not-icky body-builder.

# NIV Faithgirlz! Bible, Revised Edition

*Nancy Rue*

Every girl wants to know she's totally unique and special. This Bible says that with Faithgirlz! sparkle. Through the many in-text features found only in the Faithgirlz! Bible, girls will grow closer to God as they discover the journey of a lifetime.

Features include:

- Book introductions—Read about the who, when, where, and what of each book.

- Dream Girl—Use your imagination to put yourself in the story.

- Bring It On!—Take quizzes to really get to know yourself.

- Is There a Little (Eve, Ruth, Isaiah) in You?—See for yourself what you have in common.

- Words to Live By—Check out these Bible verses that are great for memorizing.

- What Happens Next?—Create a list of events to tell a Bible story in your own words.

- Oh, I Get It!—Find answers to Bible questions you've wondered about.

- The complete NIV translation

- Features written by bestselling author Nancy Rue

*Available in stores and online!*

# Talk It Up!

*Want free books?*
*First looks at the best new fiction?*
*Awesome exclusive merchandise?*

We want to hear from you!

Give us your opinions on titles, covers, and stories.
Join the Z Street Team.

Email us at zstreetteam@zondervan.com
to sign up today!

Also—Friend us on Facebook!

www.facebook.com/goodteenreads

- Video Trailers
- Connect with your favorite authors
- Sneak peeks at new releases
- Giveaways
- Fun discussions
- And much more!

ZONDERVAN®
.com